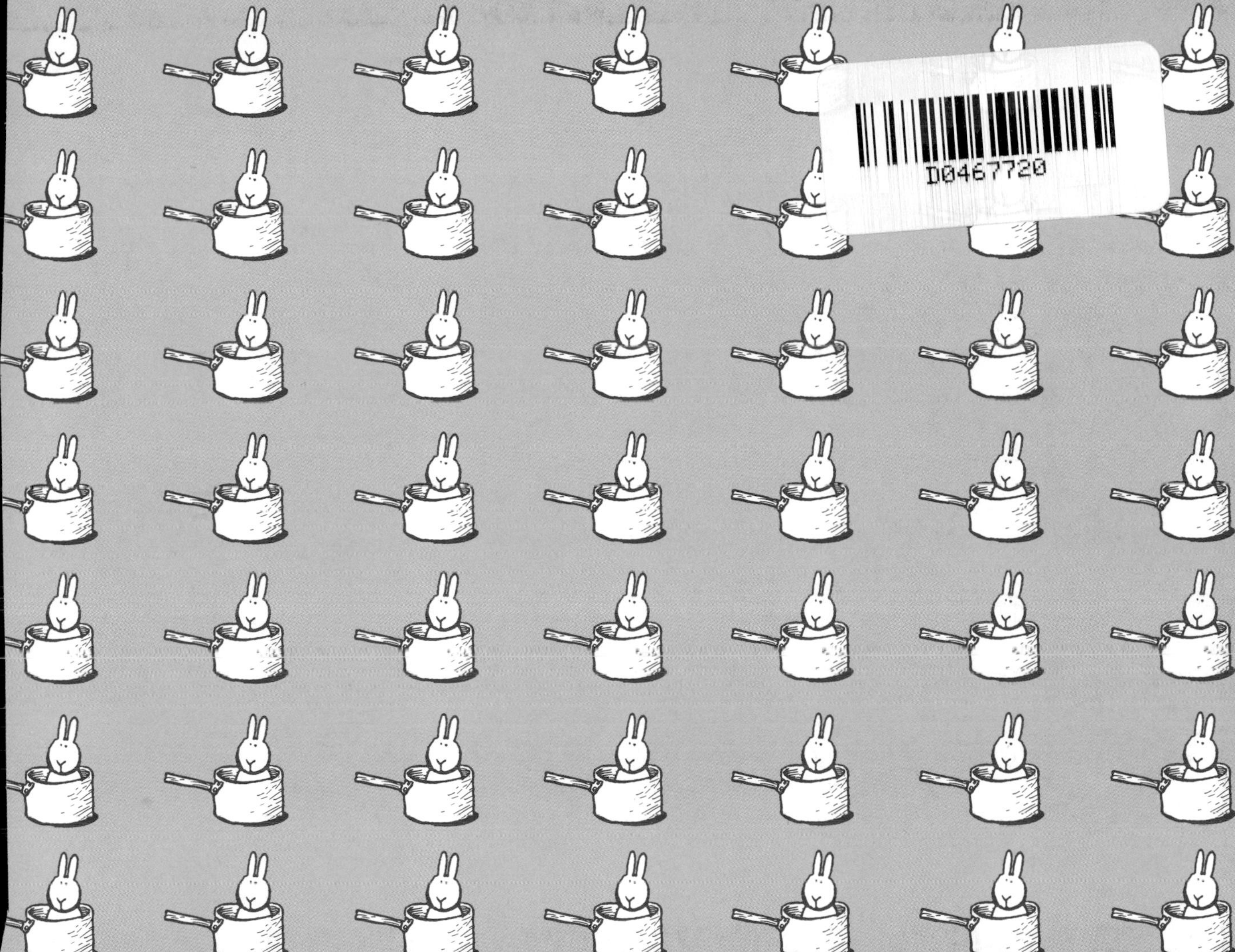

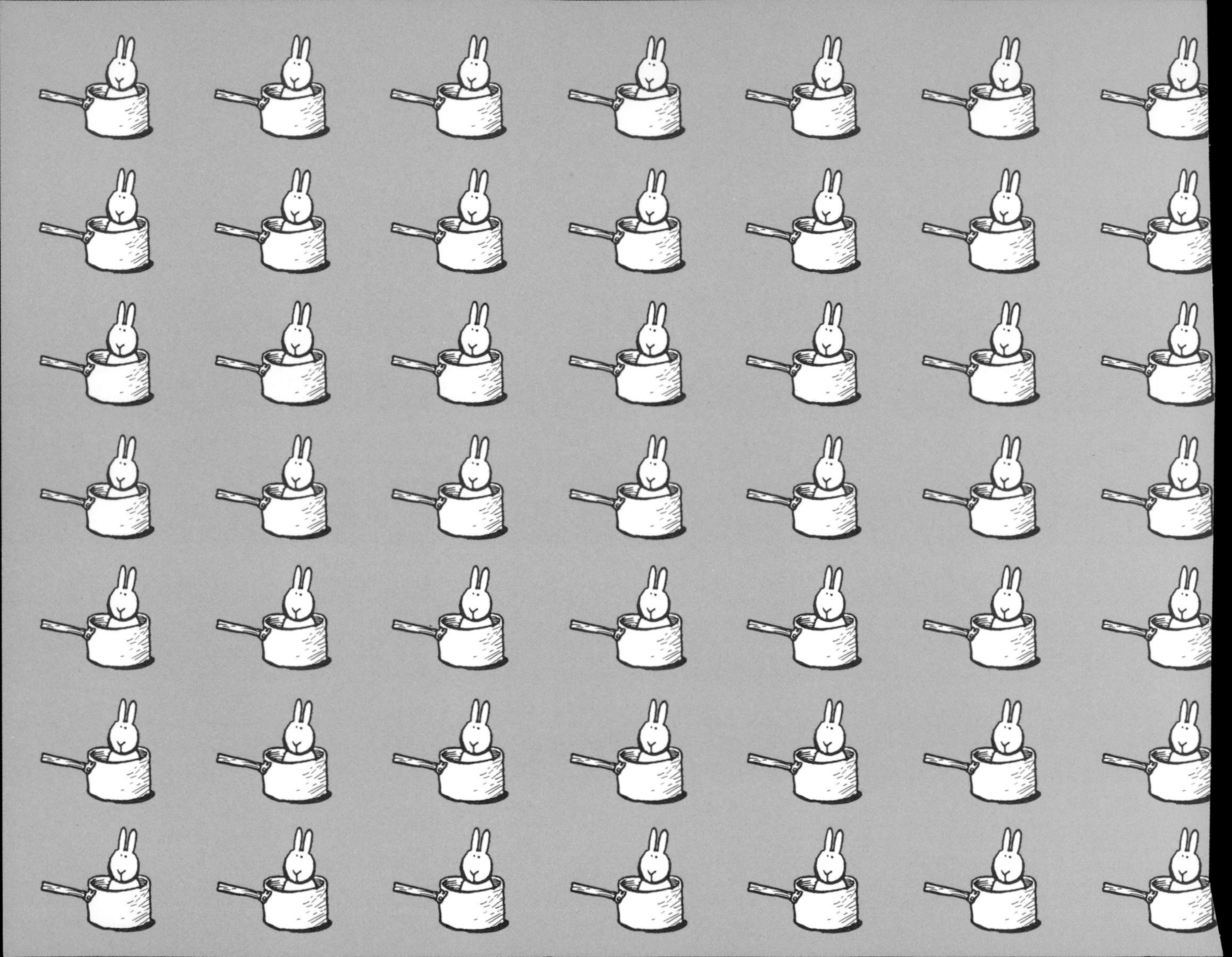

DAWN OF THE BUNNY SUICIDES

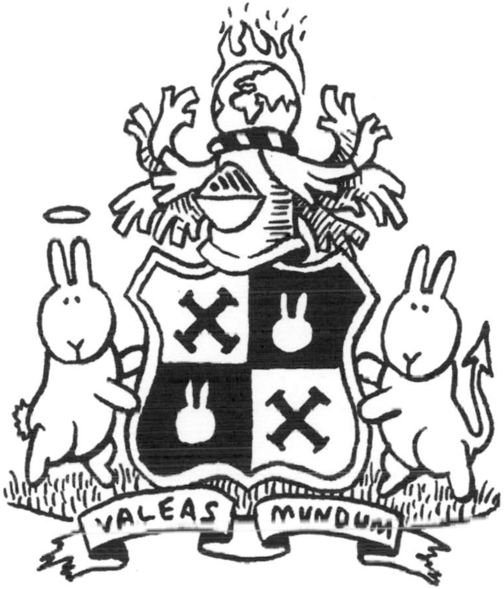
VALEAS
MUNDUM

Dawn of the Bunny Suicides

Andy Riley

CHRONICLE BOOKS

SAN FRANCISCO

ANDY RILEY IS THE AUTHOR/ARTIST OF:

THE BOOK OF BUNNY SUICIDES, RETURN OF THE BUNNY SUICIDES, GREAT LIES TO TELL SMALL KIDS, LOADS MORE LIES TO TELL SMALL KIDS, SELFISH PIGS, D.I.Y. DENTISTRY (AND OTHER ALARMING INVENTIONS), AND THE BUMPER BOOK OF BUNNY SUICIDES. ROASTED, HIS STRIP IN THE OBSERVER MAGAZINE, IS COLLECTED AS A HODDER & STOUGHTON HARDBACK.

HIS SCRIPTWRITING WORK INCLUDES BLACK BOOKS, THE GREAT OUTDOORS, HYPERDRIVE, LITTLE BRITAIN, THE ARMSTRONG & MILLER SHOW, THE ARMANDO IANNUCCI SHOWS, SLACKER CATS, JET, THE 99p CHALLENGE, BIG TRAIN, THE FRIDAY NIGHT ARMISTICE, SPITTING IMAGE, SMACK THE PONY, GNOMEO AND JULIET, SO GRAHAM NORTON, HARRY AND PAUL AND THE BAFTA-WINNING ANIMATION ROBBIE THE REINDEER.

LOOK OUT FOR NEW CARTOONS AT:
misterandyriley.com

ON TWITTER:
@andyrileyish

WITH THANKS TO:

POLLY FABER, GORDON WISE, CAMILLA HORNBY, LISA HIGHTON & ALL AT CHRONICLE BOOKS, KEVIN CECIL, ARTHUR MATHEWS AND ELLIOTT MILLER

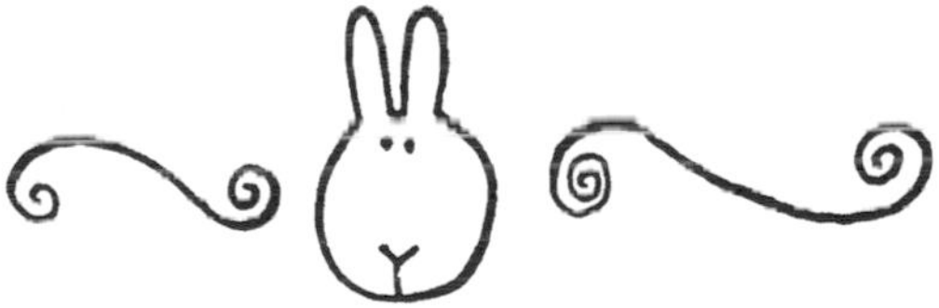

First published in the United States in 2011 by Chronicle Books.

First published in the United Kingdom in 2011 by Hodder & Stoughton, 338 Euston Road, London NW1 3BH, England.

Library of Congress Cataloging-in-Publication Data is available.

ISBN: 978-1-4521-0498-0

Manufactured in China

10 9 8 7 6 5 4 3 2 1

Chronicle Books
680 Second Street
San Francisco, California 94107
www.chroniclebooks.com

FOR
BILL & EDDIE

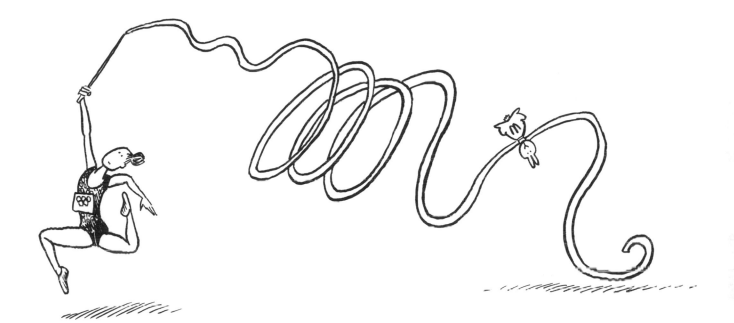

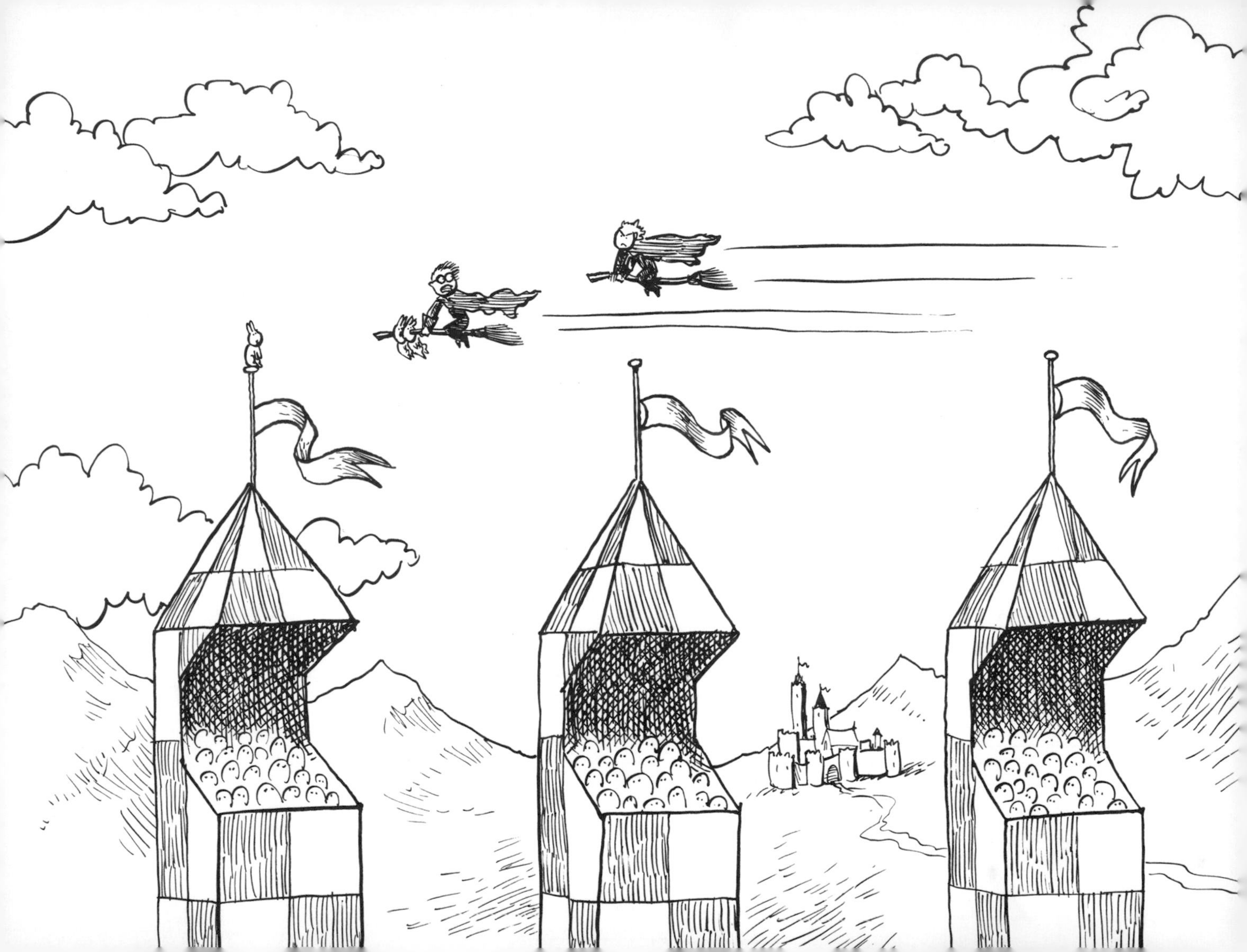

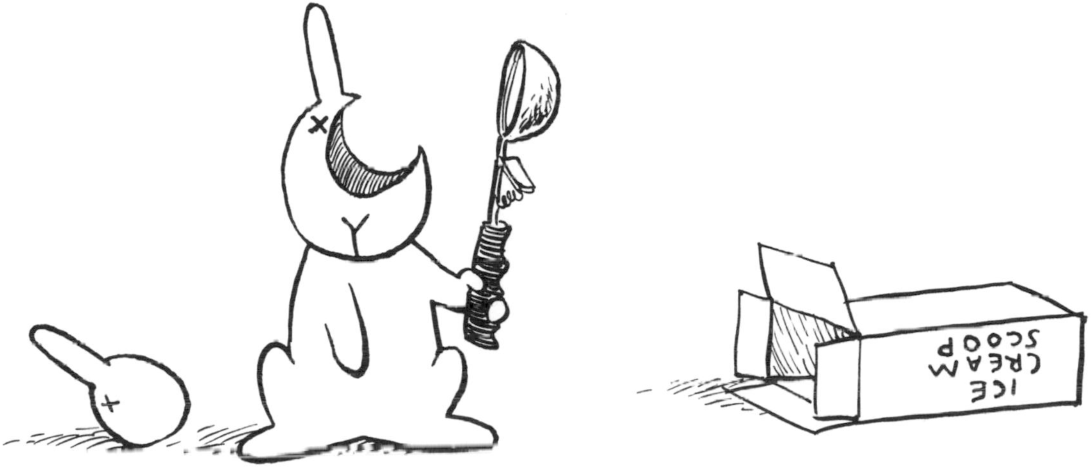
ICE
CREAM
SCOOP

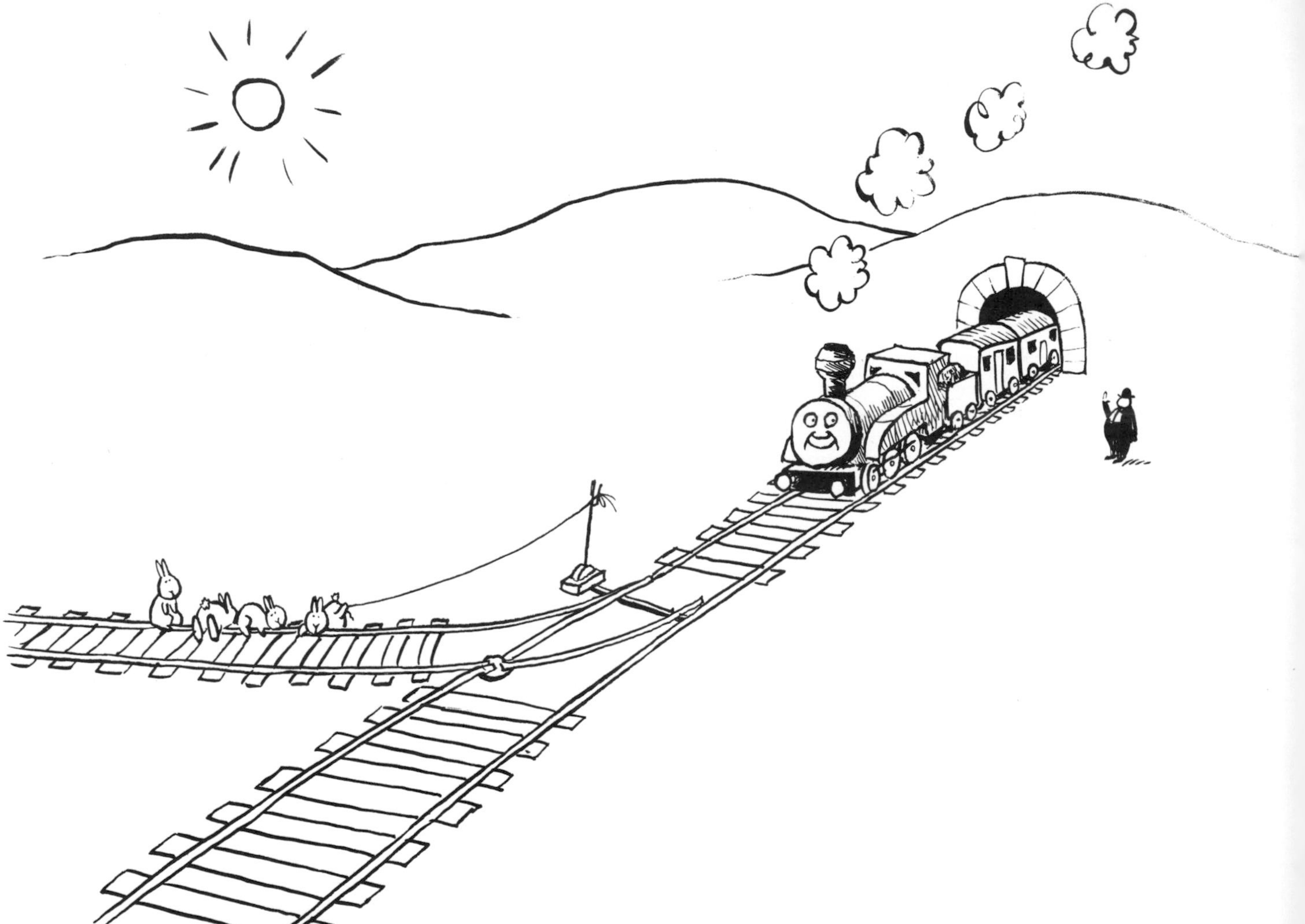

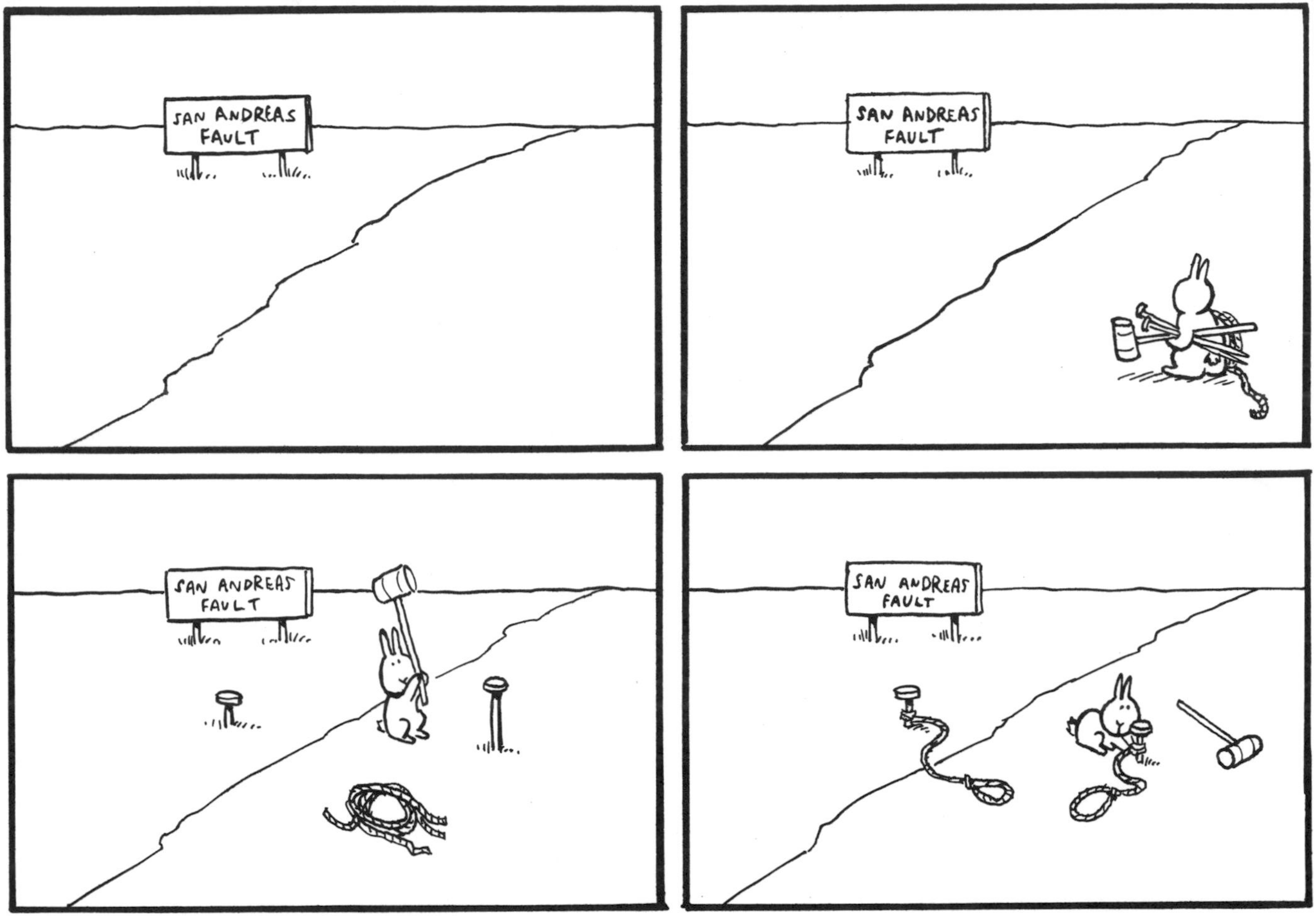
SAN ANDREAS FAULT
SAN ANDREAS FAULT
SAN ANDREAS FAULT
SAN ANDREAS FAULT

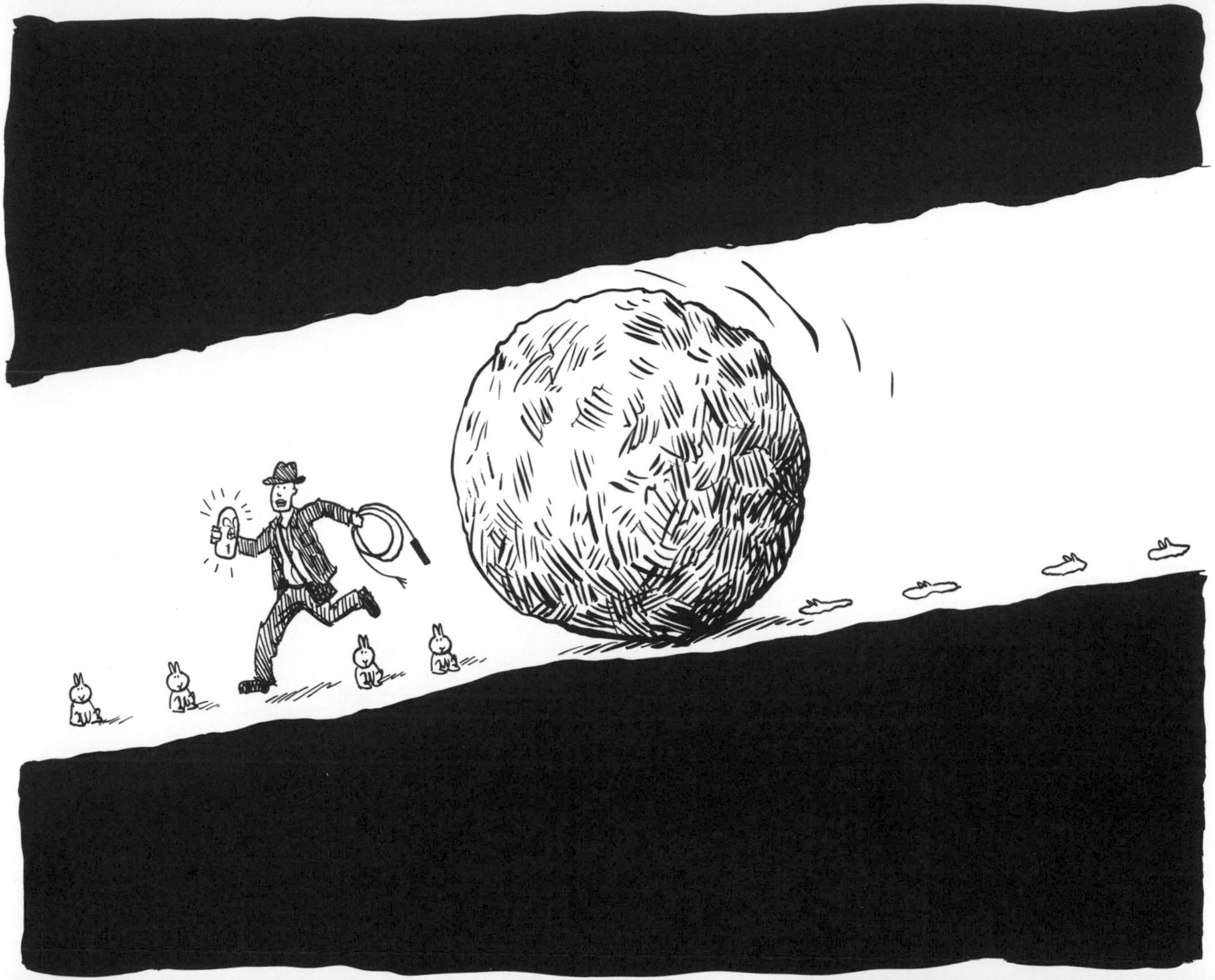

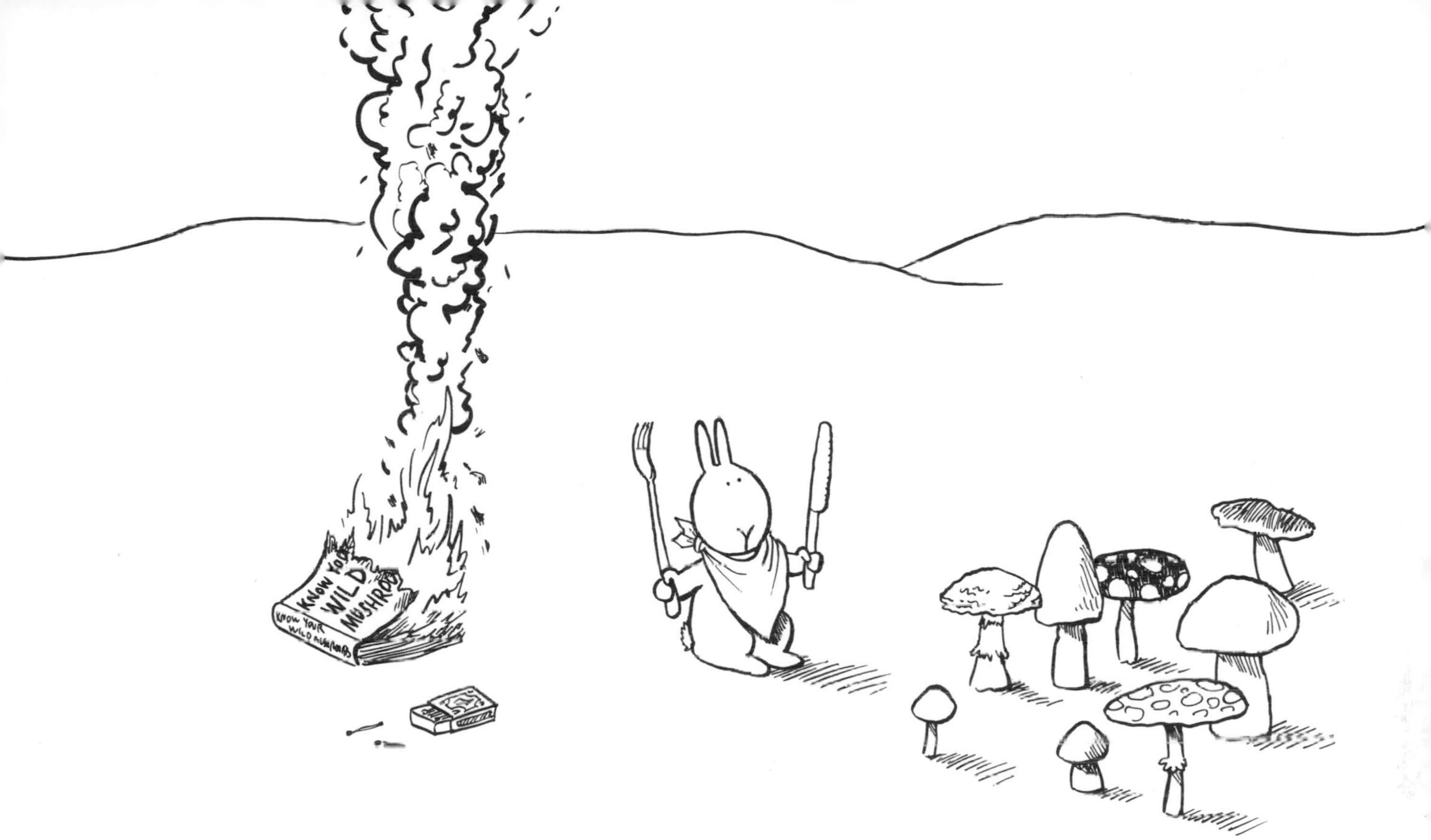
KNOW YOU
WILD
MUSHRO
KNOW YOUR
WILD MUSHROOMS

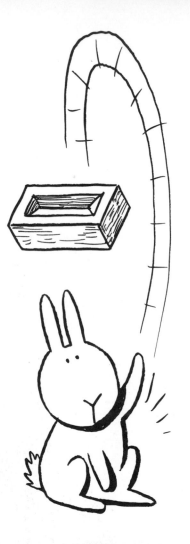

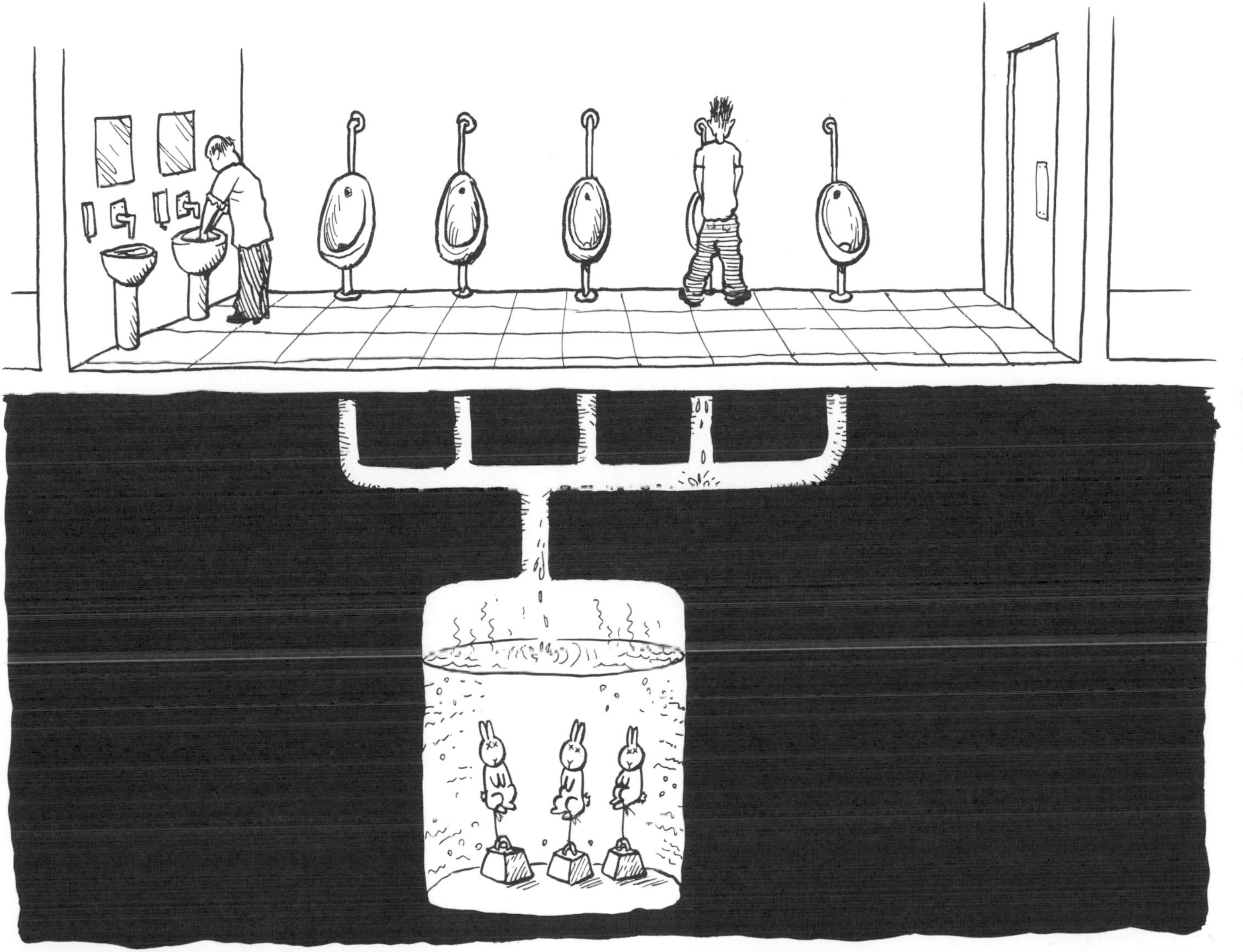

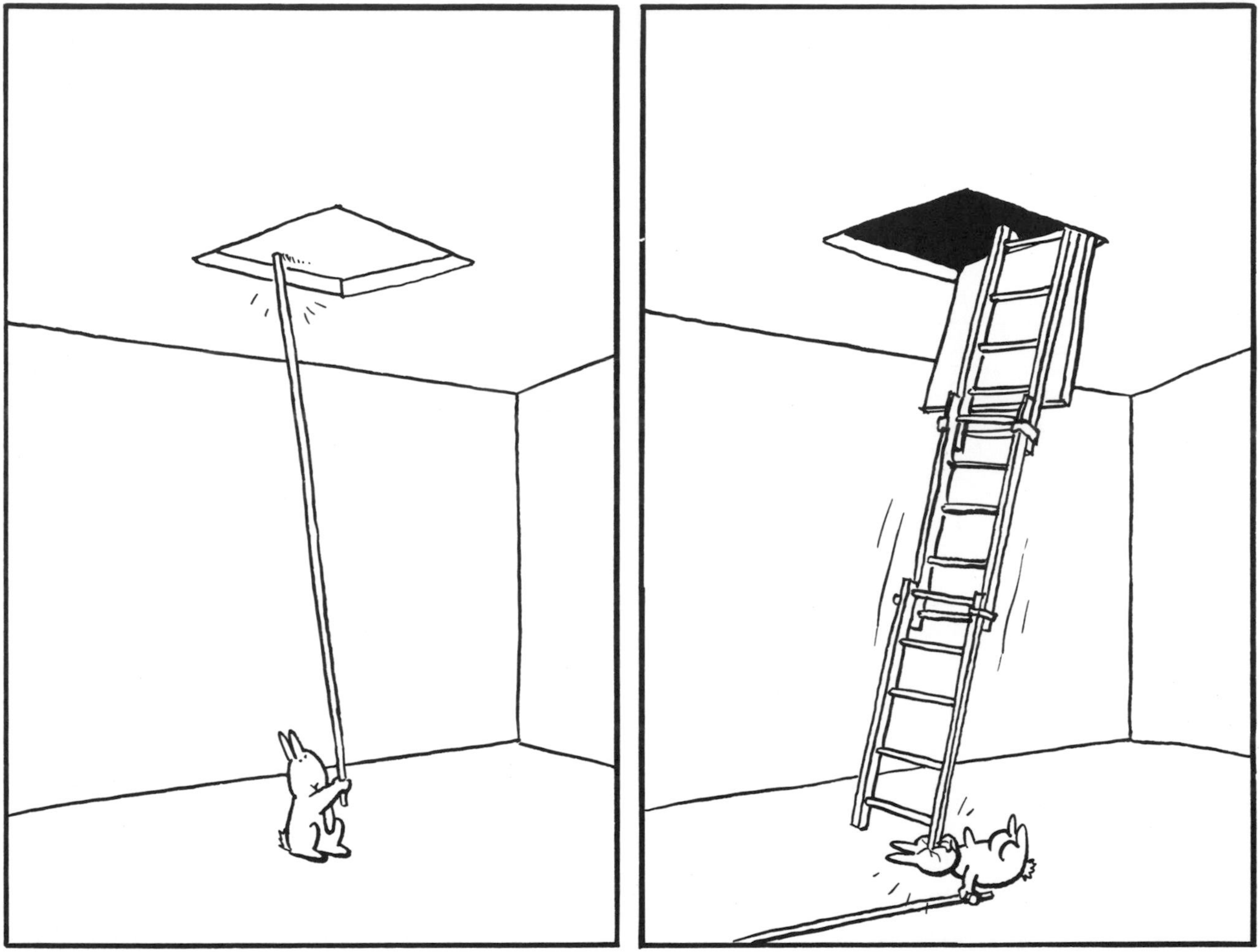

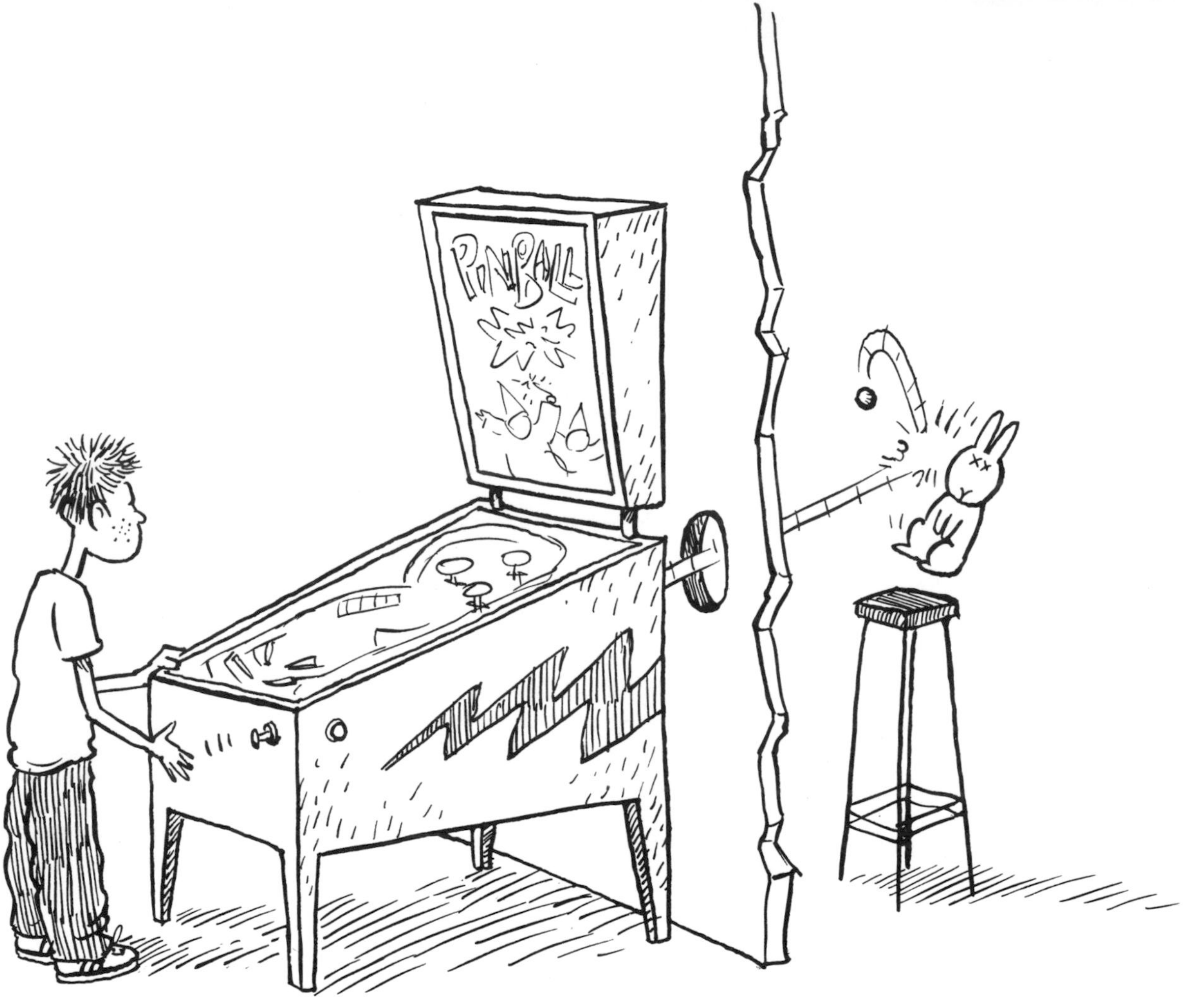
PINBALL

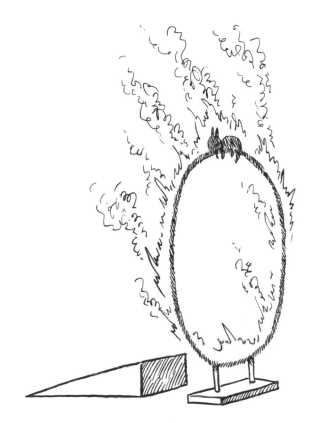

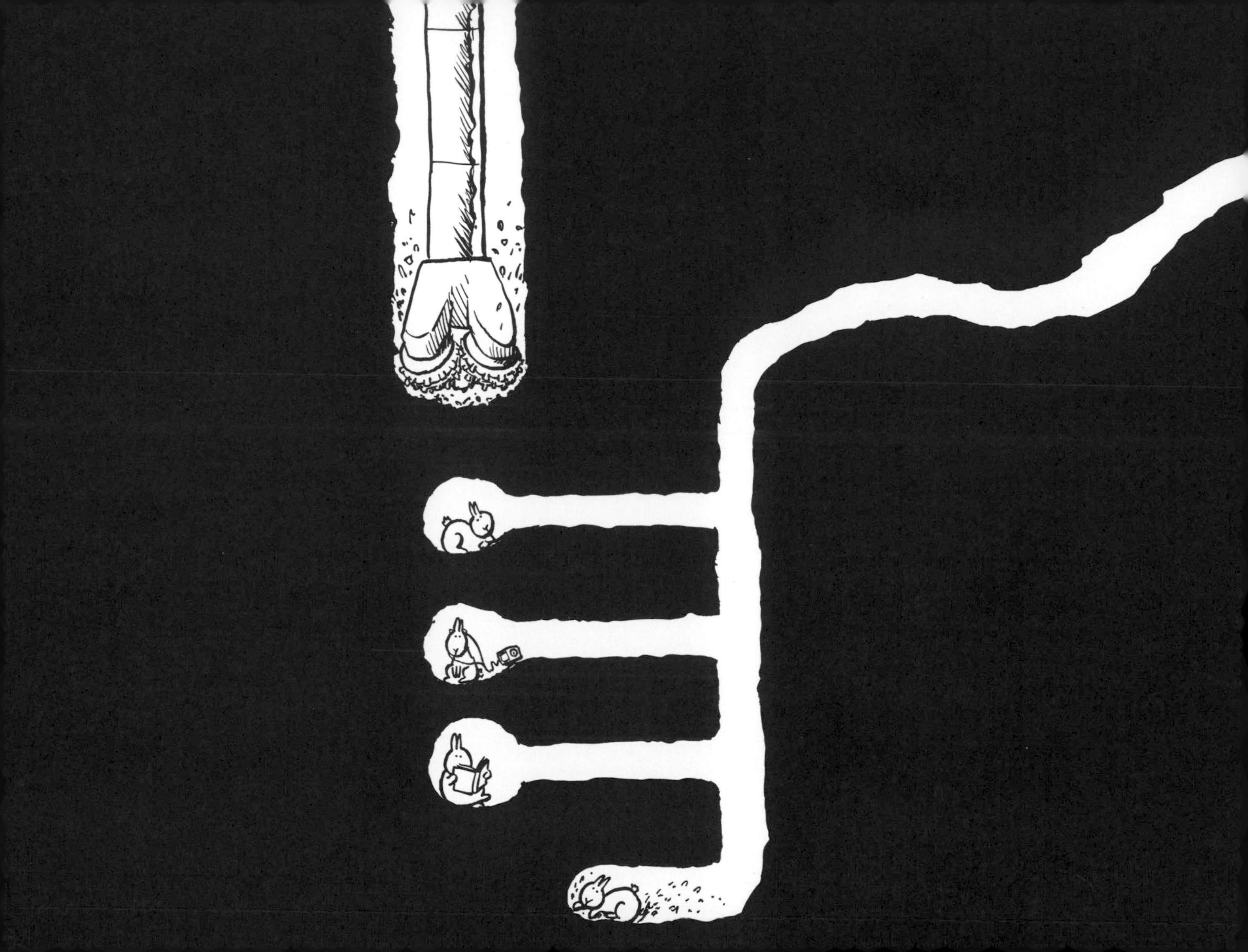

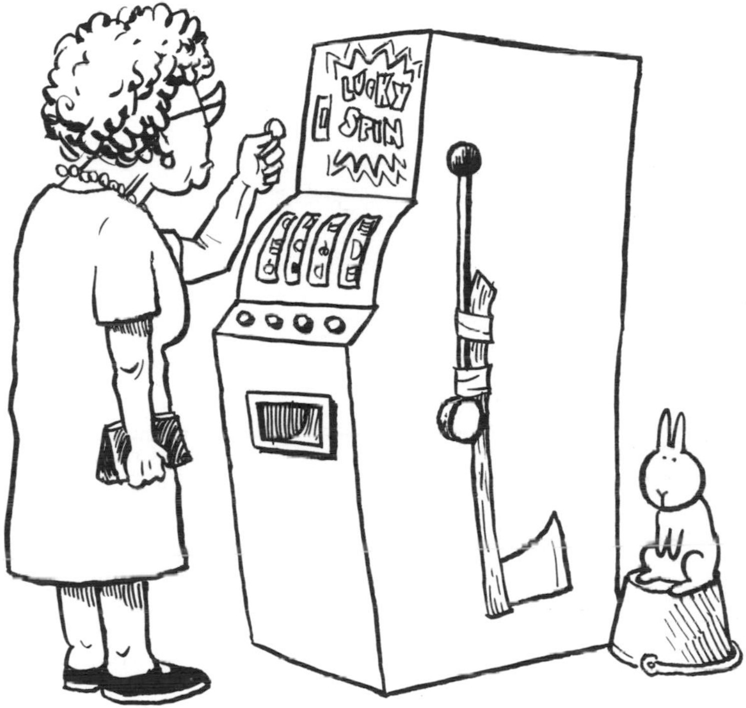
LUCKY SPIN

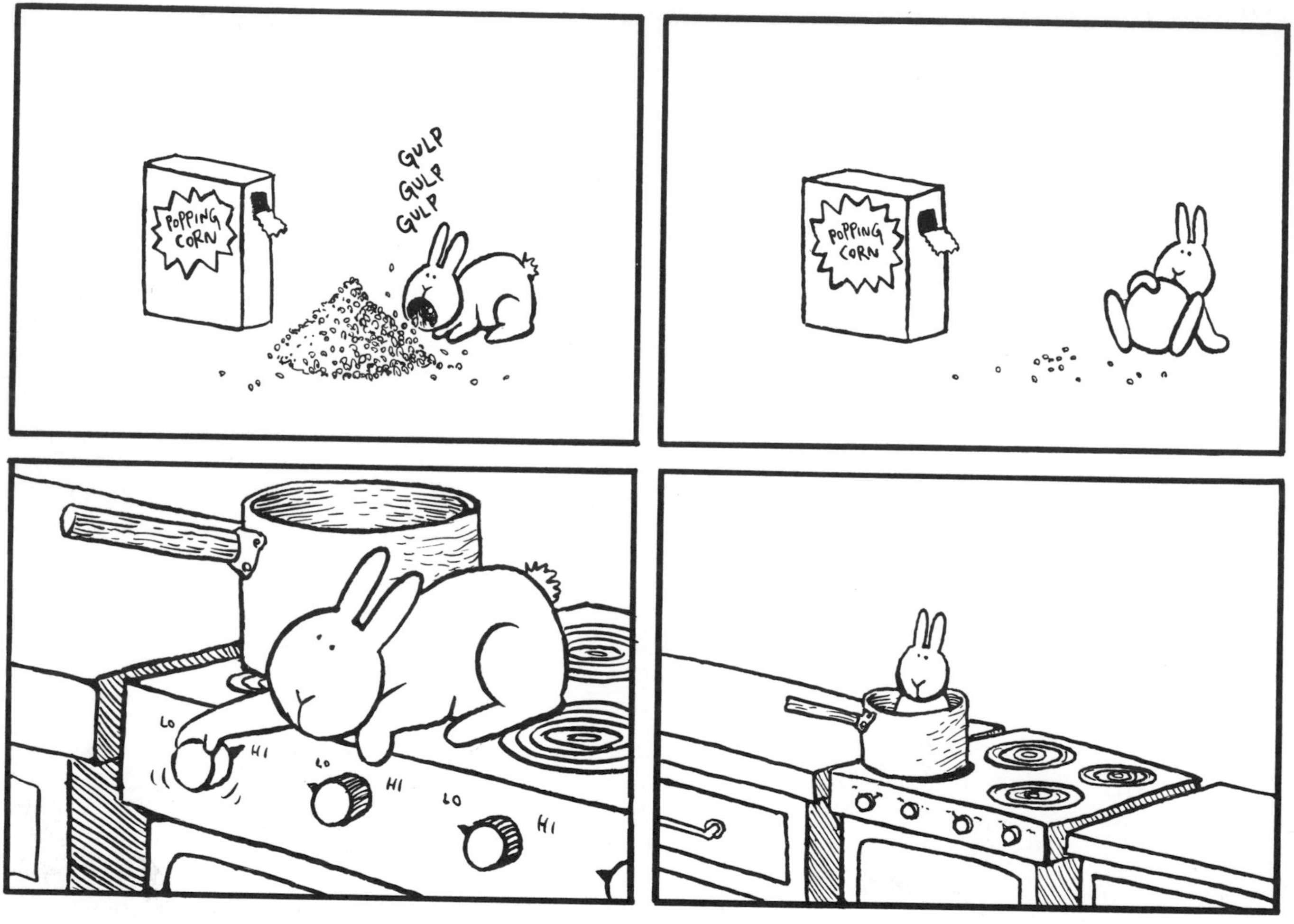
POPPING CORN
GULP
GULP
GULP
POPPING CORN
LO
HI
LO
HI
LO
HI

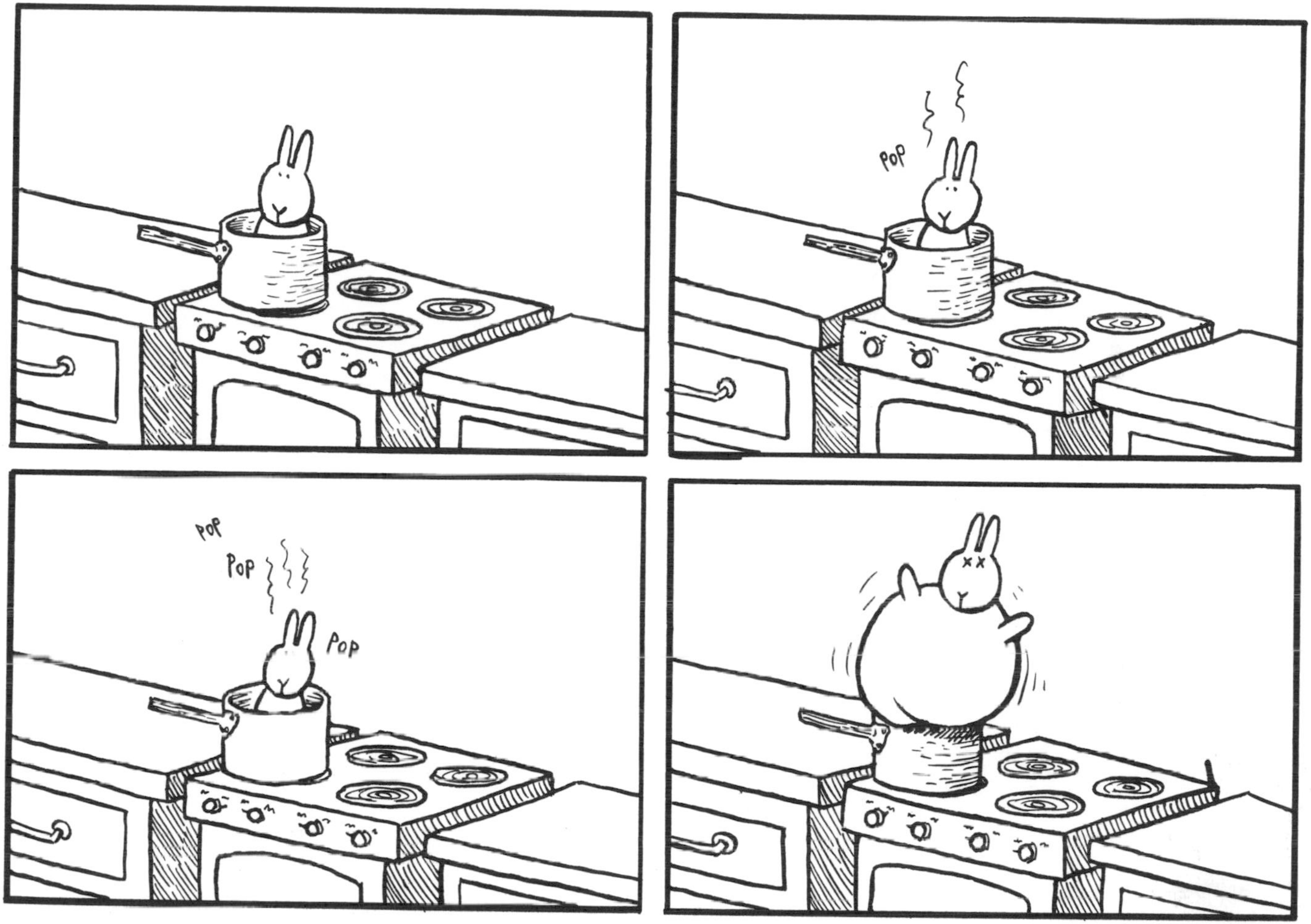
POP
POP
POP
POP

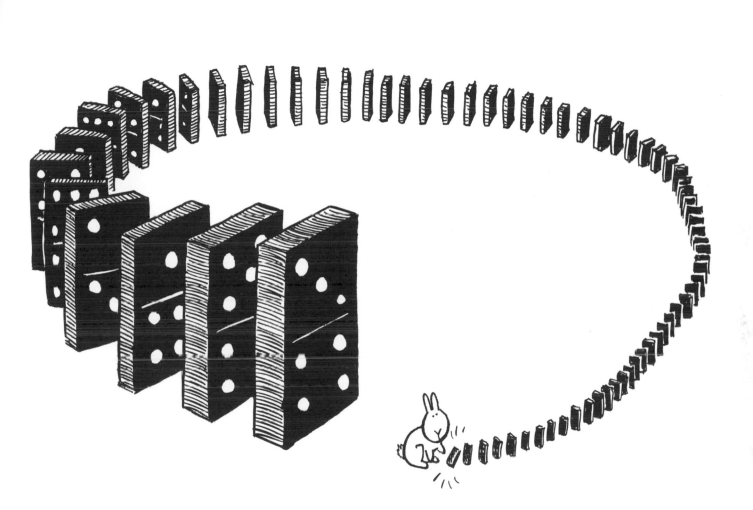

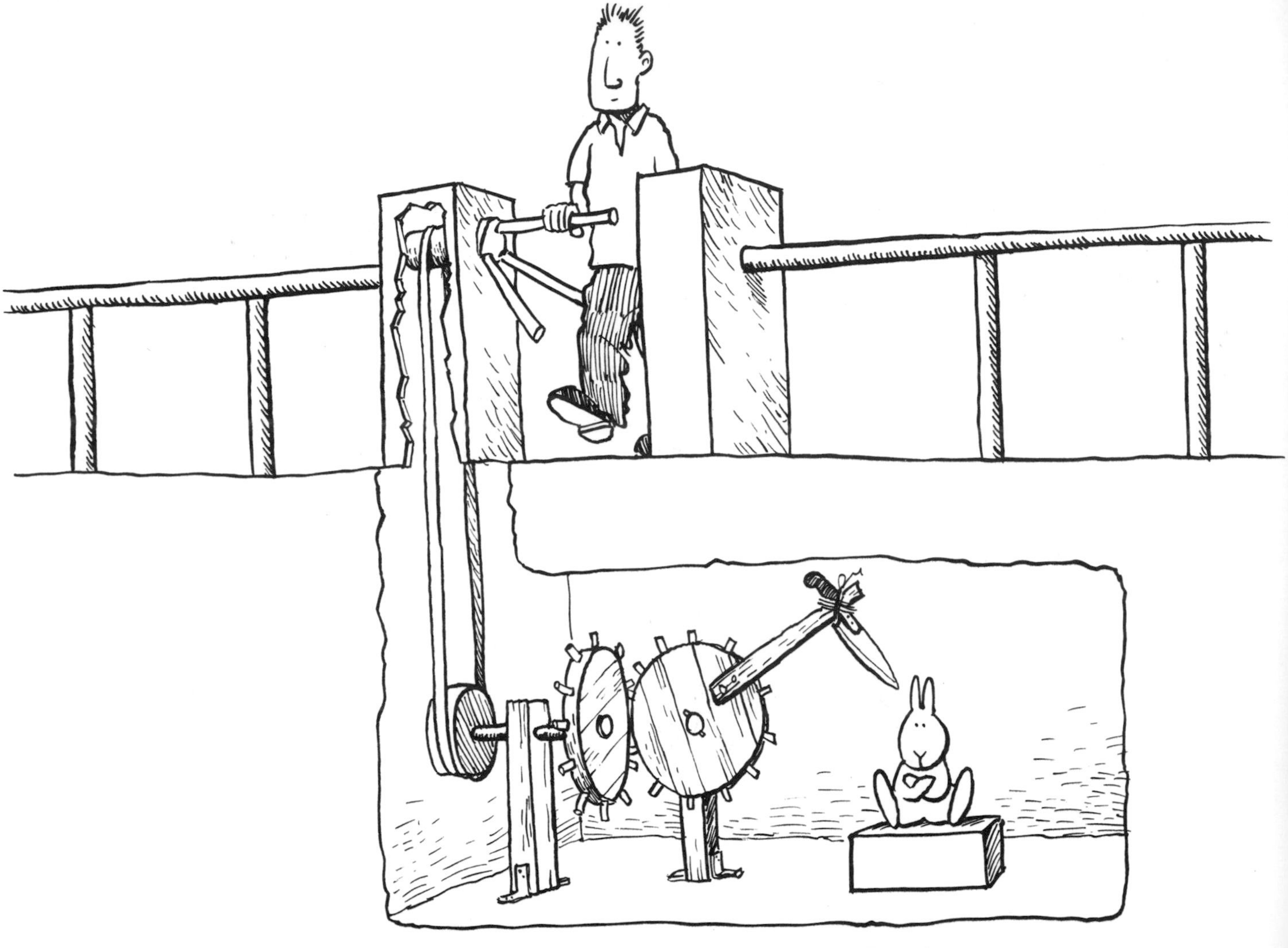

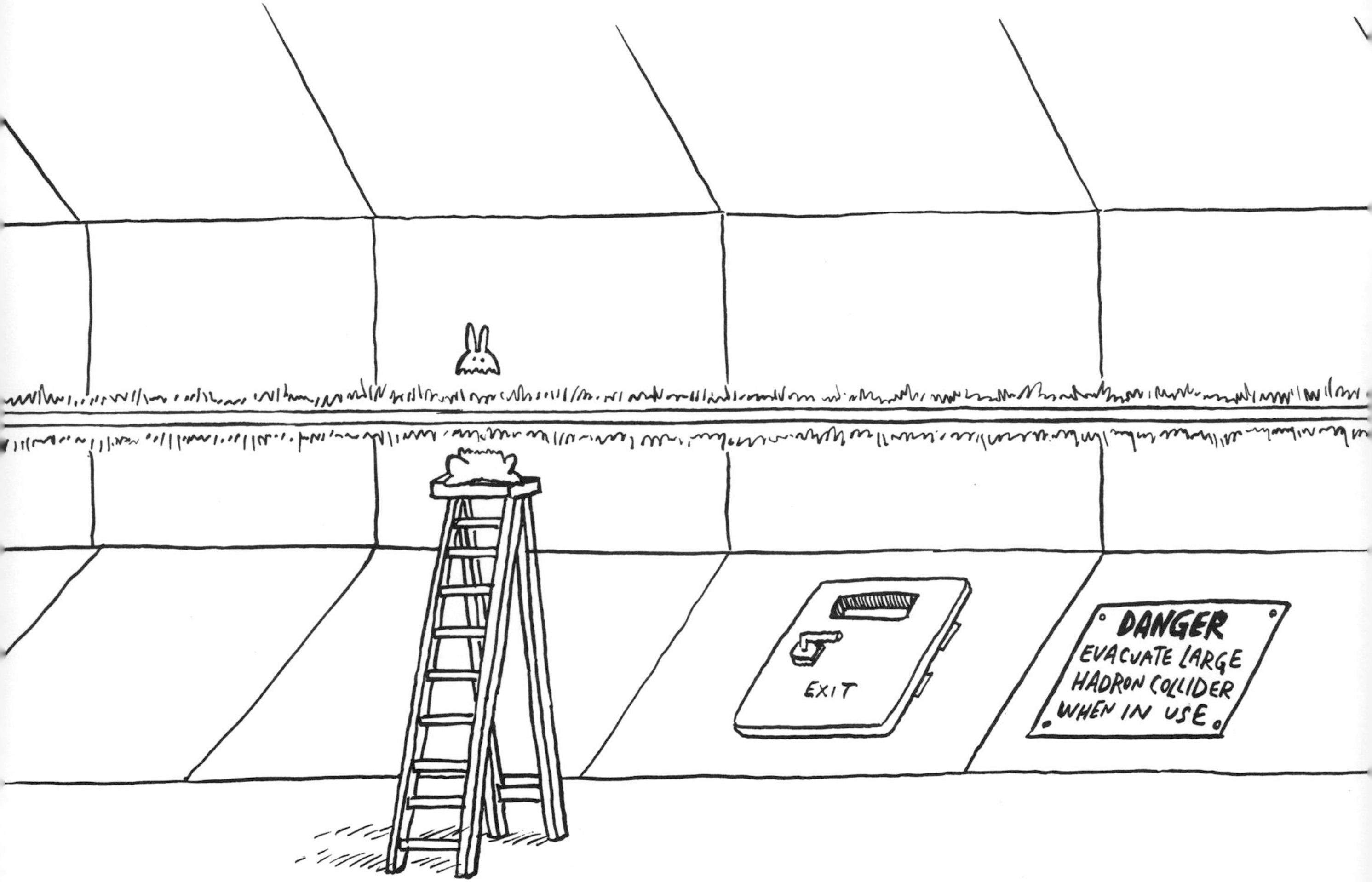
EXIT
DANGER
EVACUATE LARGE HADRON COLLIDER WHEN IN USE.

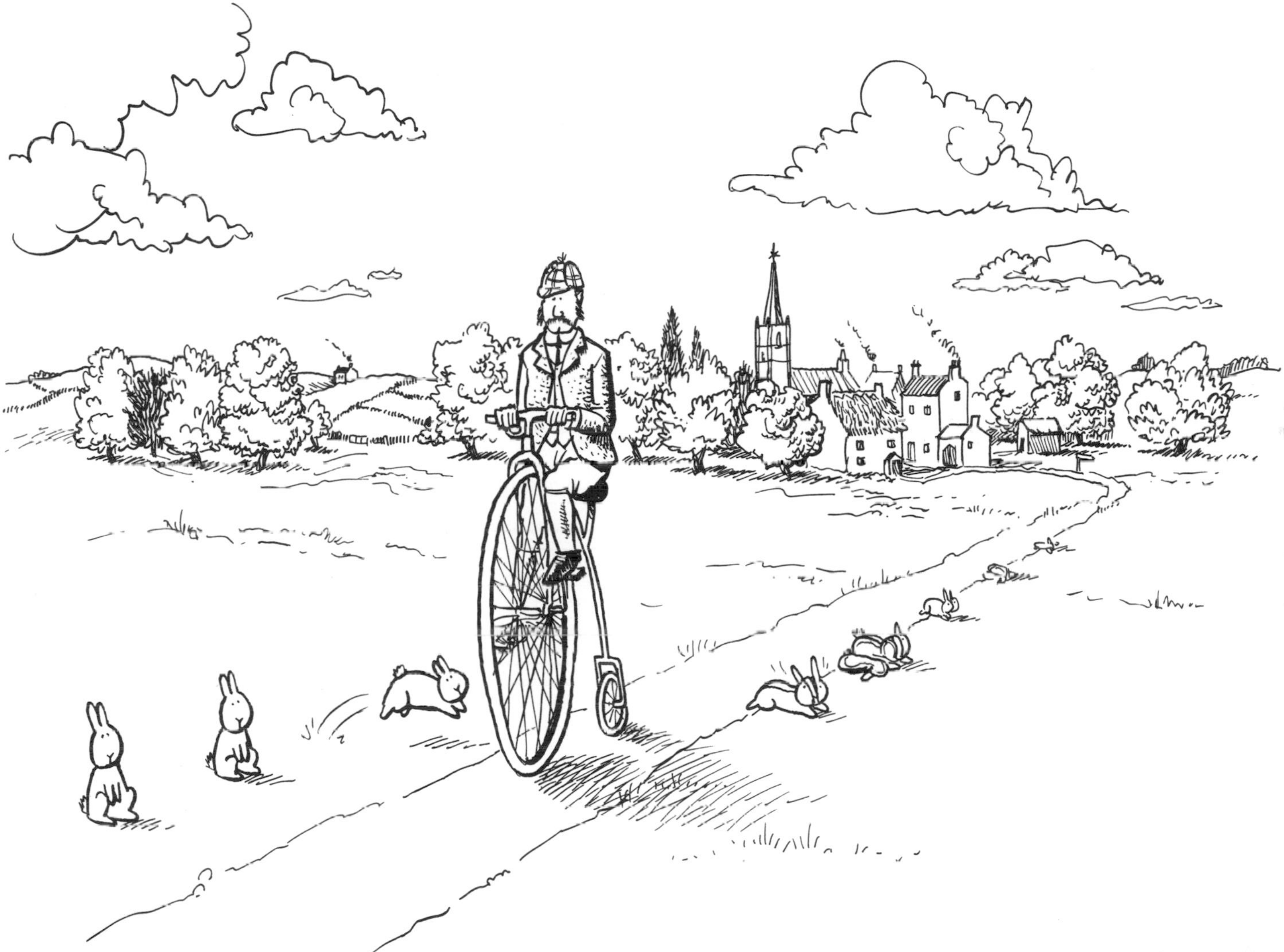

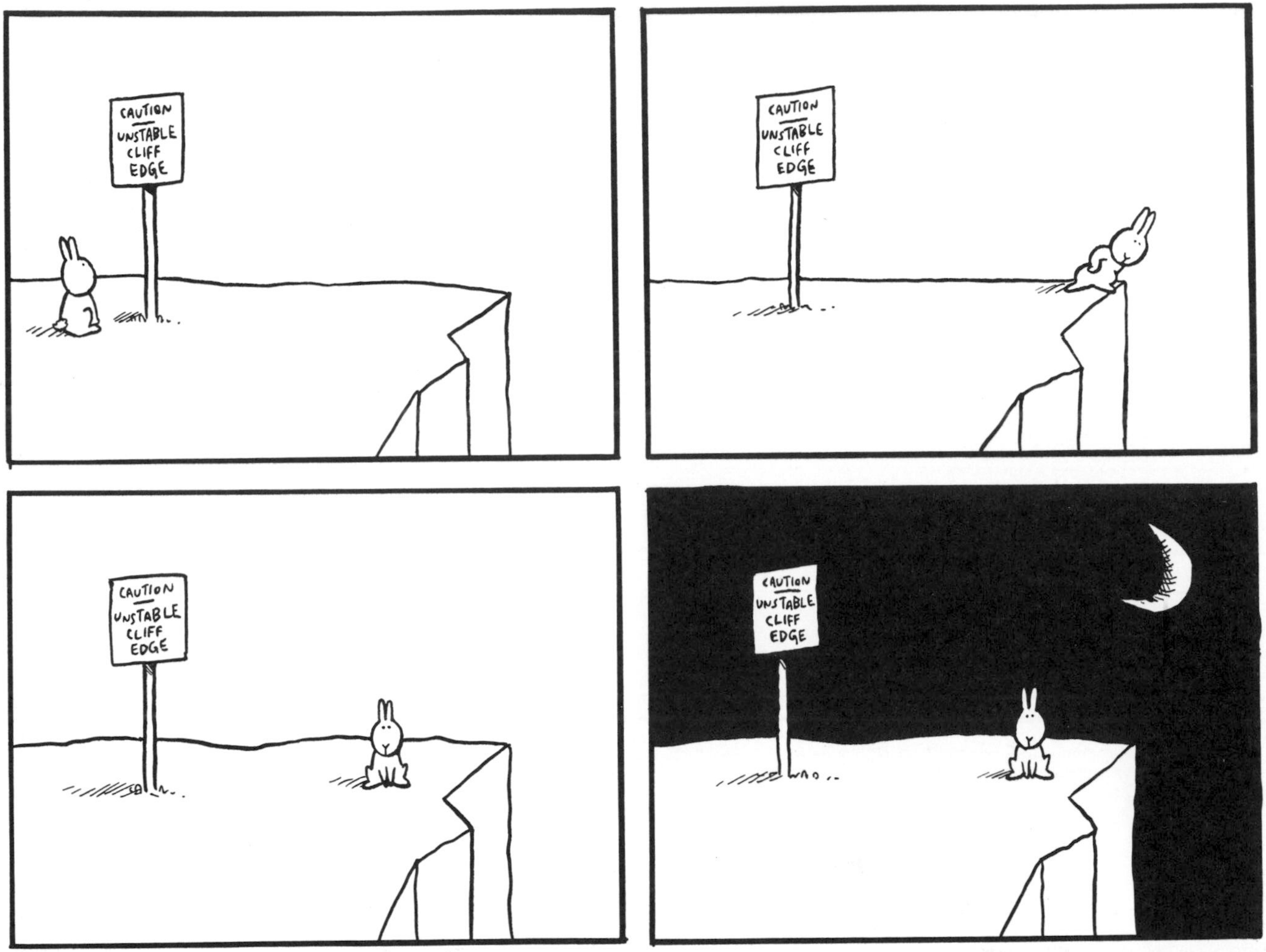

CAUTION
UNSTABLE CLIFF EDGE
CAUTION
UNSTABLE CLIFF EDGE
CAUTION
UNSTABLE CLIFF EDGE
CAUTION
UNSTABLE CLIFF EDGE

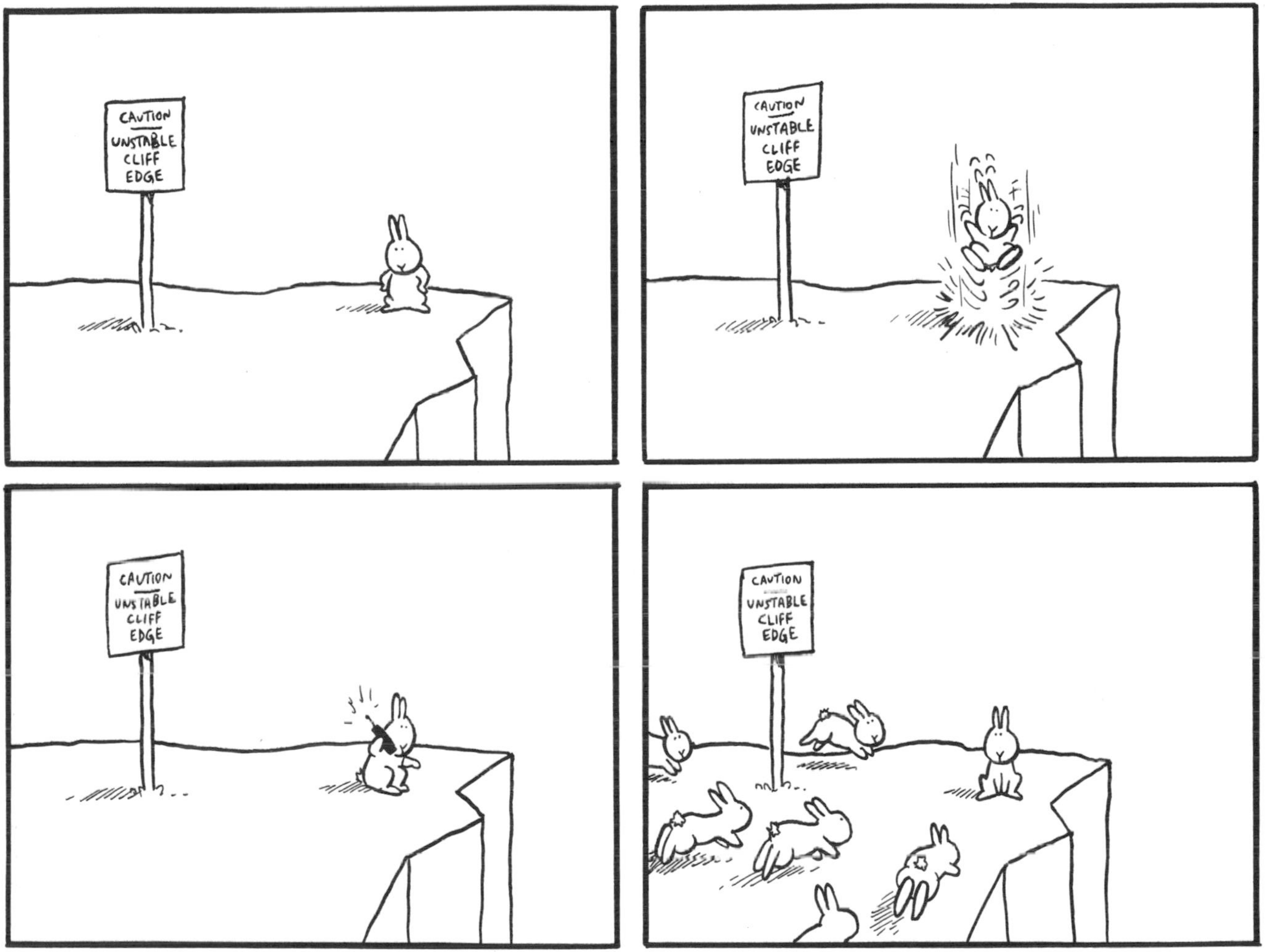
CAUTION
UNSTABLE
CLIFF
EDGE
CAUTION
UNSTABLE
CLIFF
EDGE
CAUTION
UNSTABLE
CLIFF
EDGE
CAUTION
UNSTABLE
CLIFF
EDGE

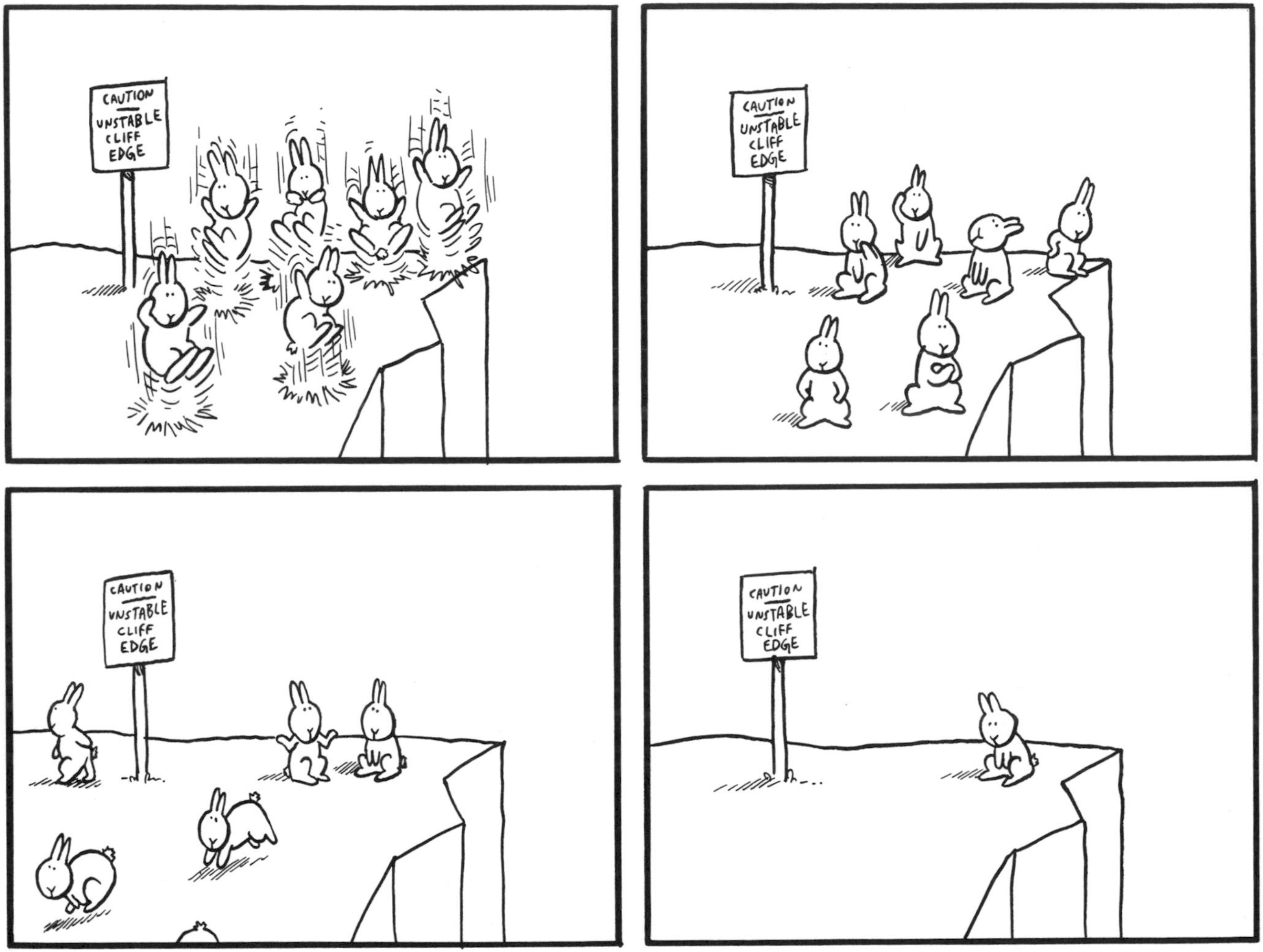
CAUTION
UNSTABLE CLIFF EDGE
CAUTION
UNSTABLE CLIFF EDGE
CAUTION
UNSTABLE CLIFF EDGE
CAUTION
UNSTABLE CLIFF EDGE

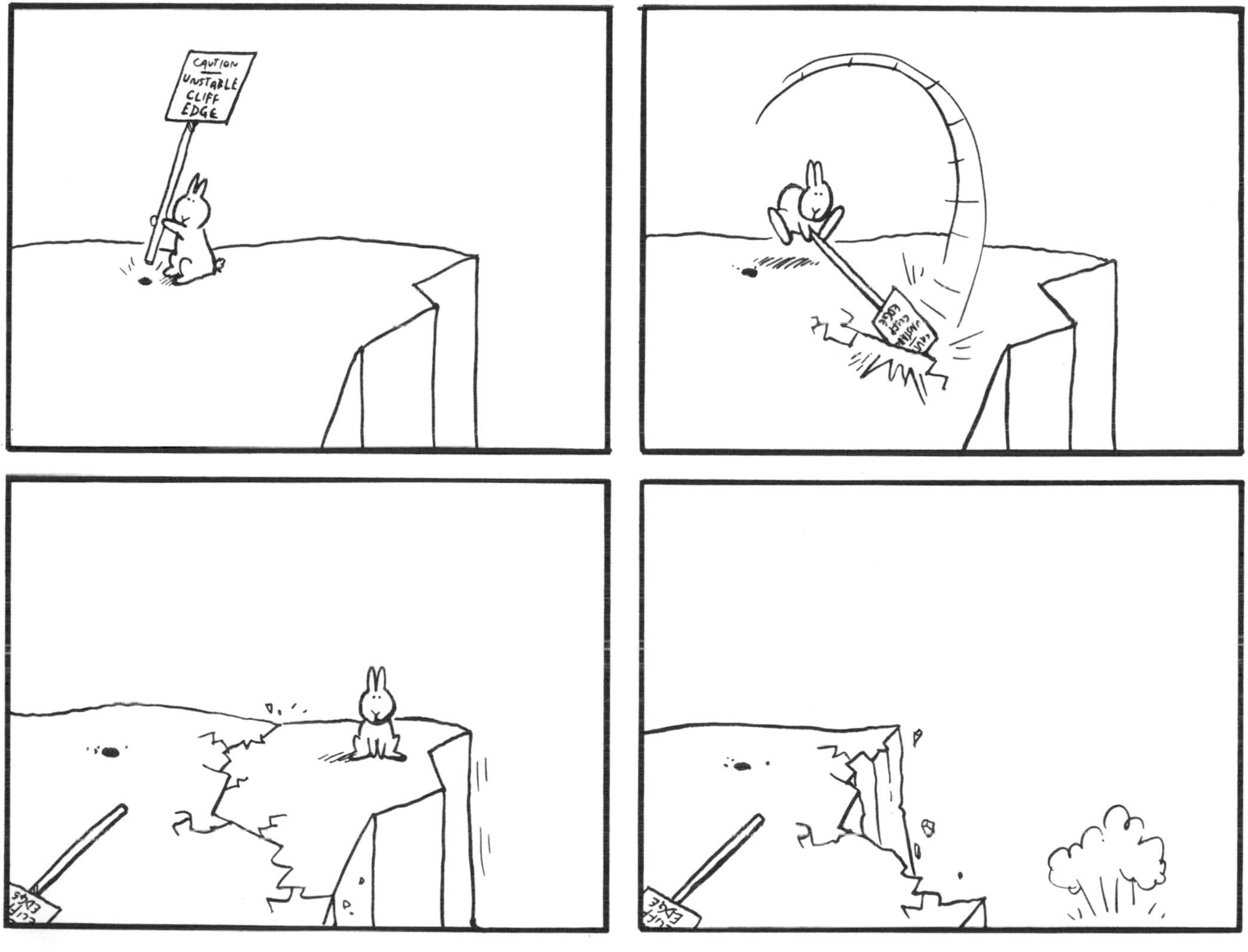
CAUTION
UNSTABLE CLIFF EDGE

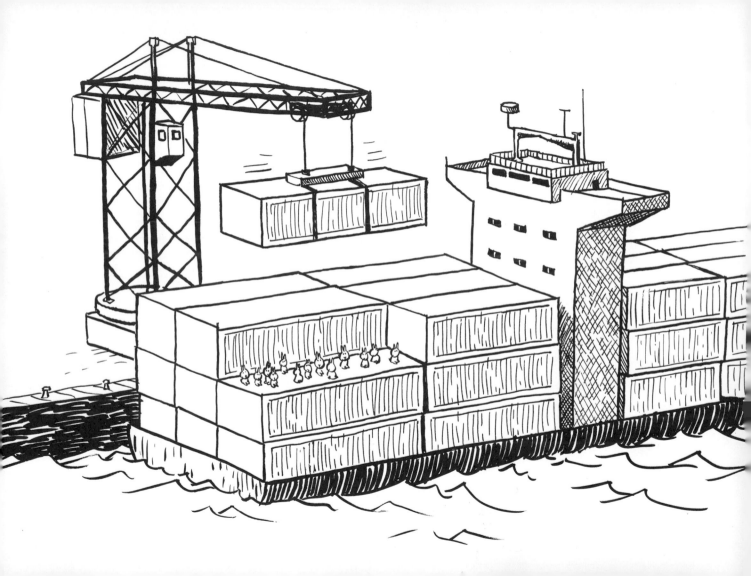

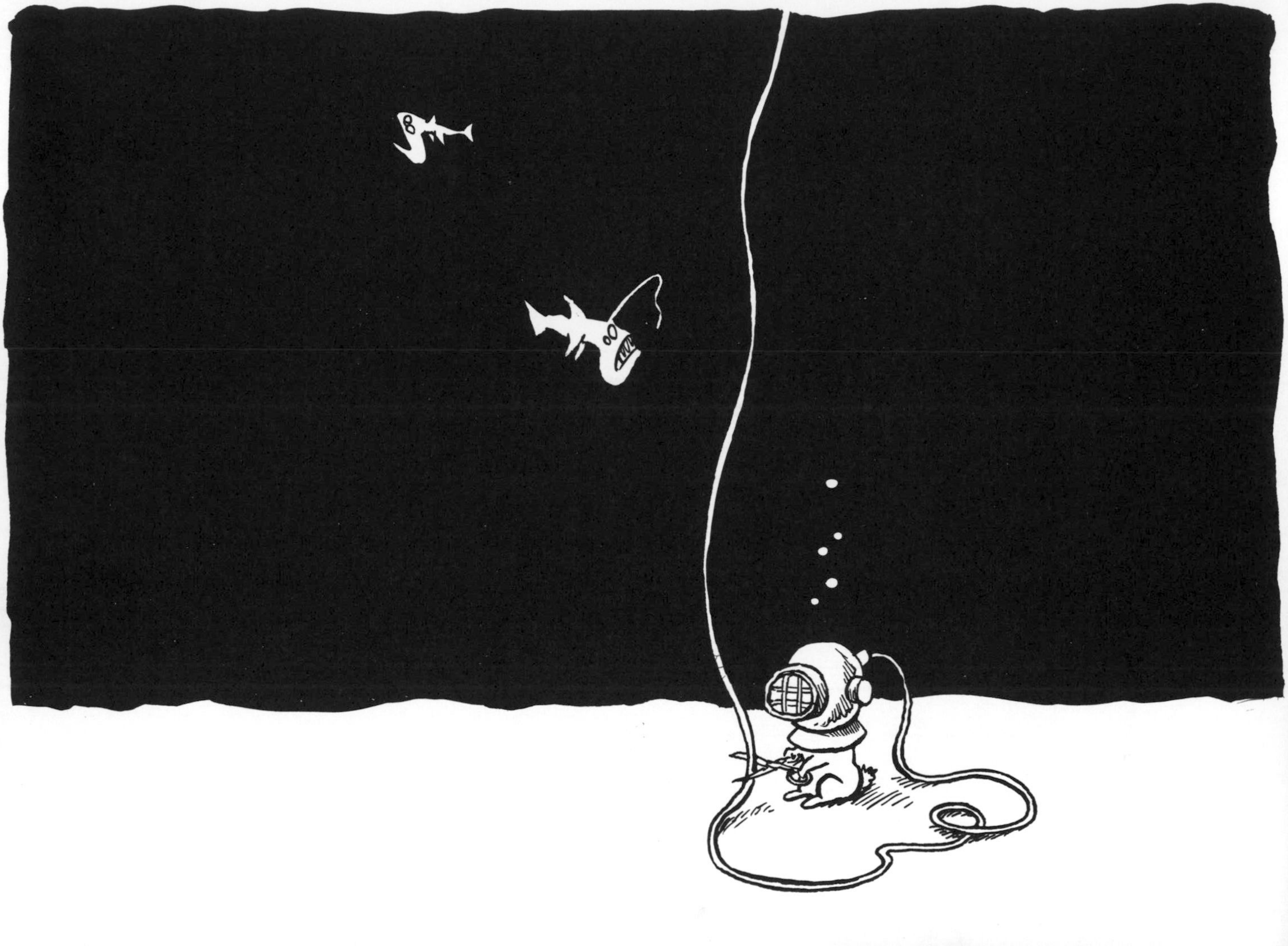

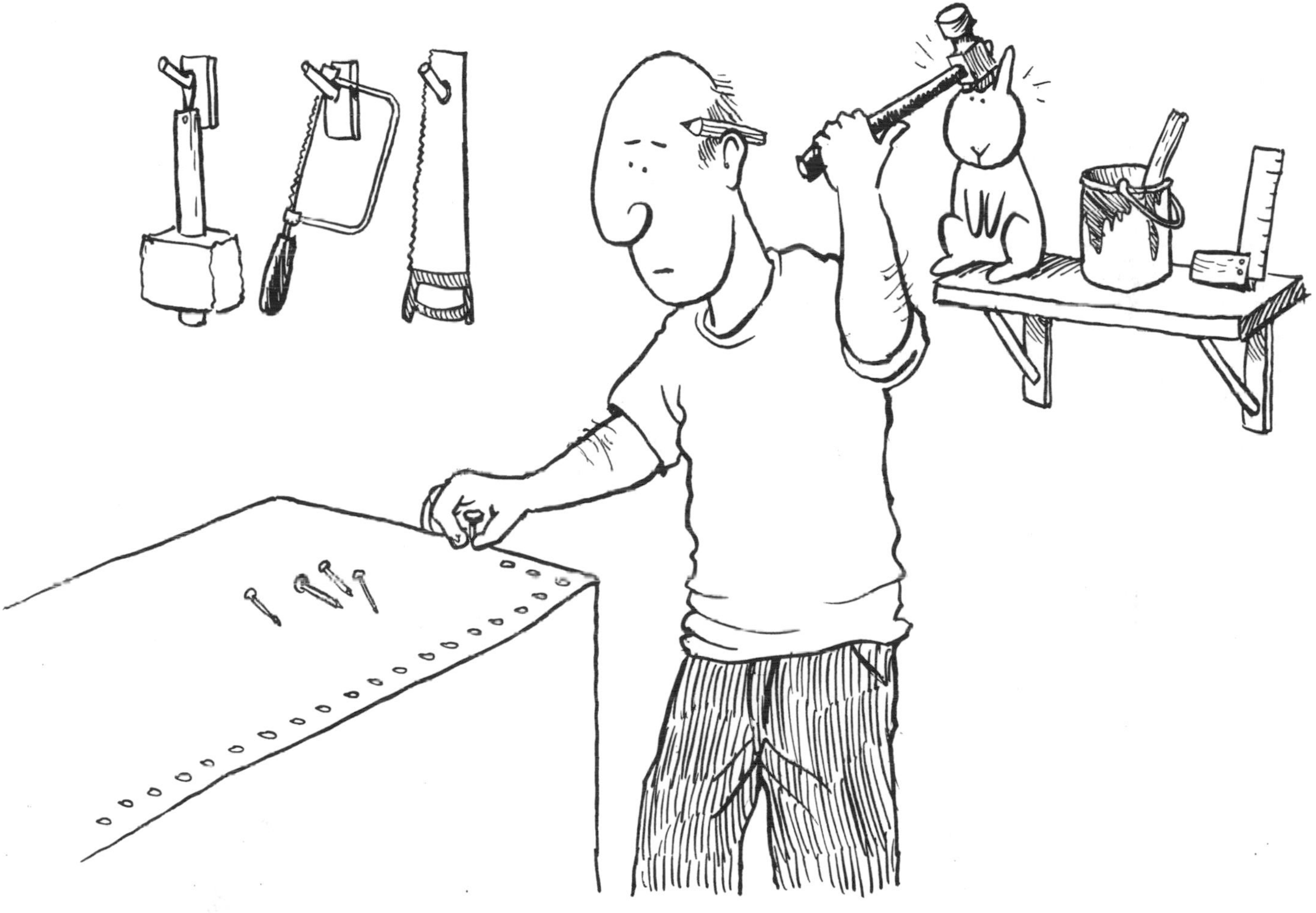

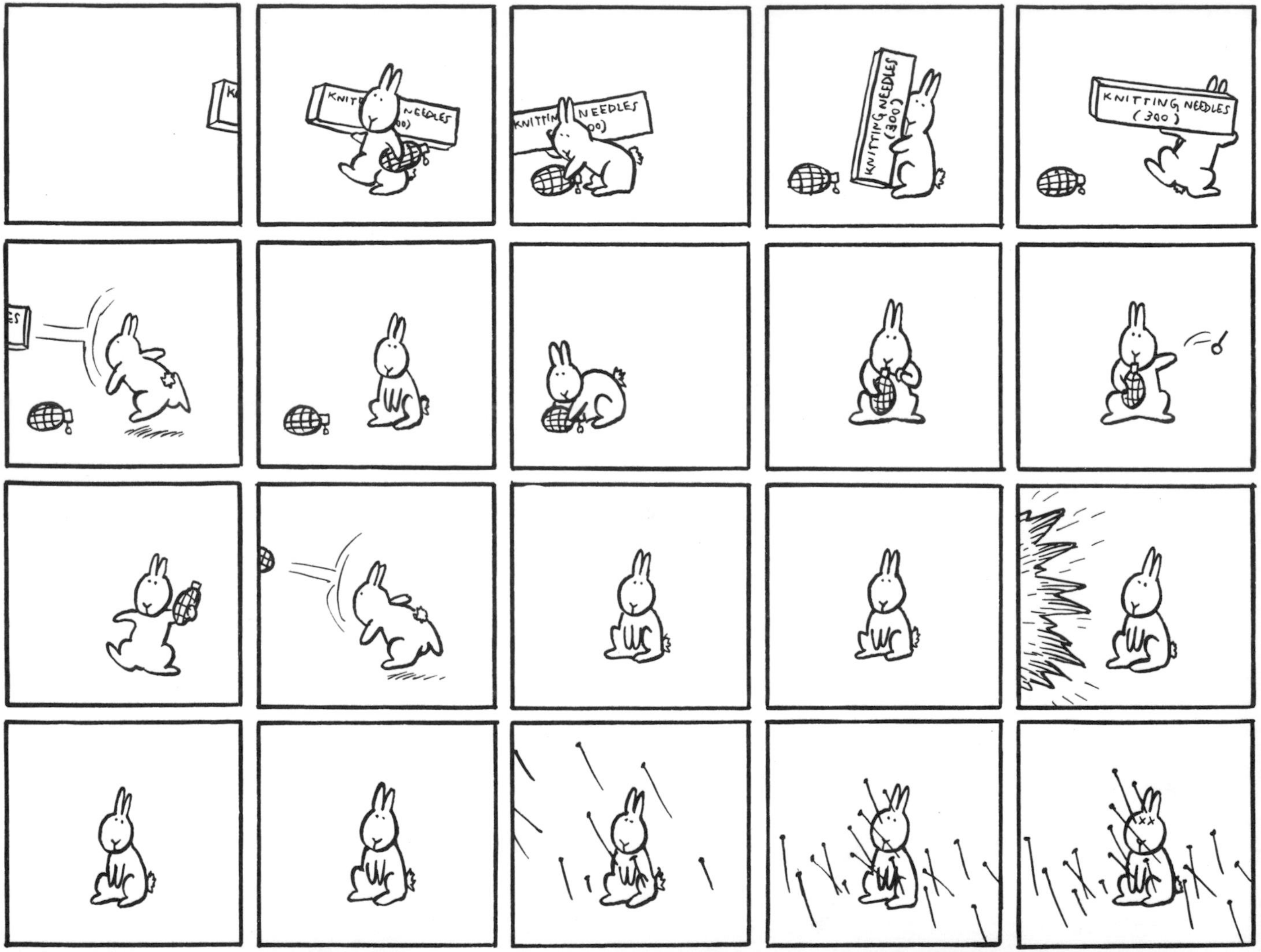

KNITTING NEEDLES (300)
KNITTING NEEDLES (300)

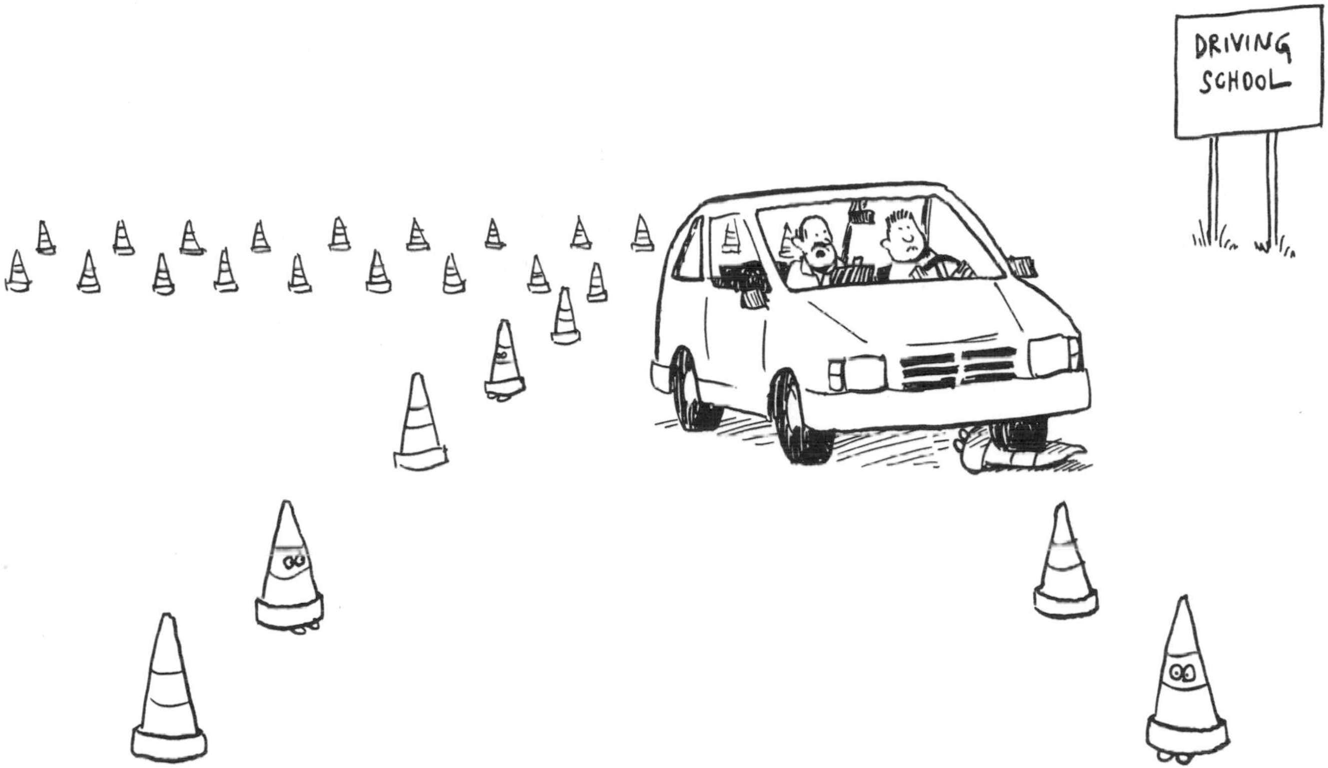
DRIVING
SCHOOL

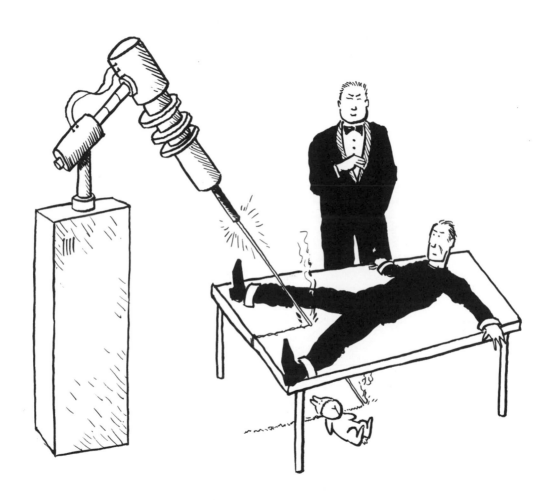

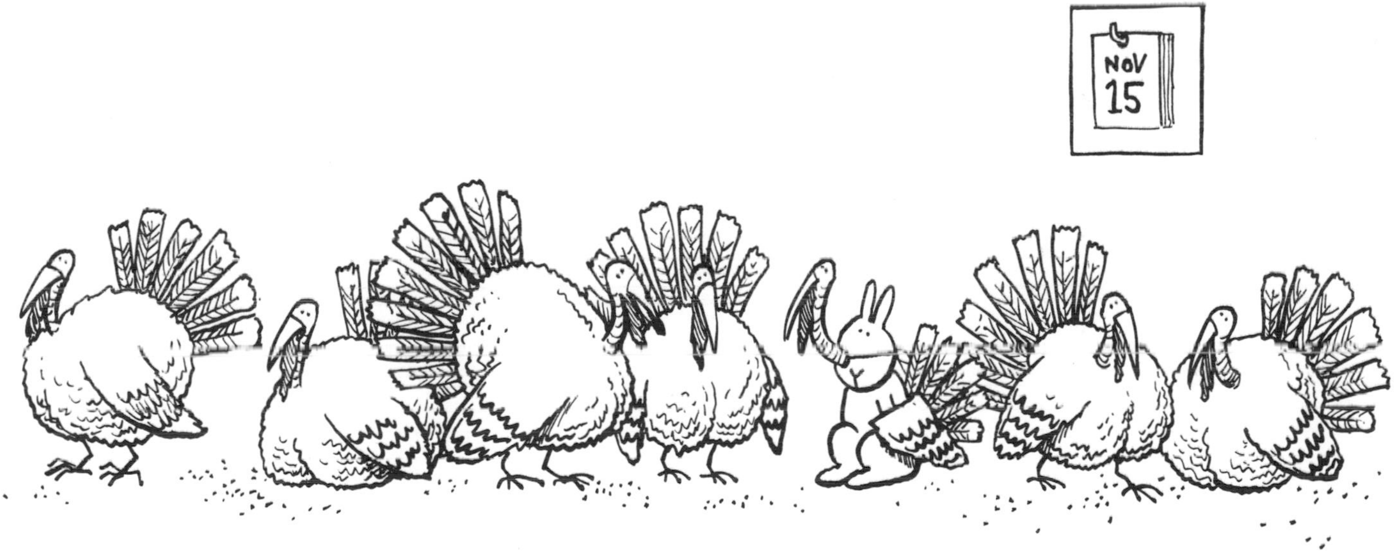
NOV
15

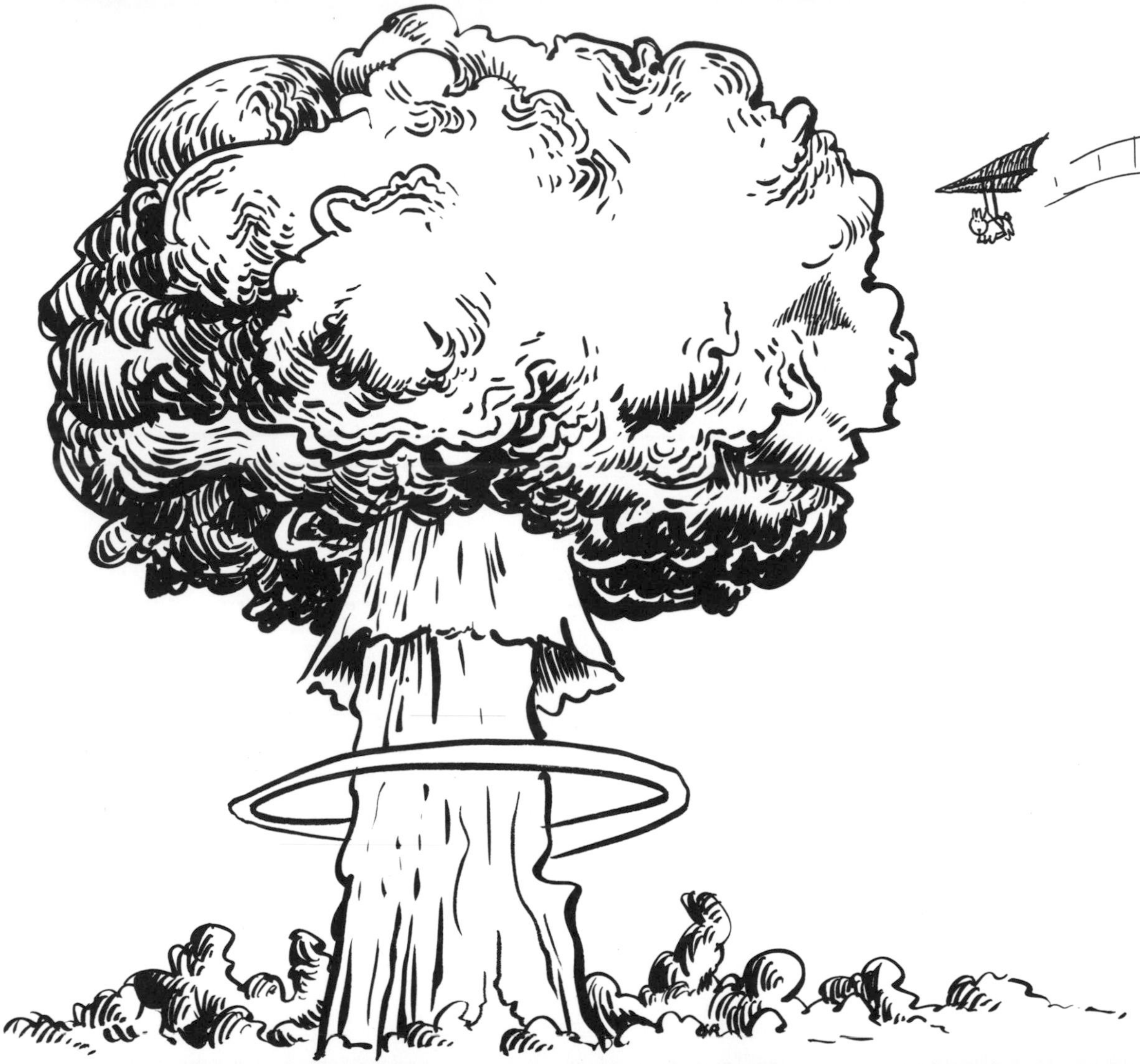

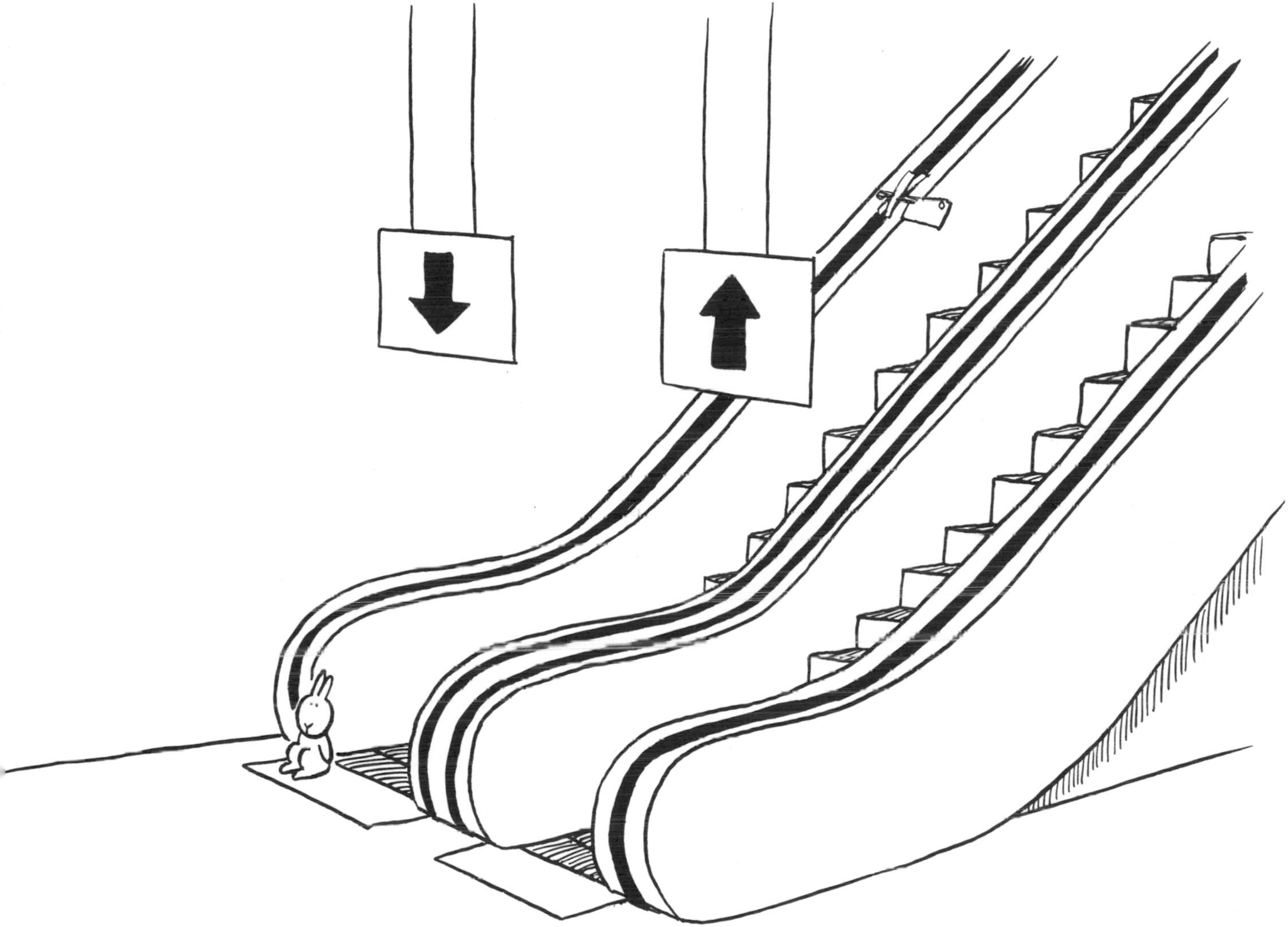

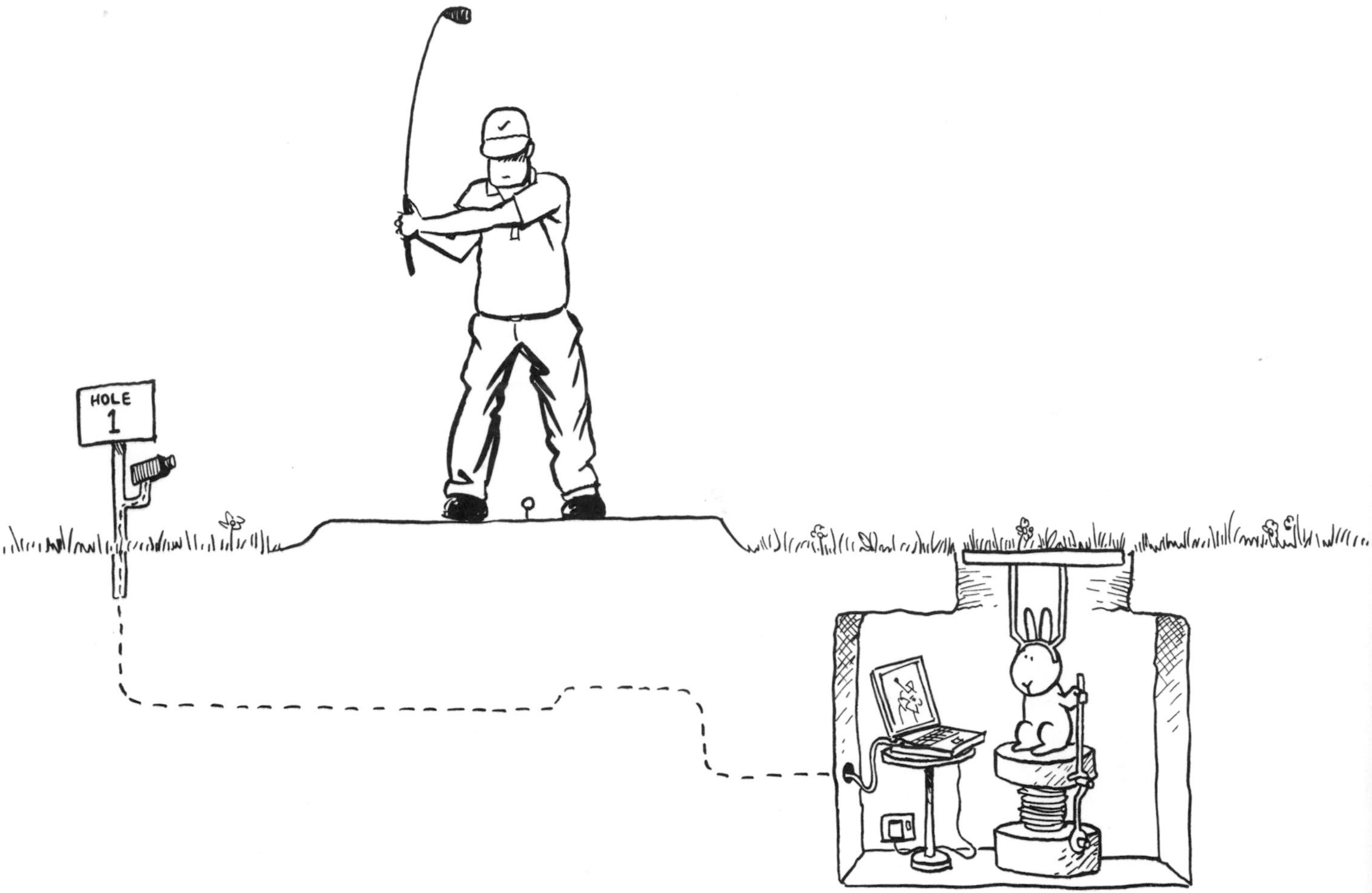
HOLE
1

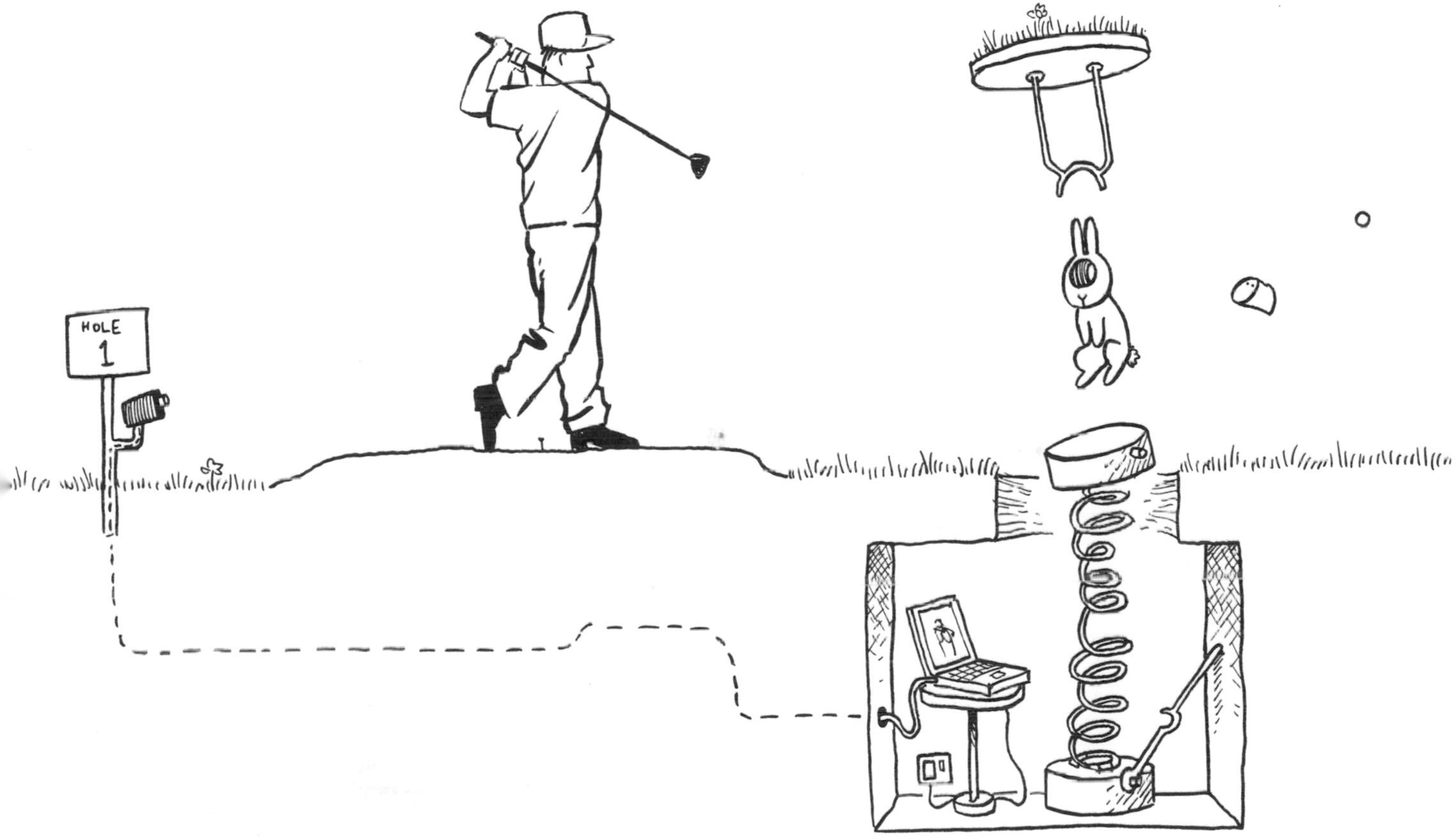
HOLE
1

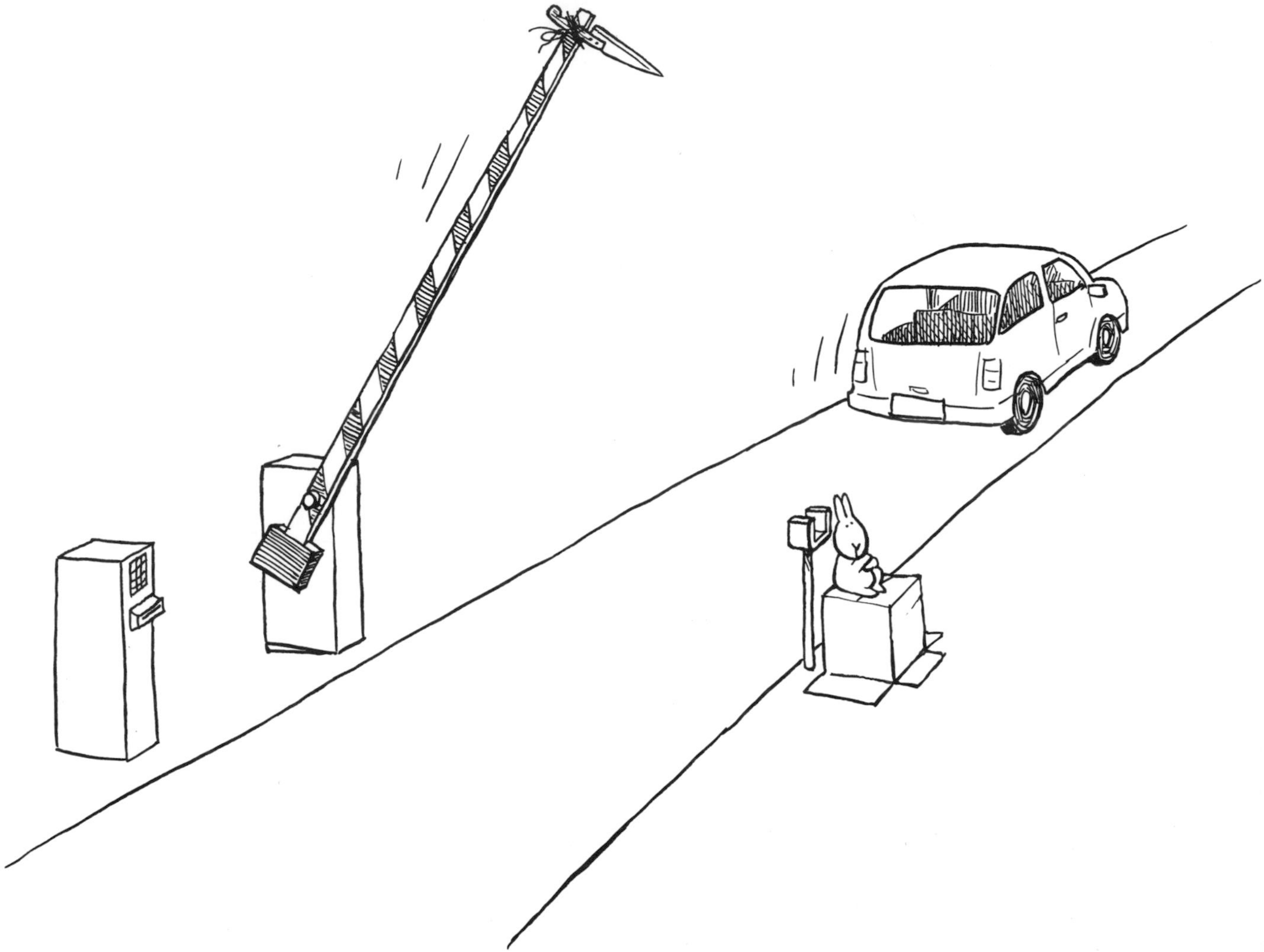

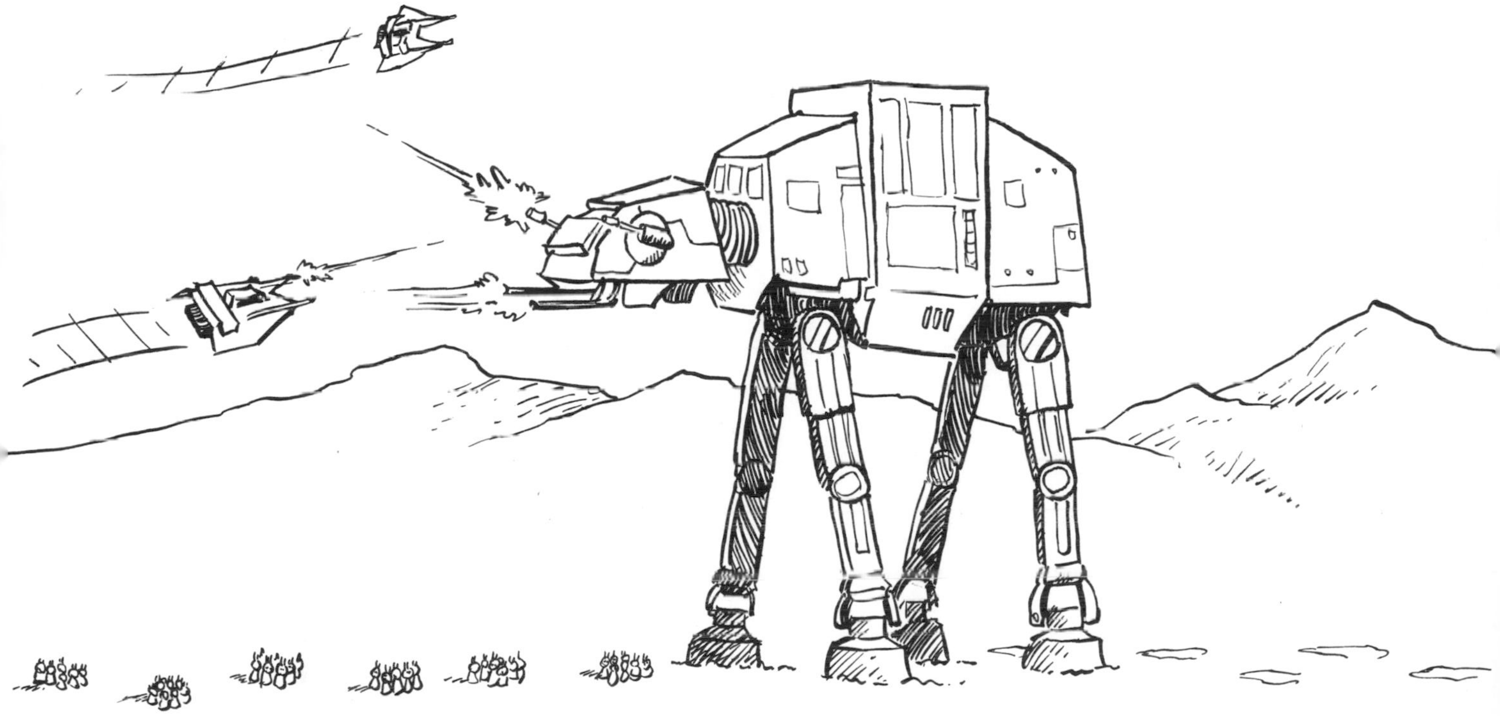

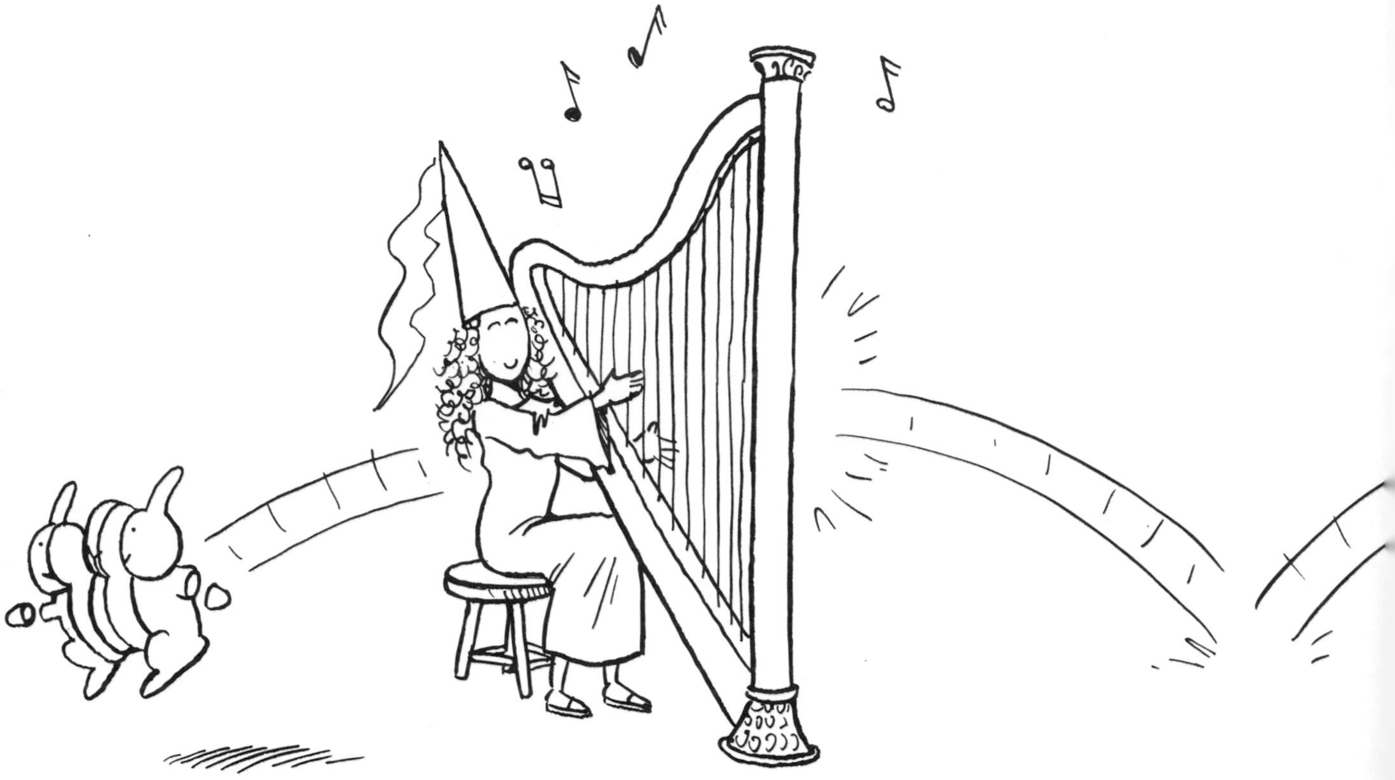

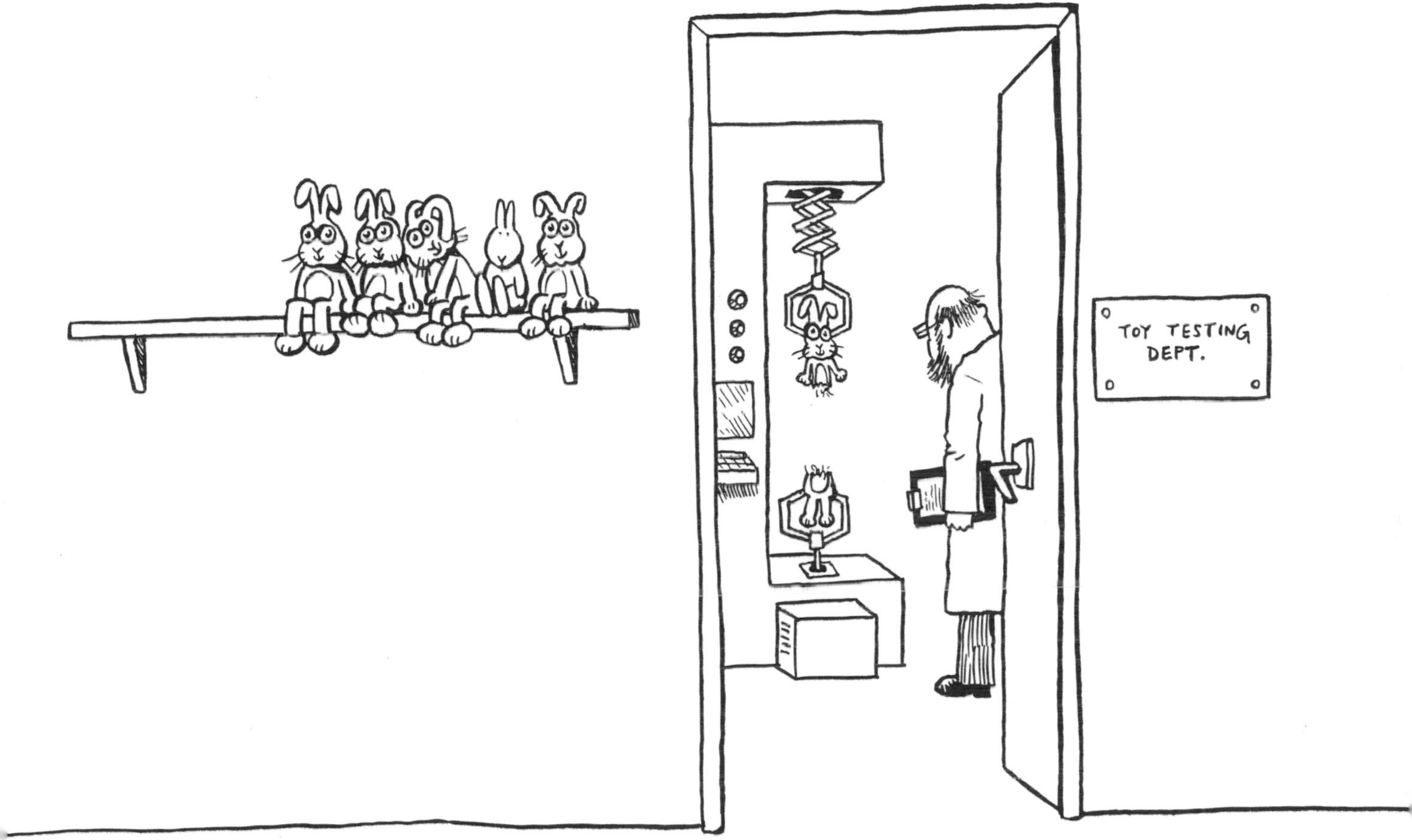
TOY TESTING
DEPT.

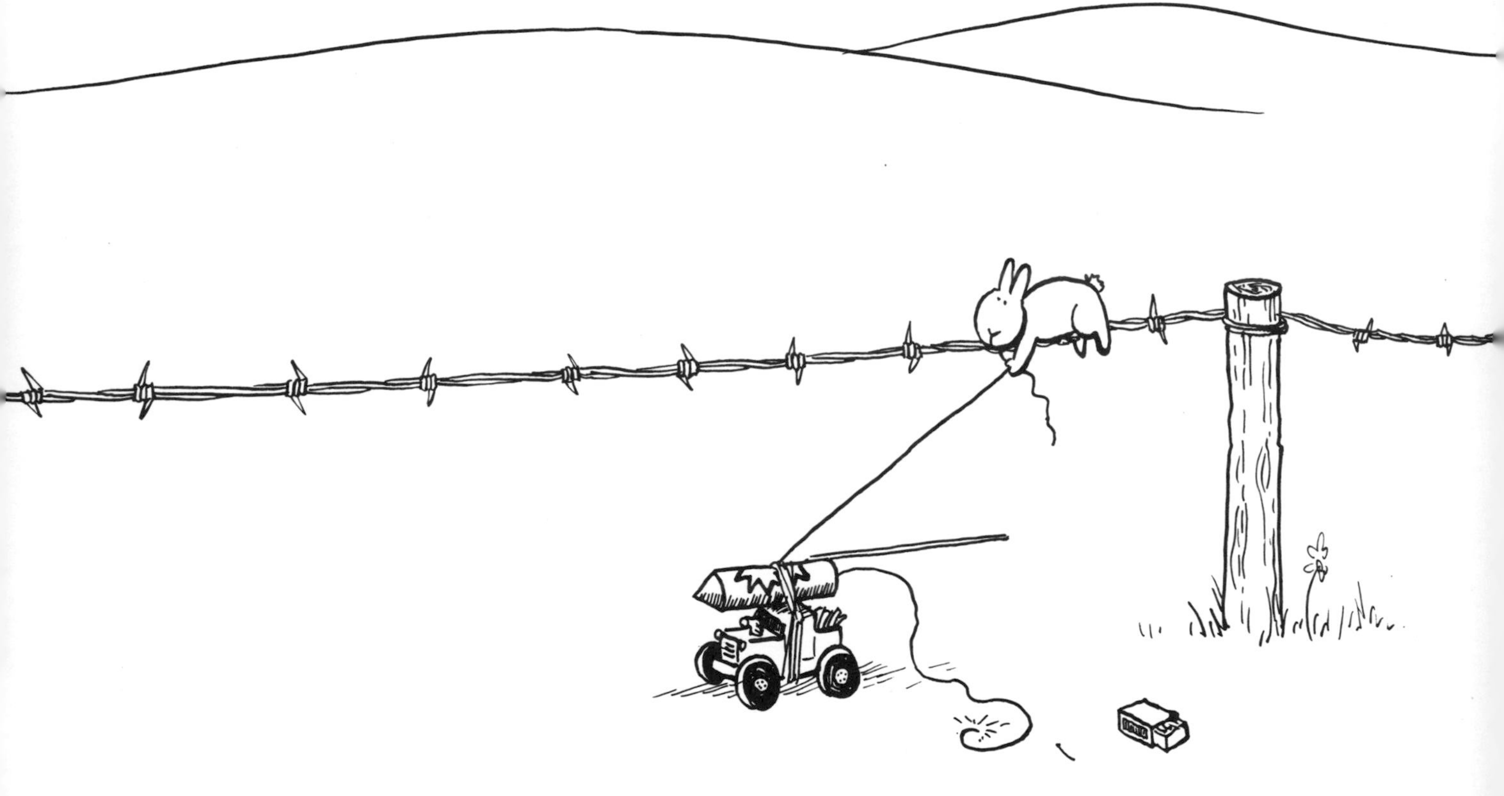

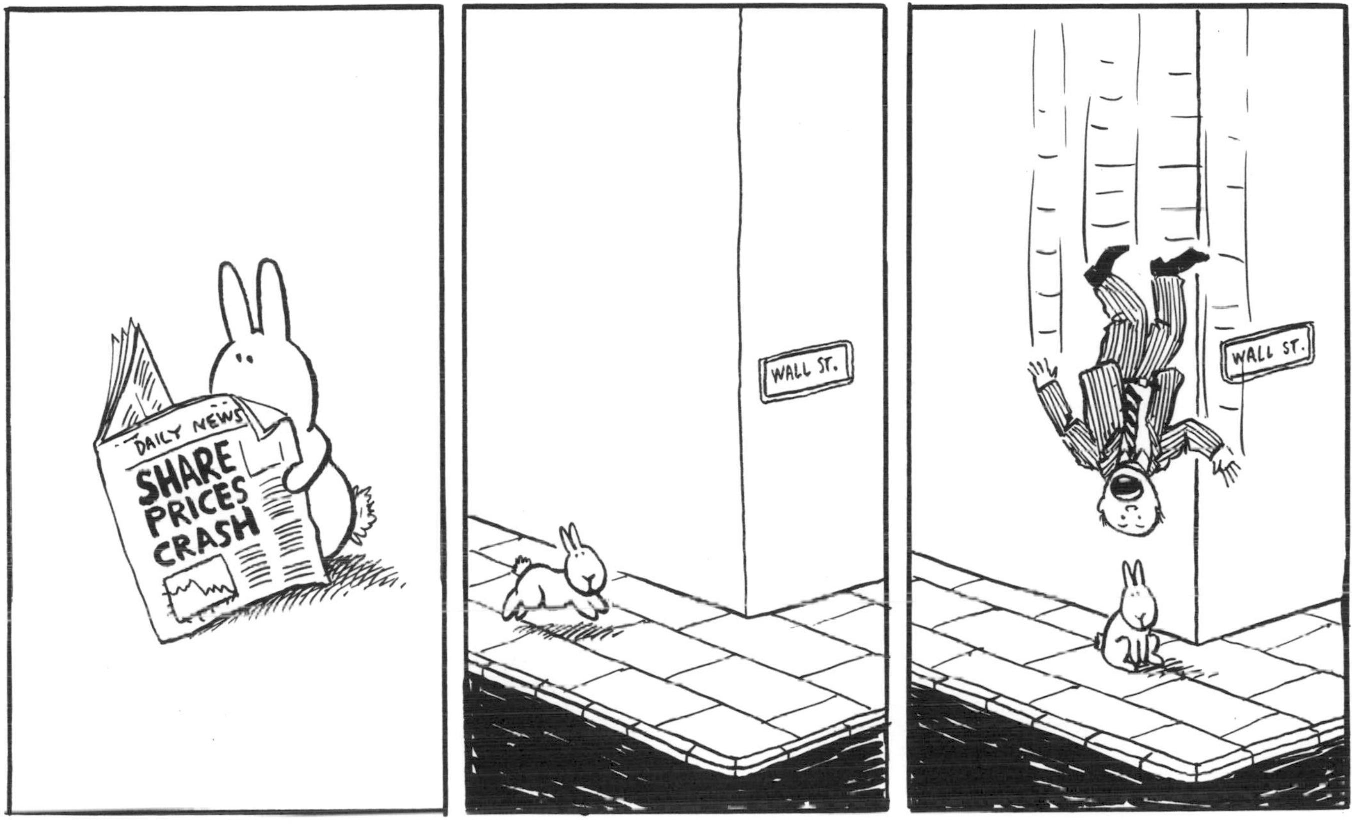
DAILY NEWS
SHARE PRICES CRASH
WALL ST.
WALL ST.

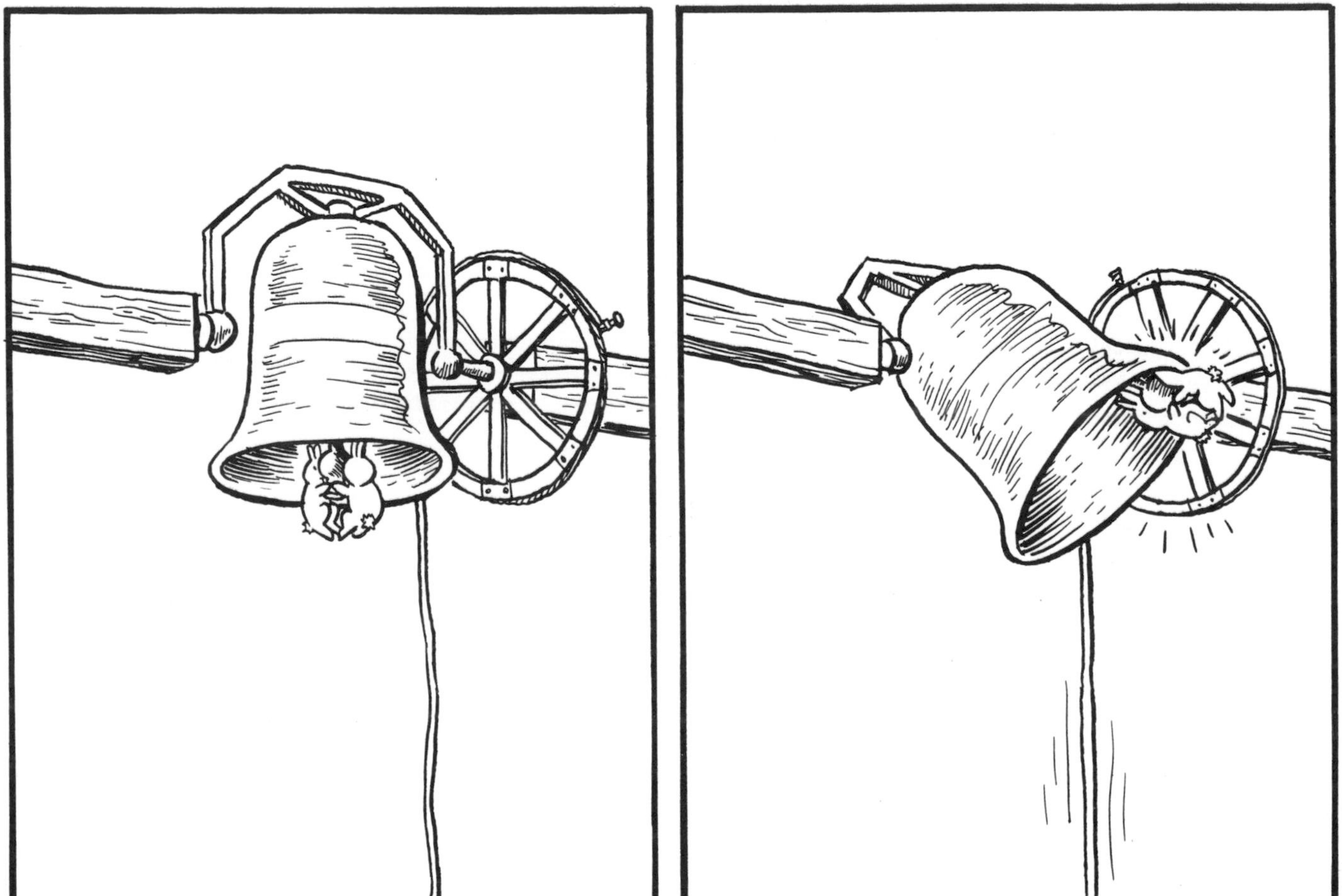

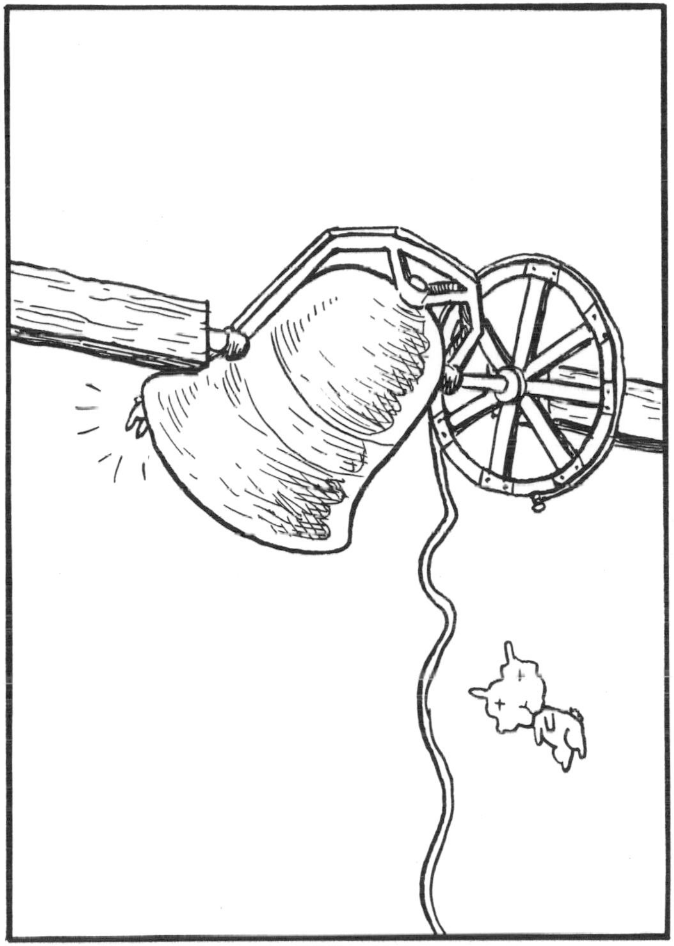
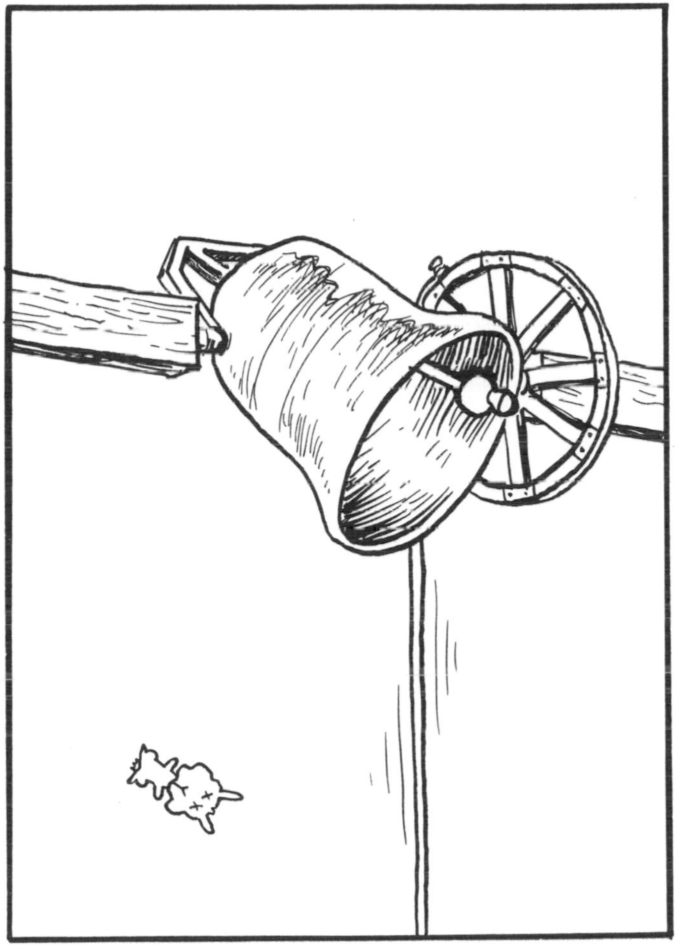

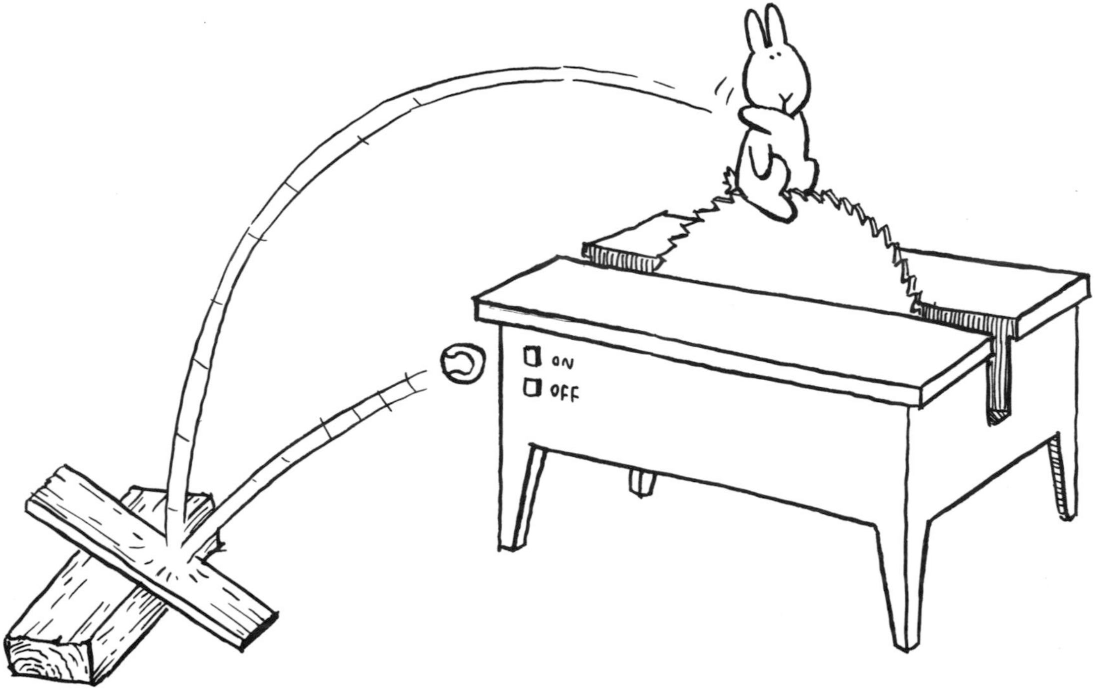
ON
OFF

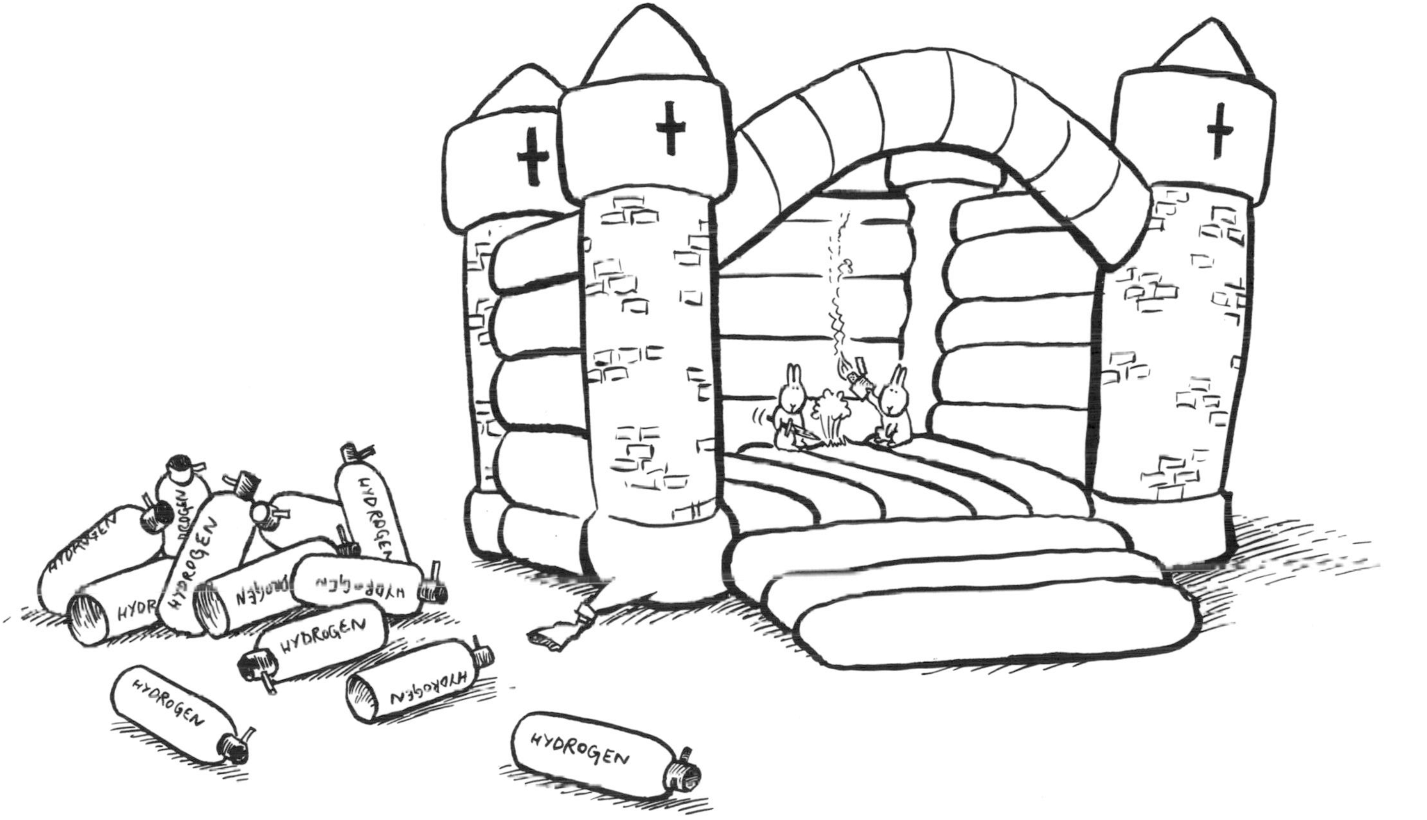

HYDROGEN
DROGEN
HYDROGEN
HYDROGEN
HYDR
HYDROGEN
HYDROGEN
HYDROGEN

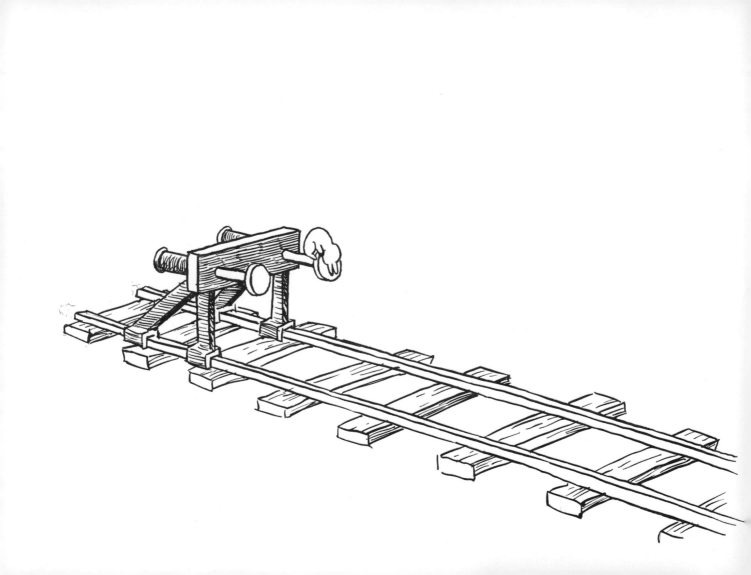

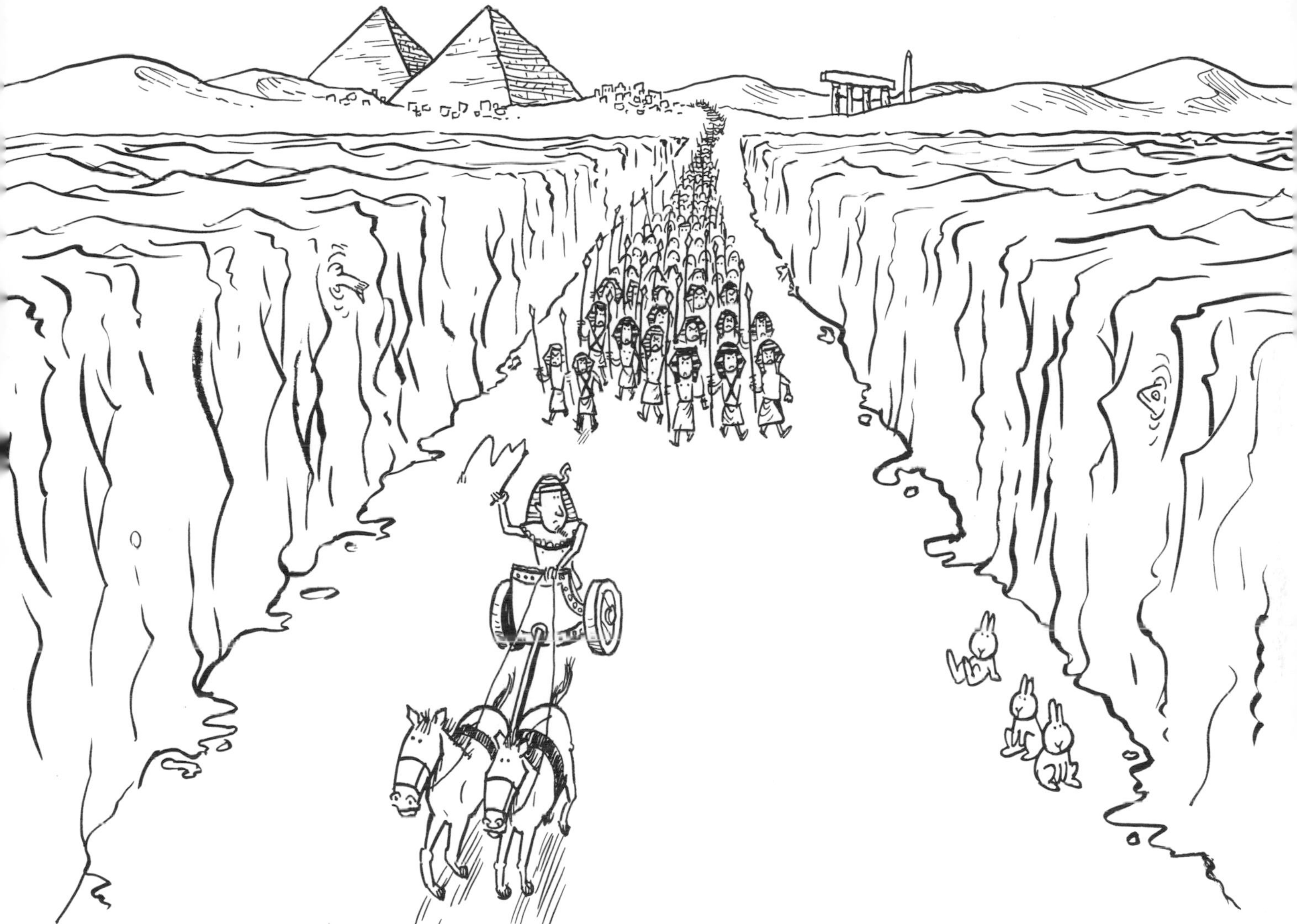

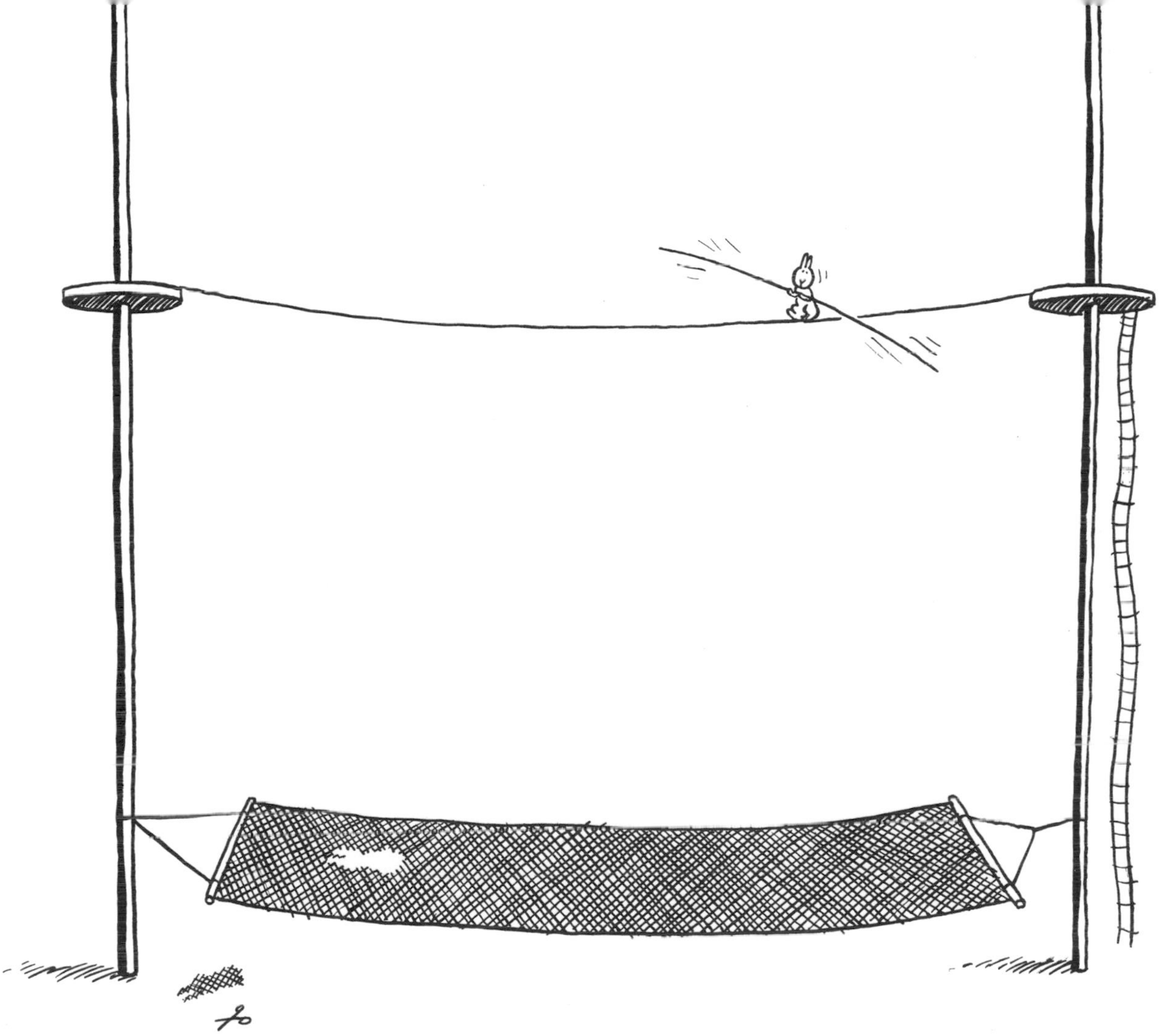

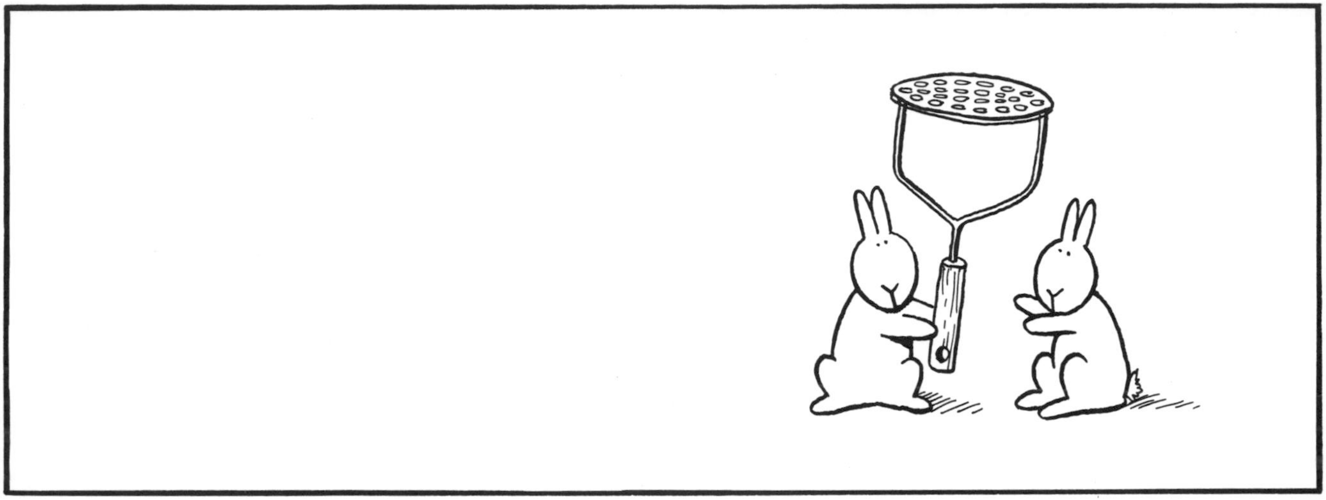

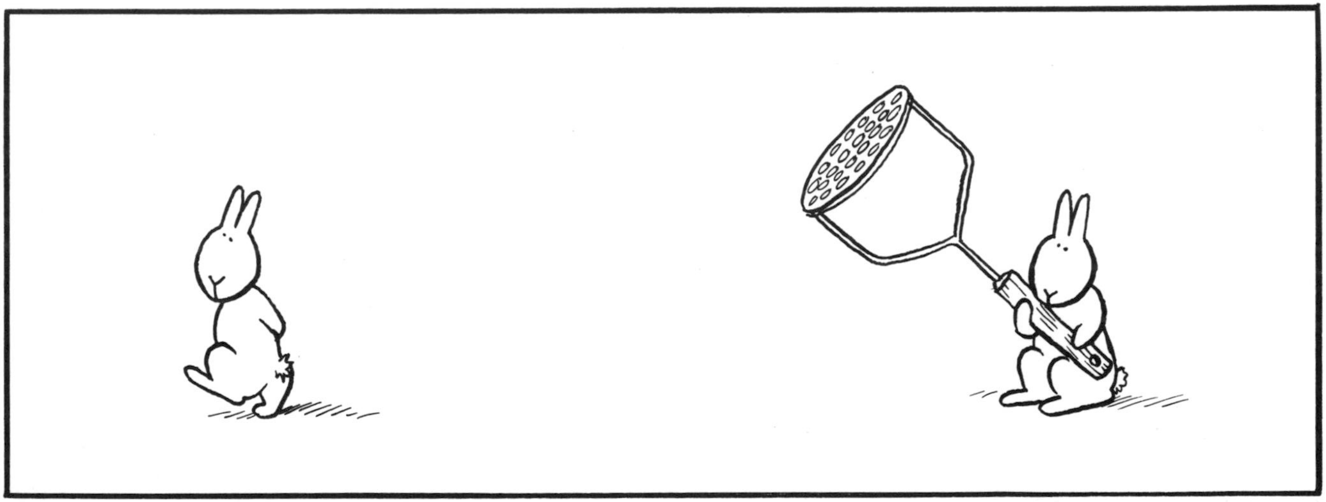

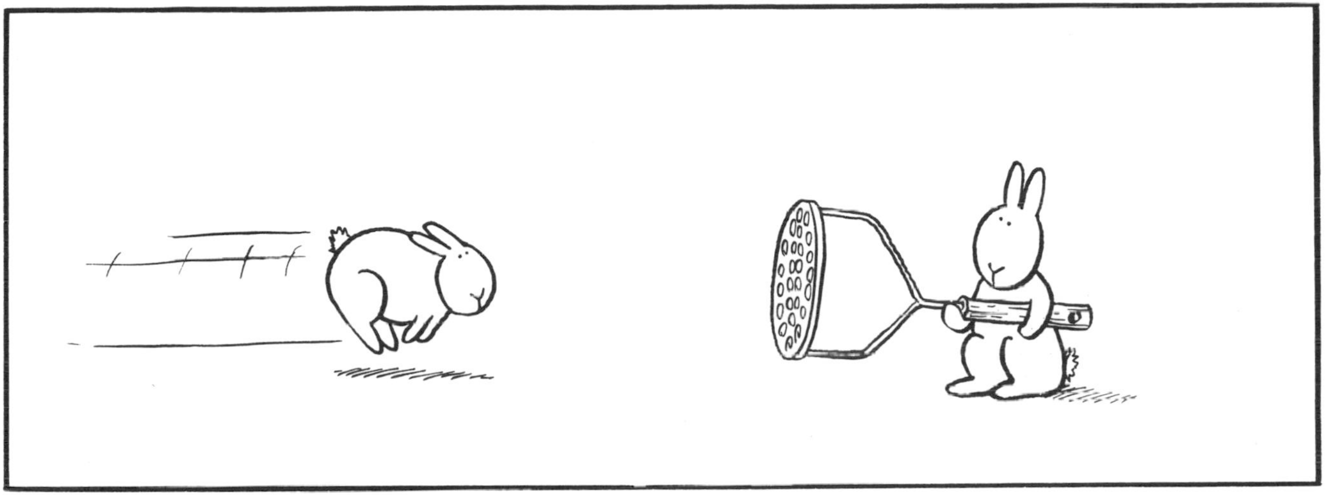

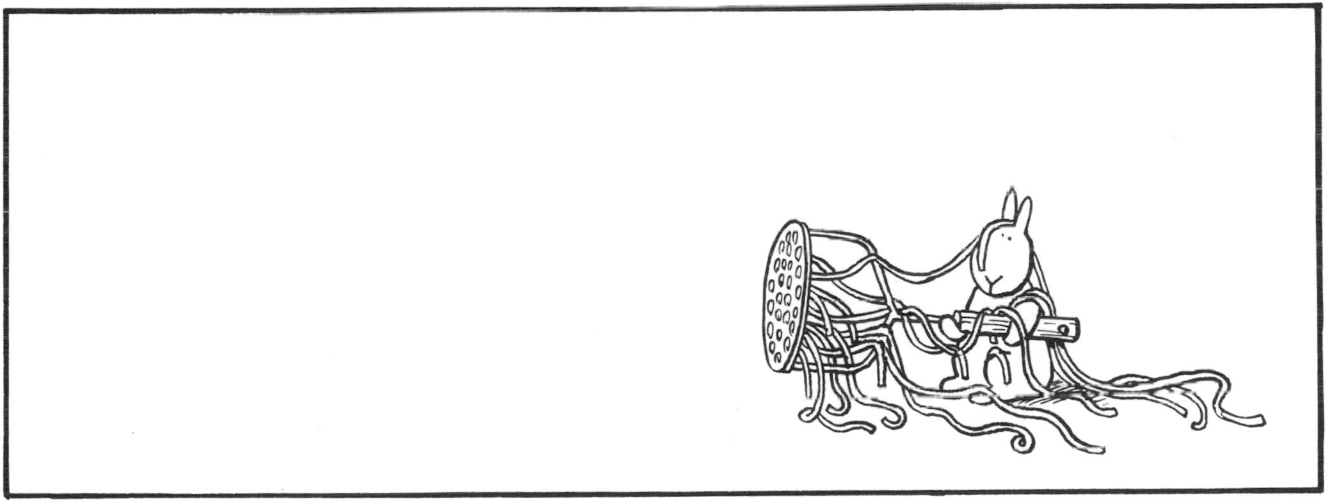

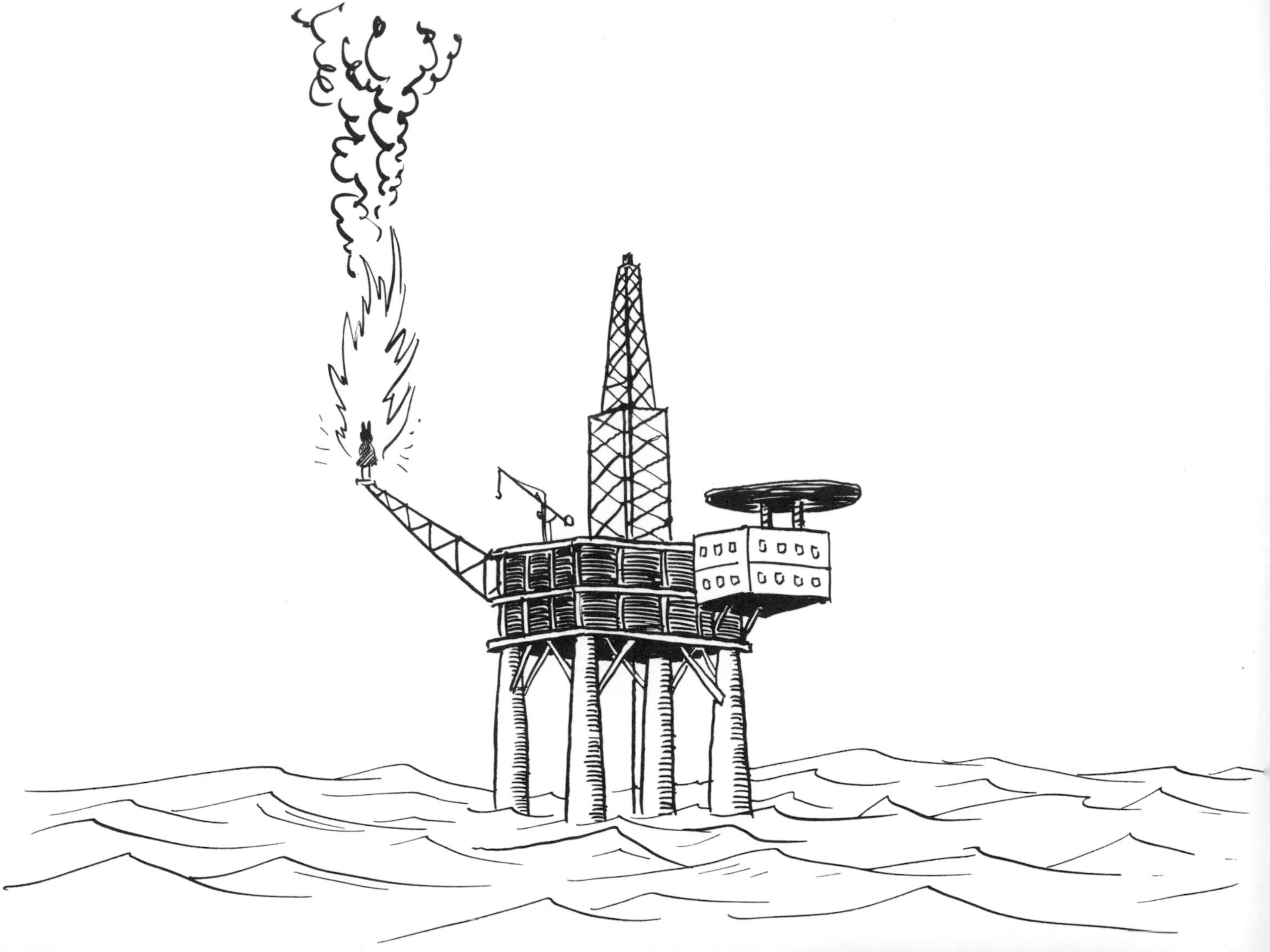

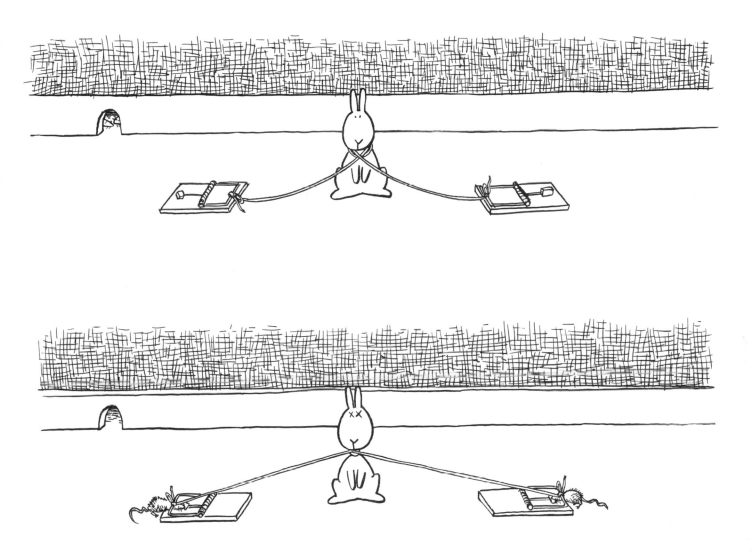

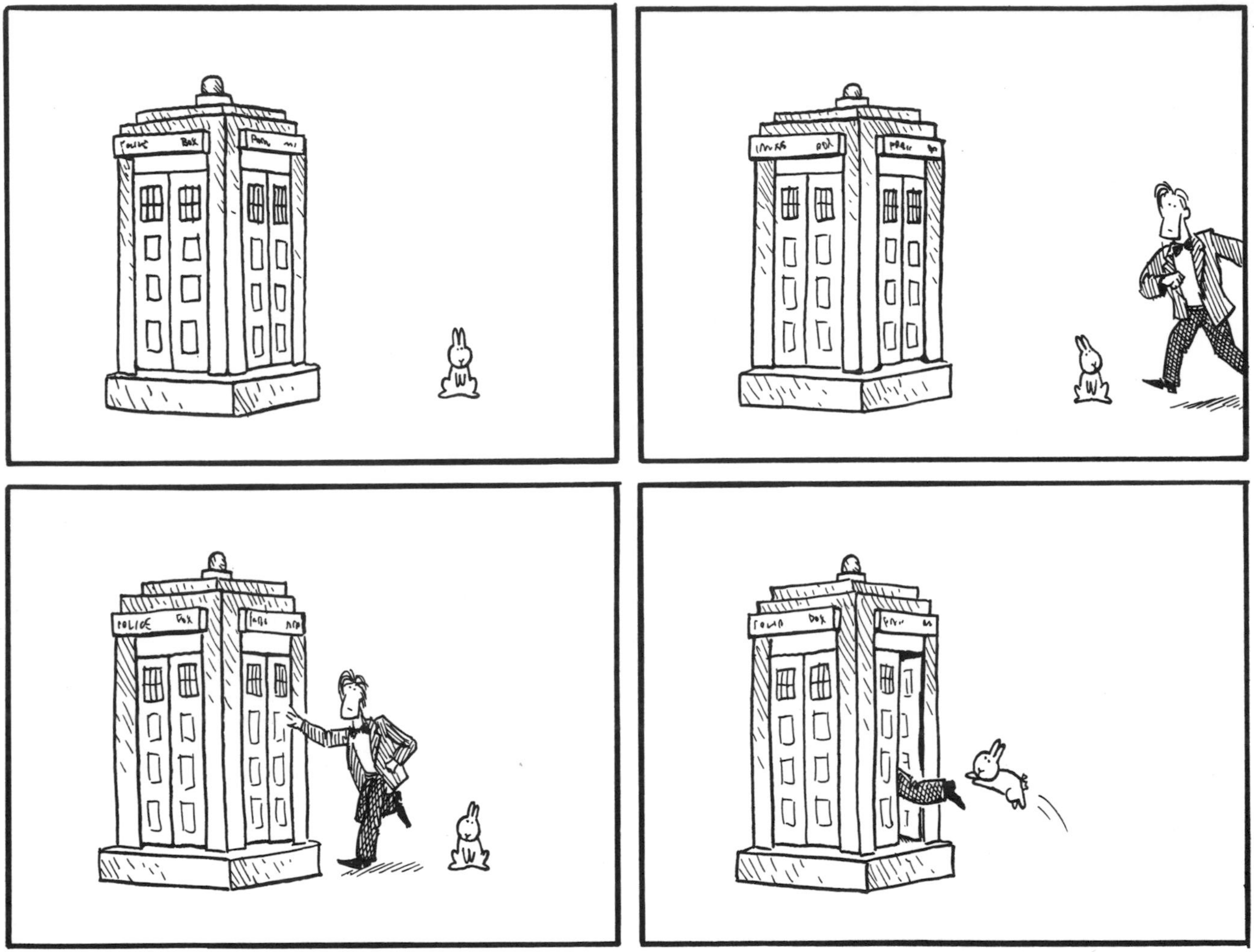
POLICE

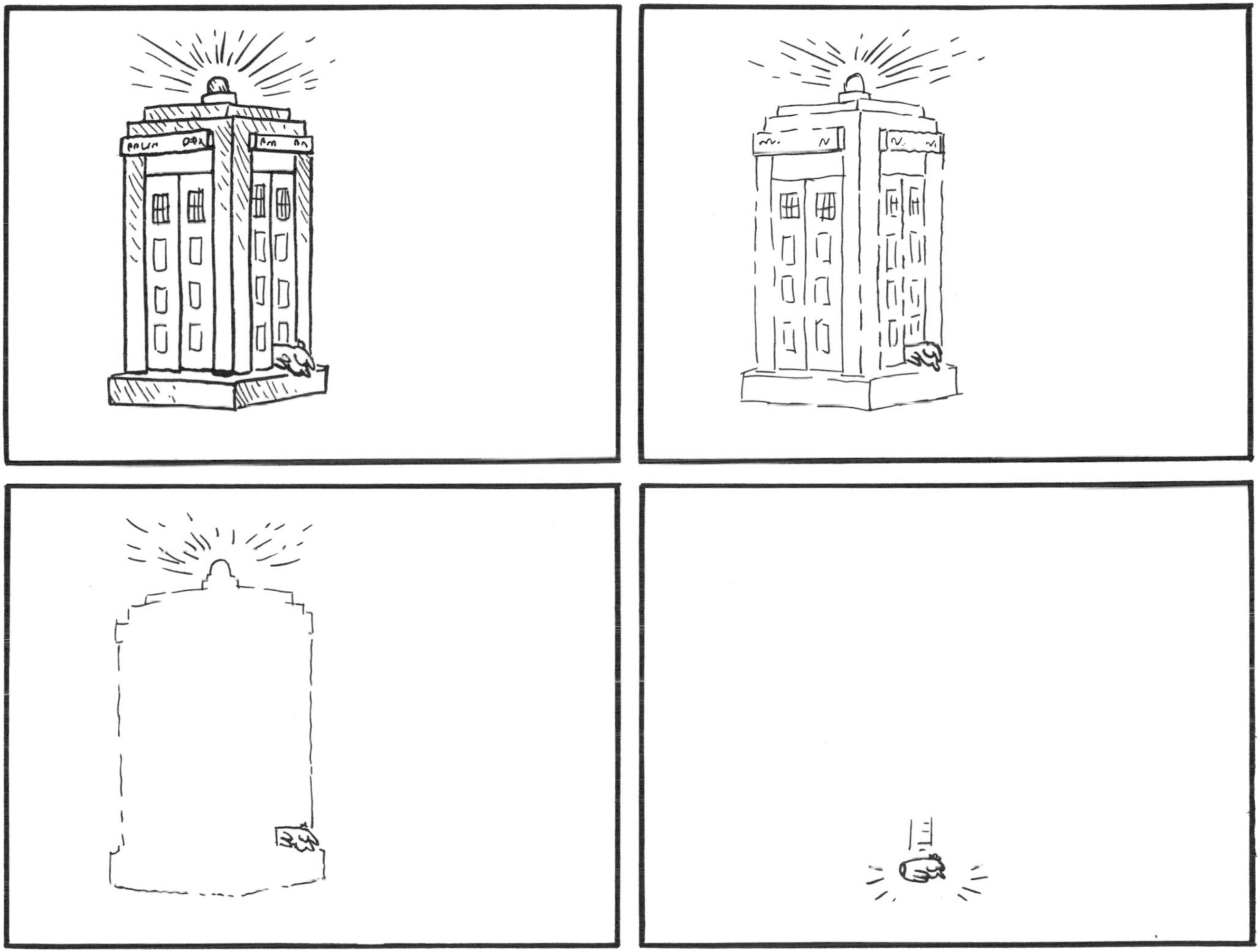

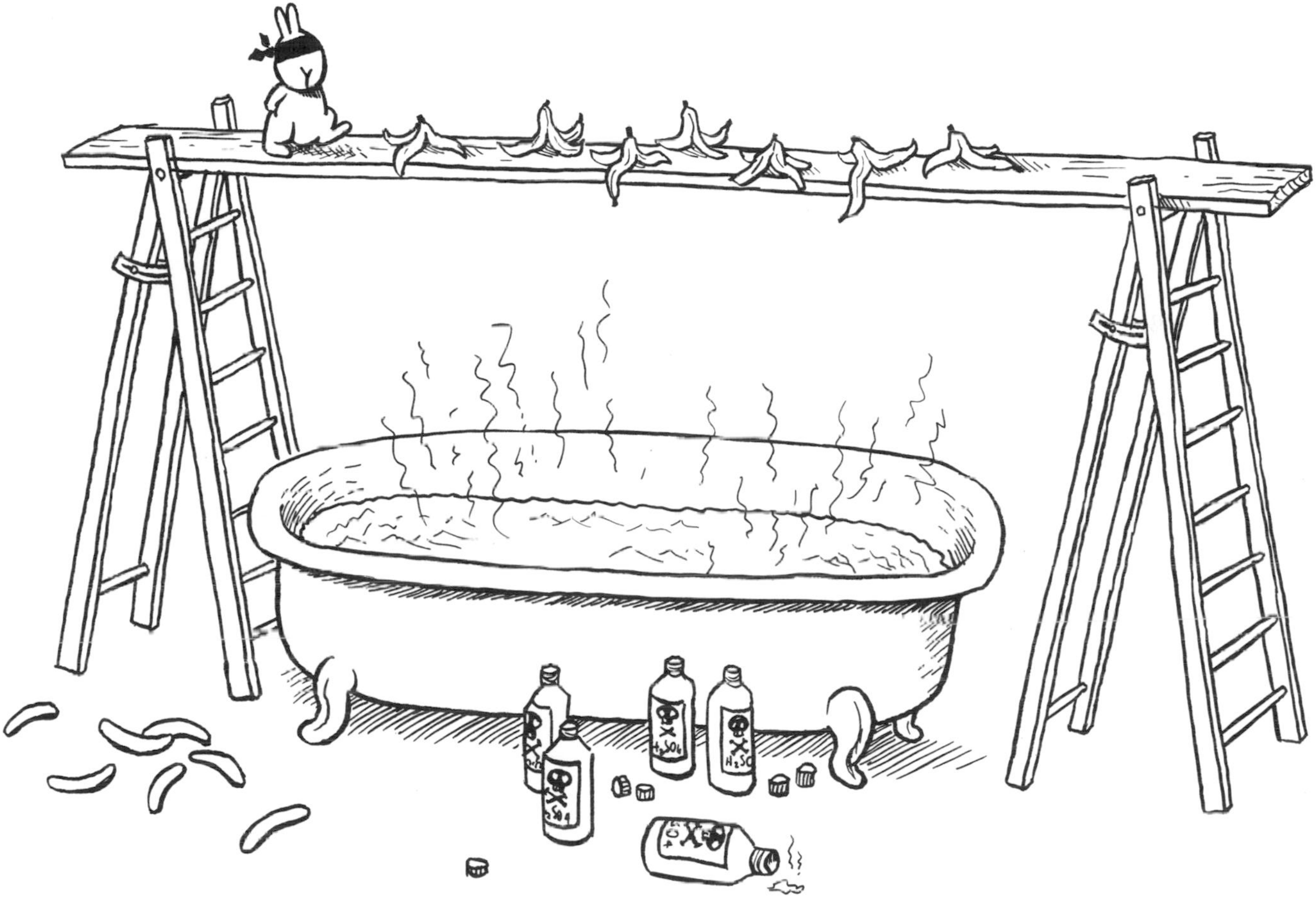
H_2SO_4

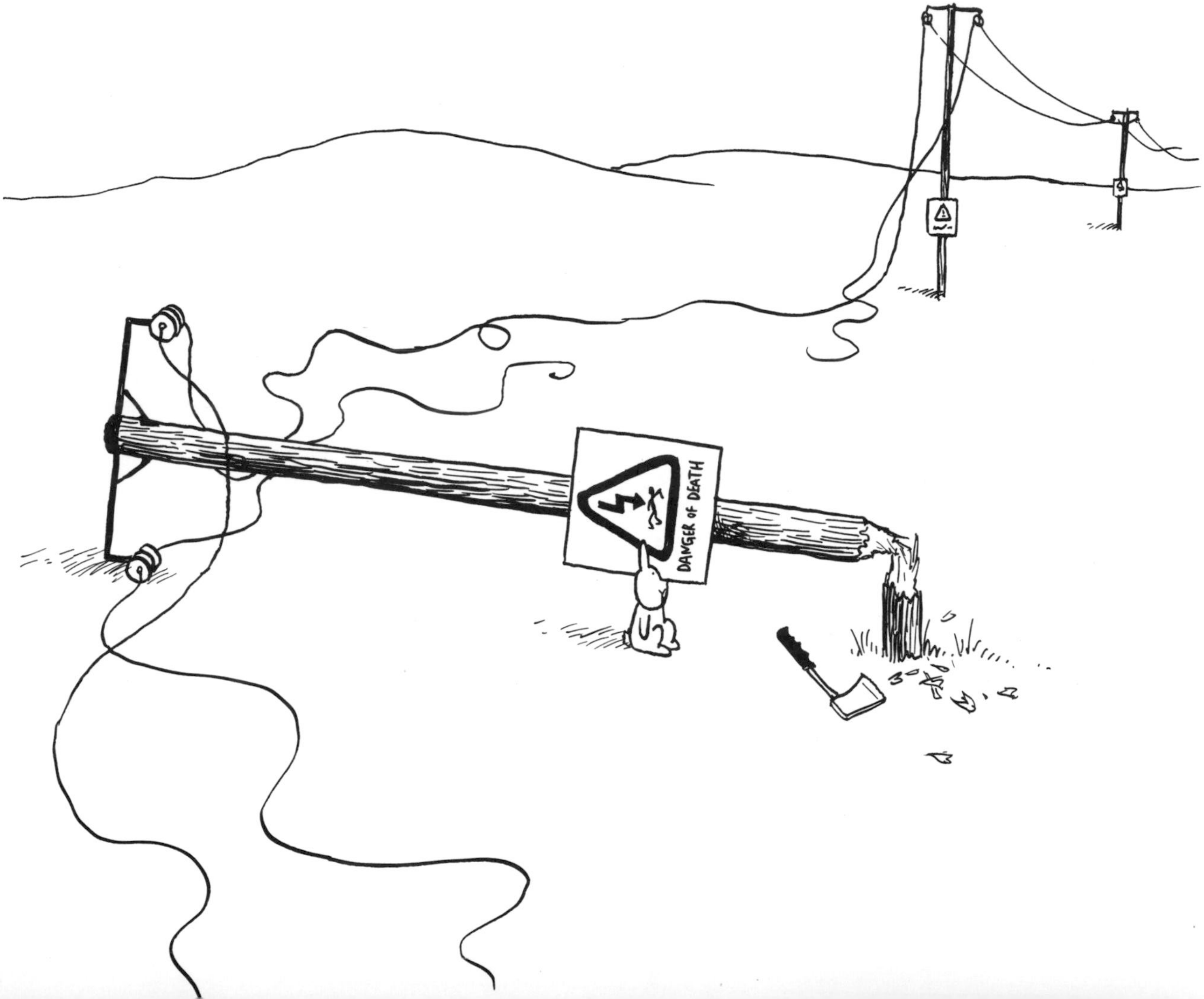
DANGER OF DEATH

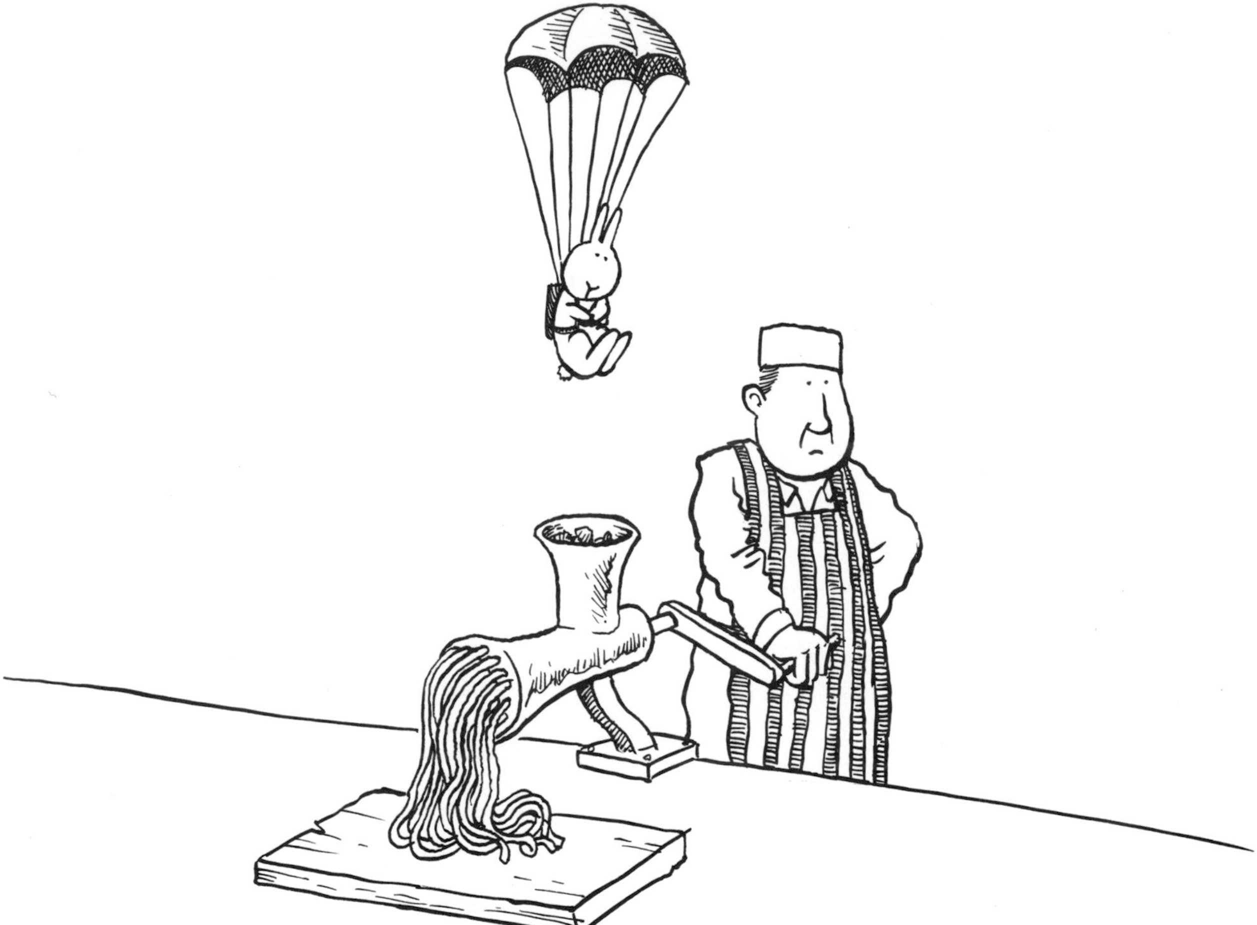

DO NOT PULL THIS LEVER
OFF
ON

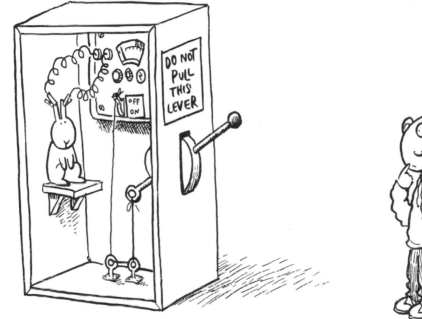

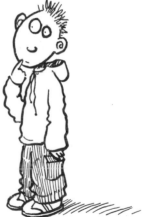

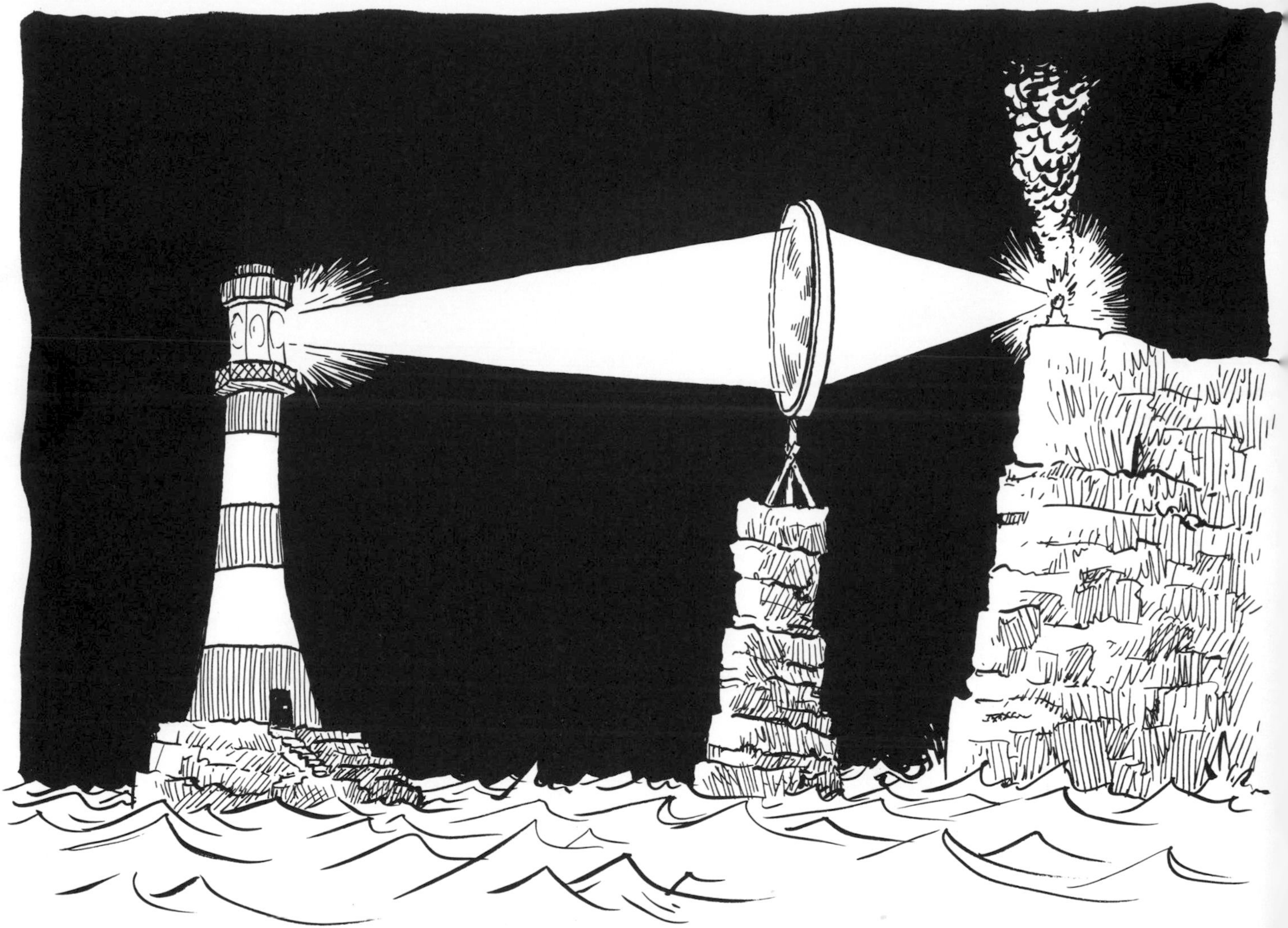

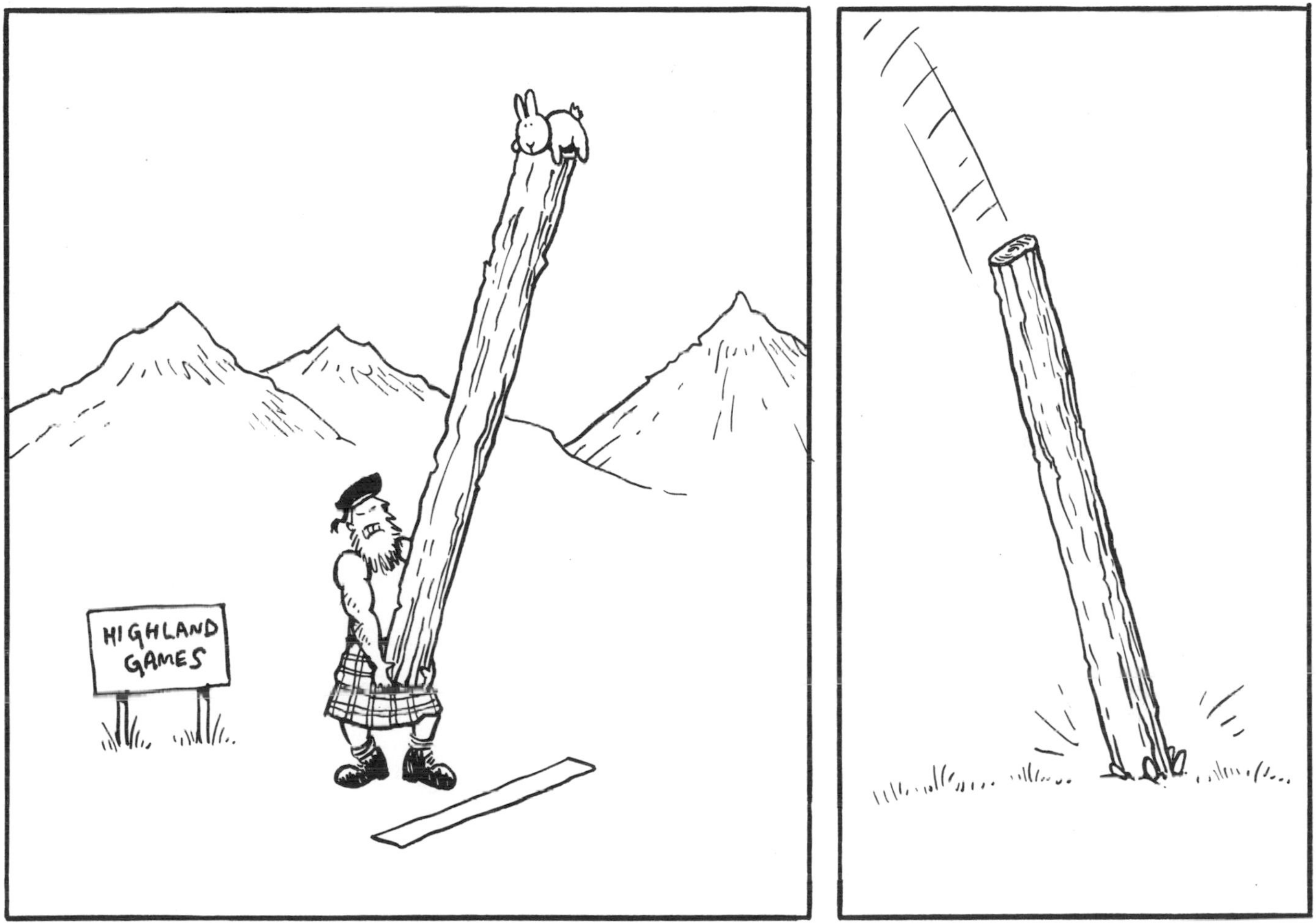
HIGHLAND GAMES

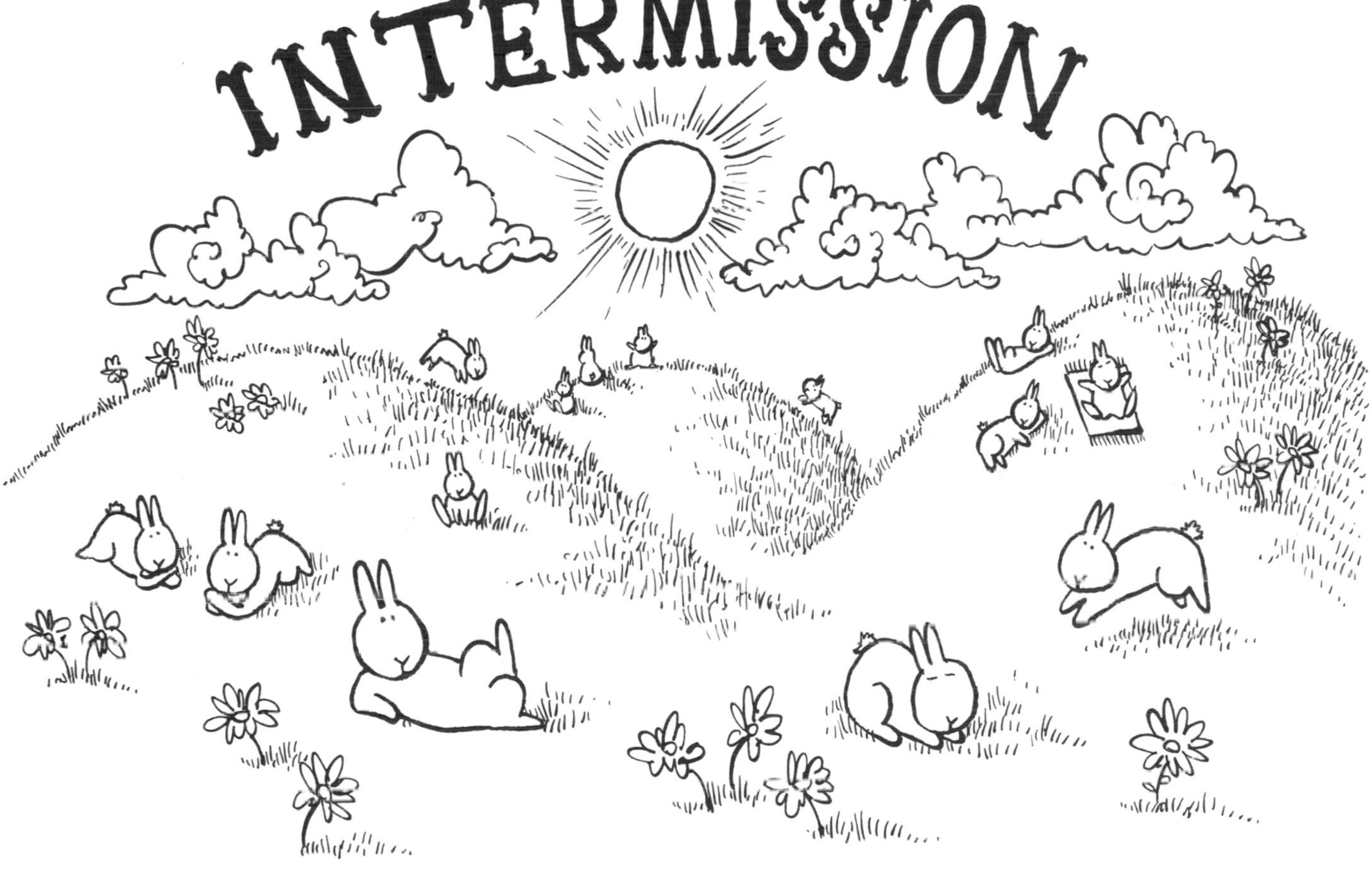
INTERMISSION

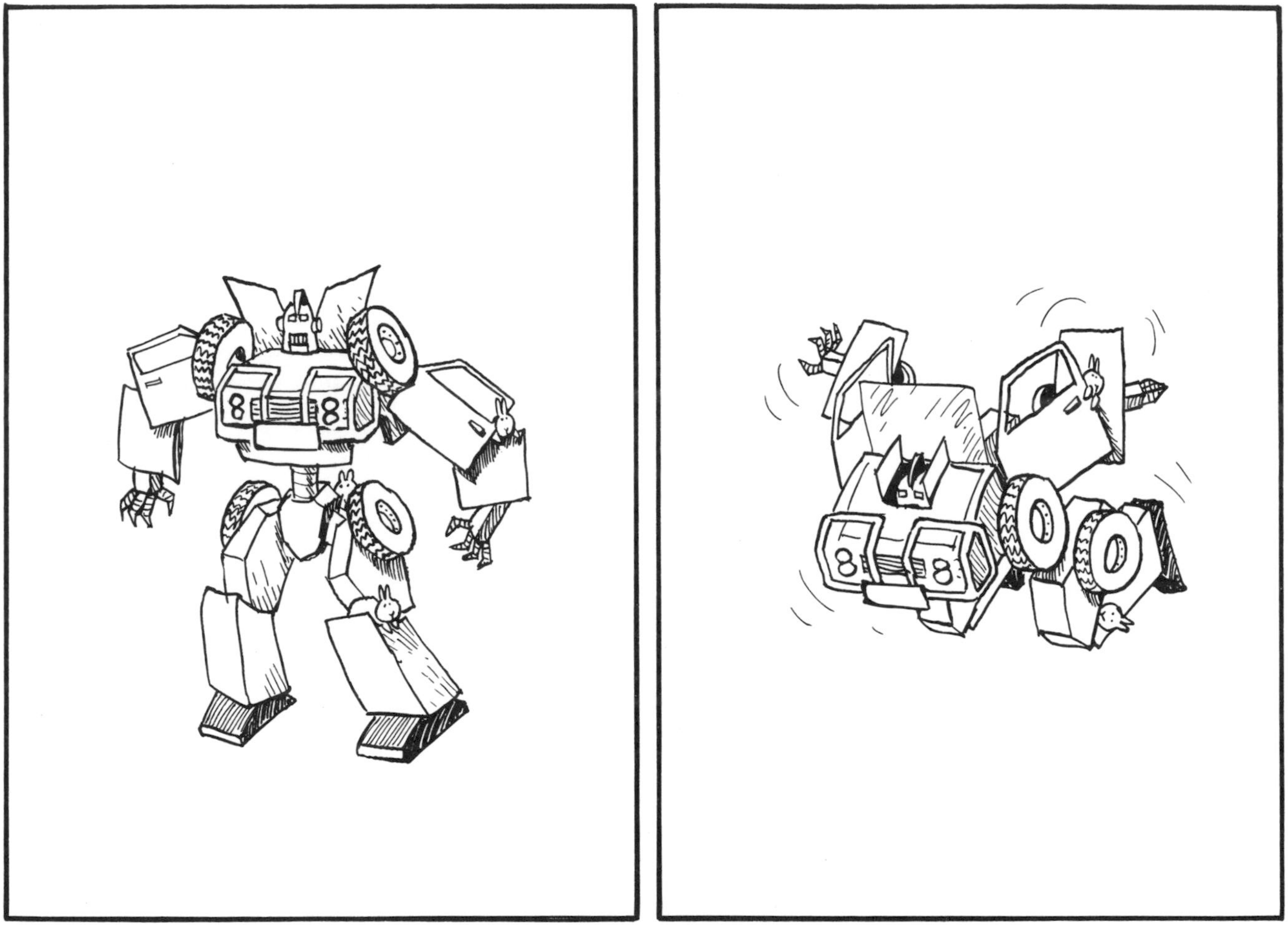

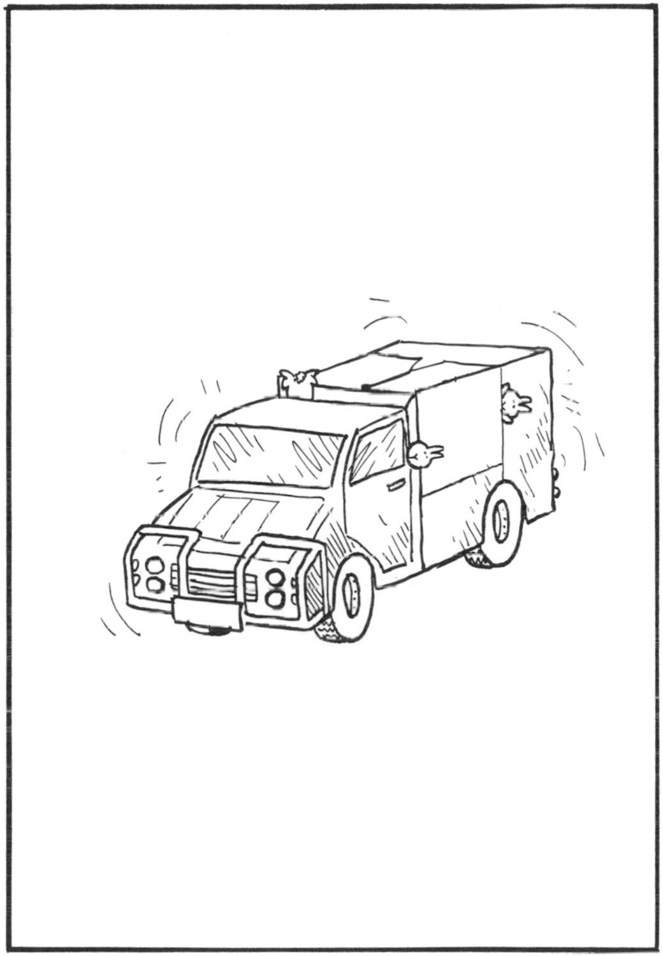
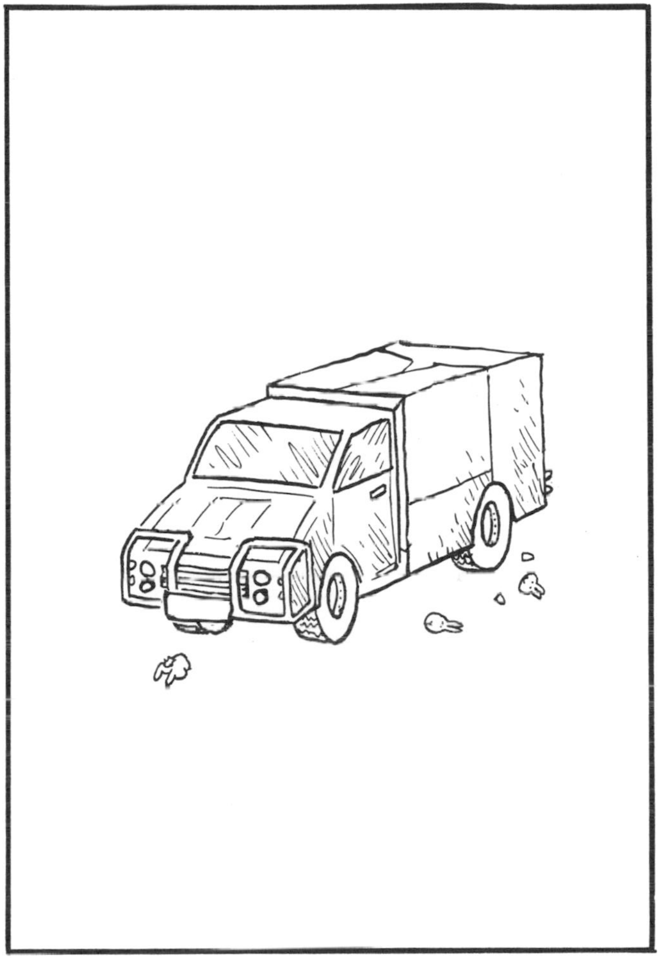

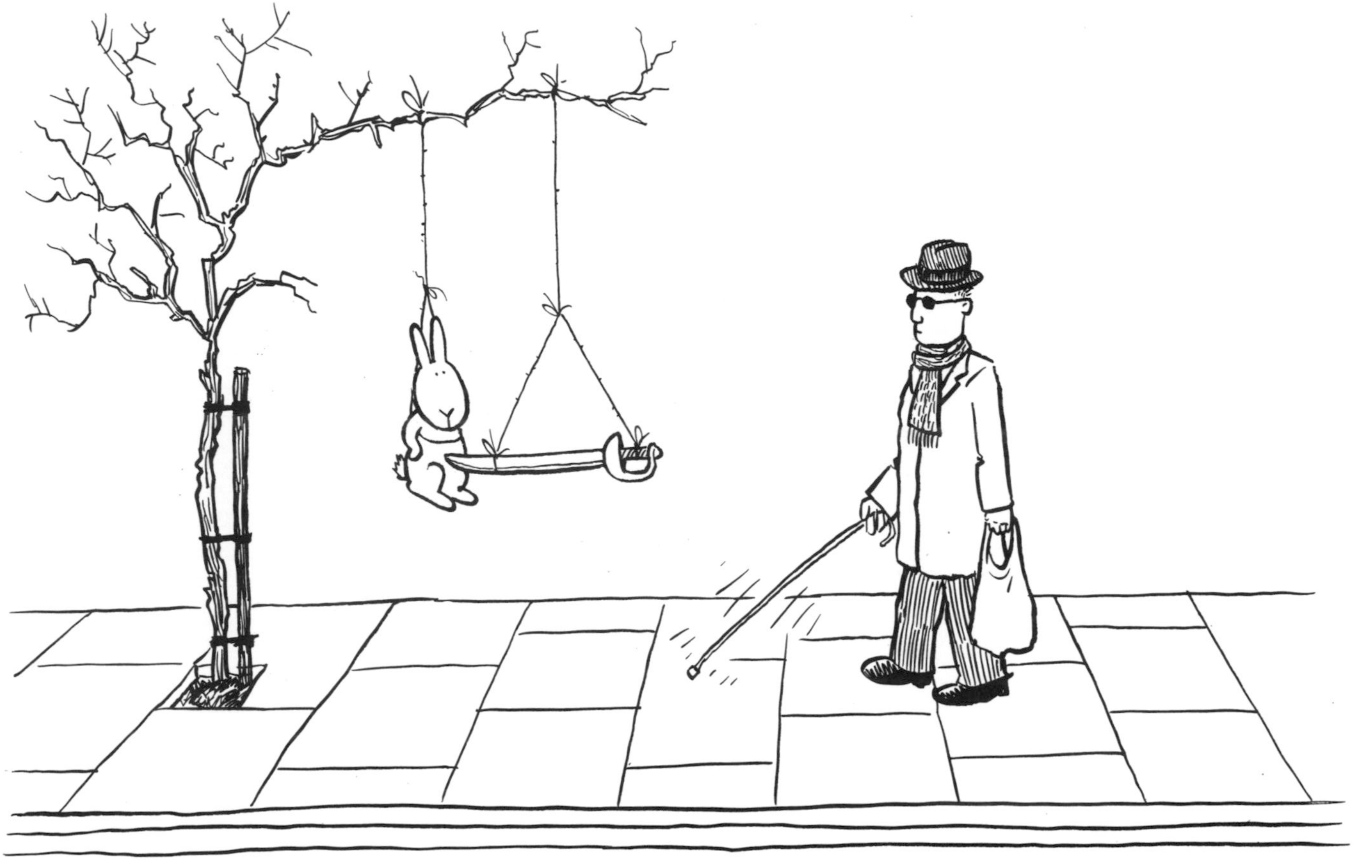

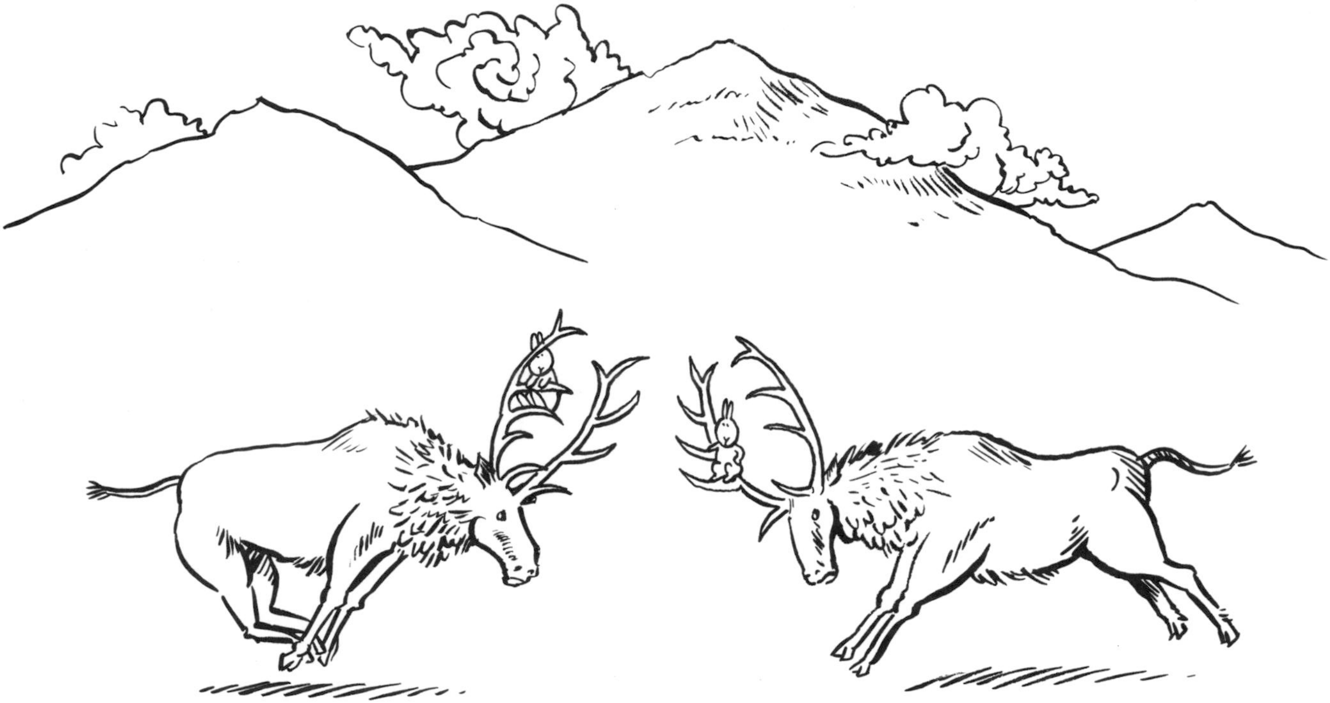

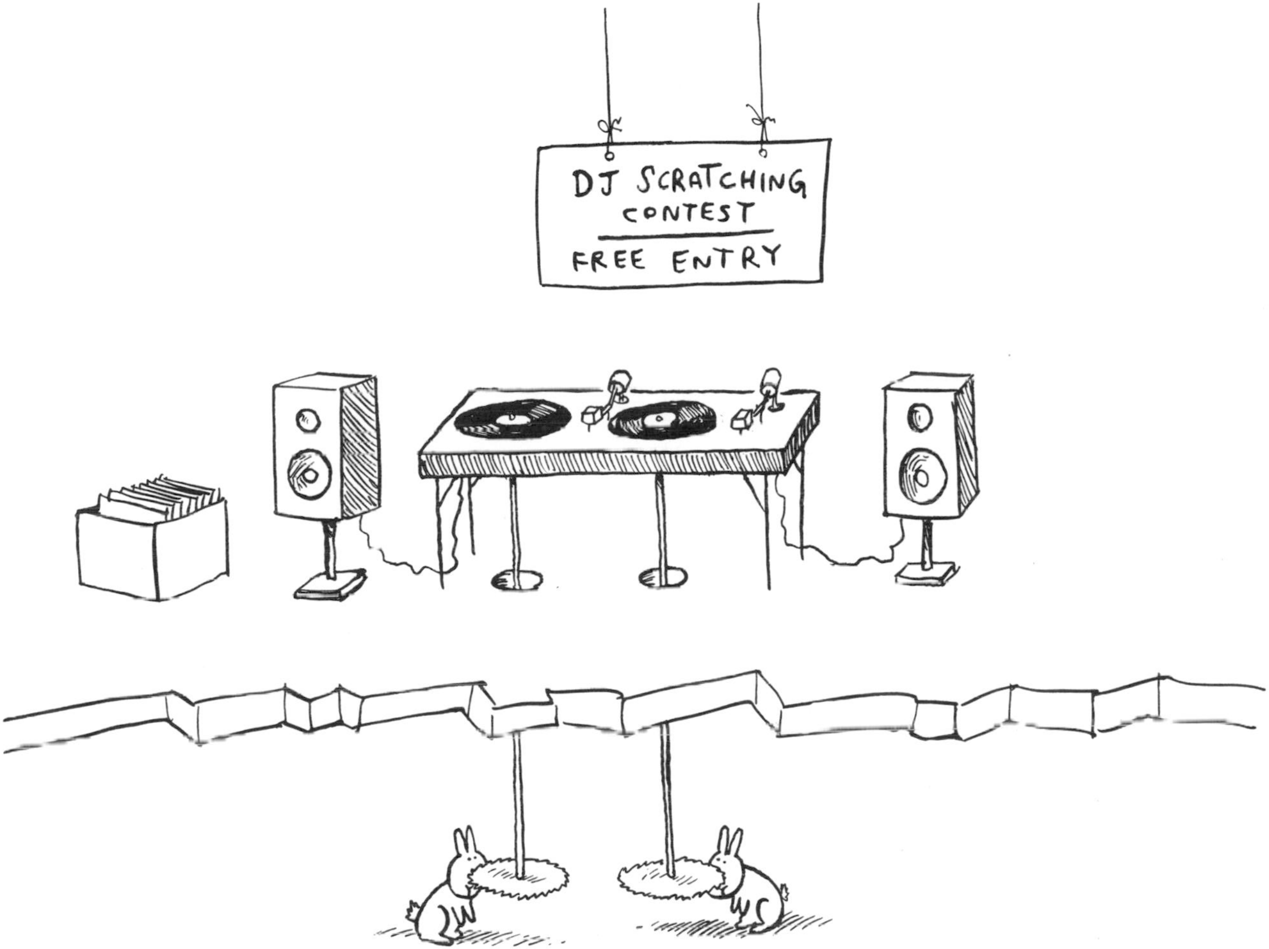
DJ SCRATCHING
CONTEST
FREE ENTRY

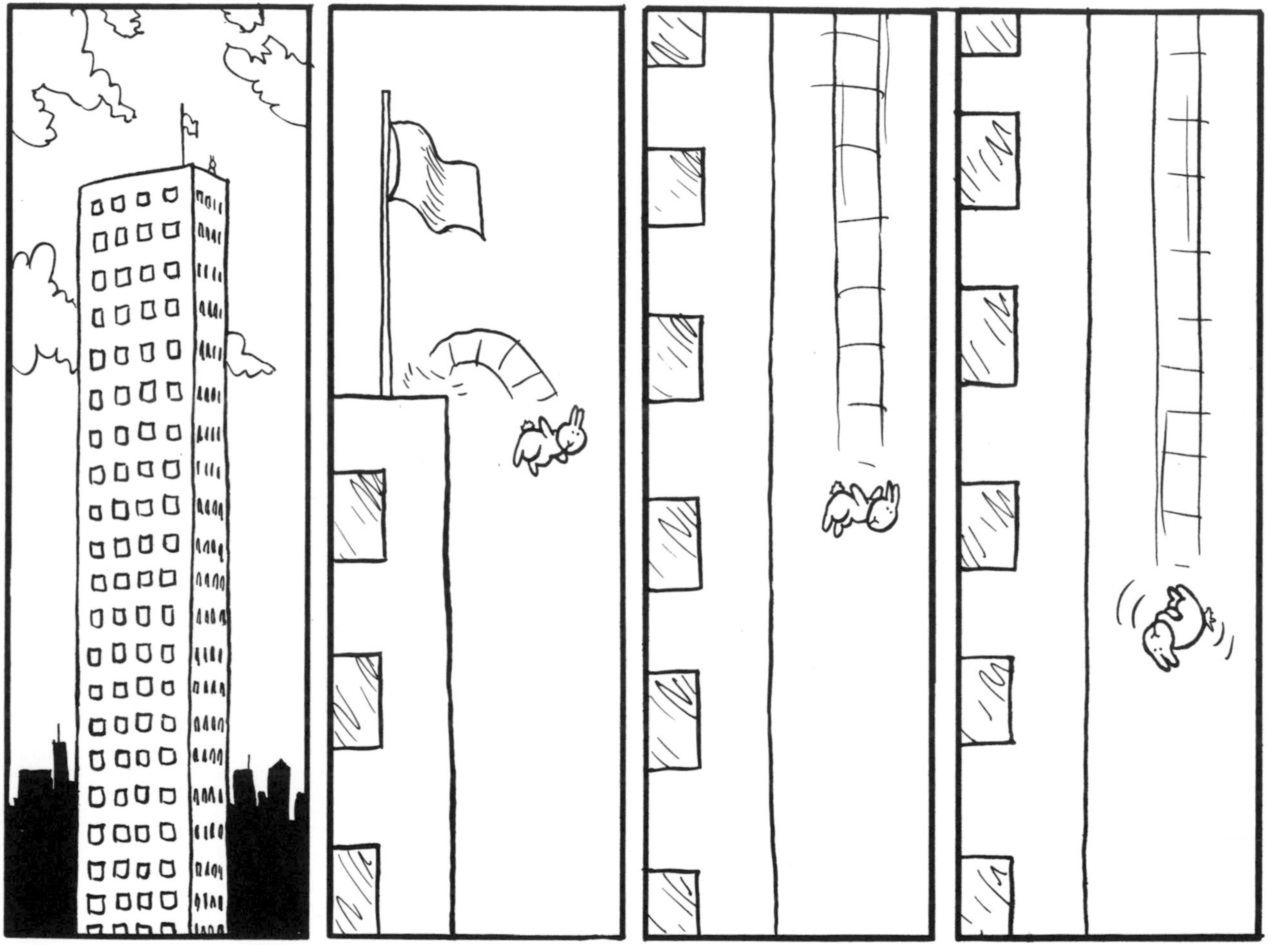

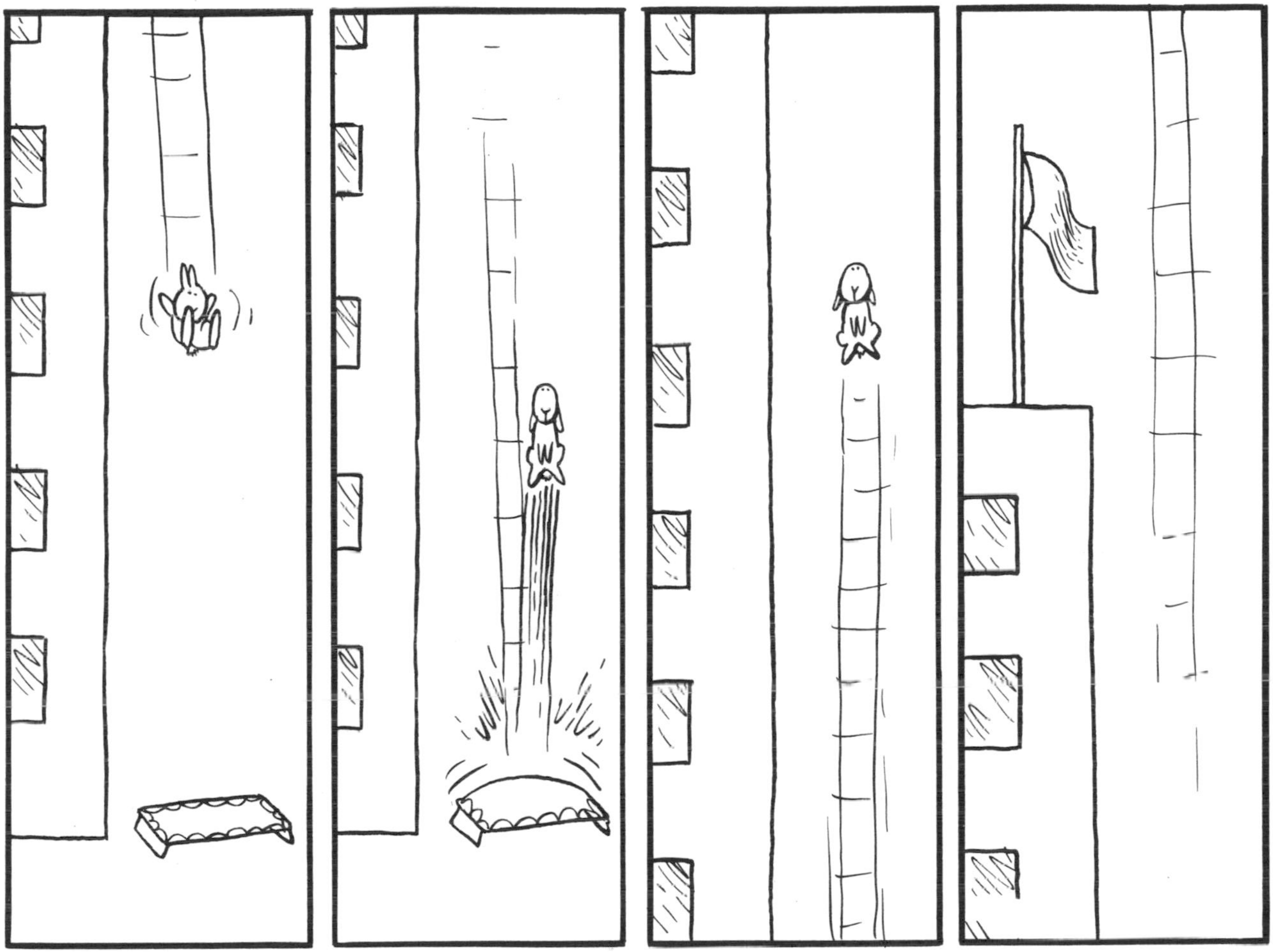

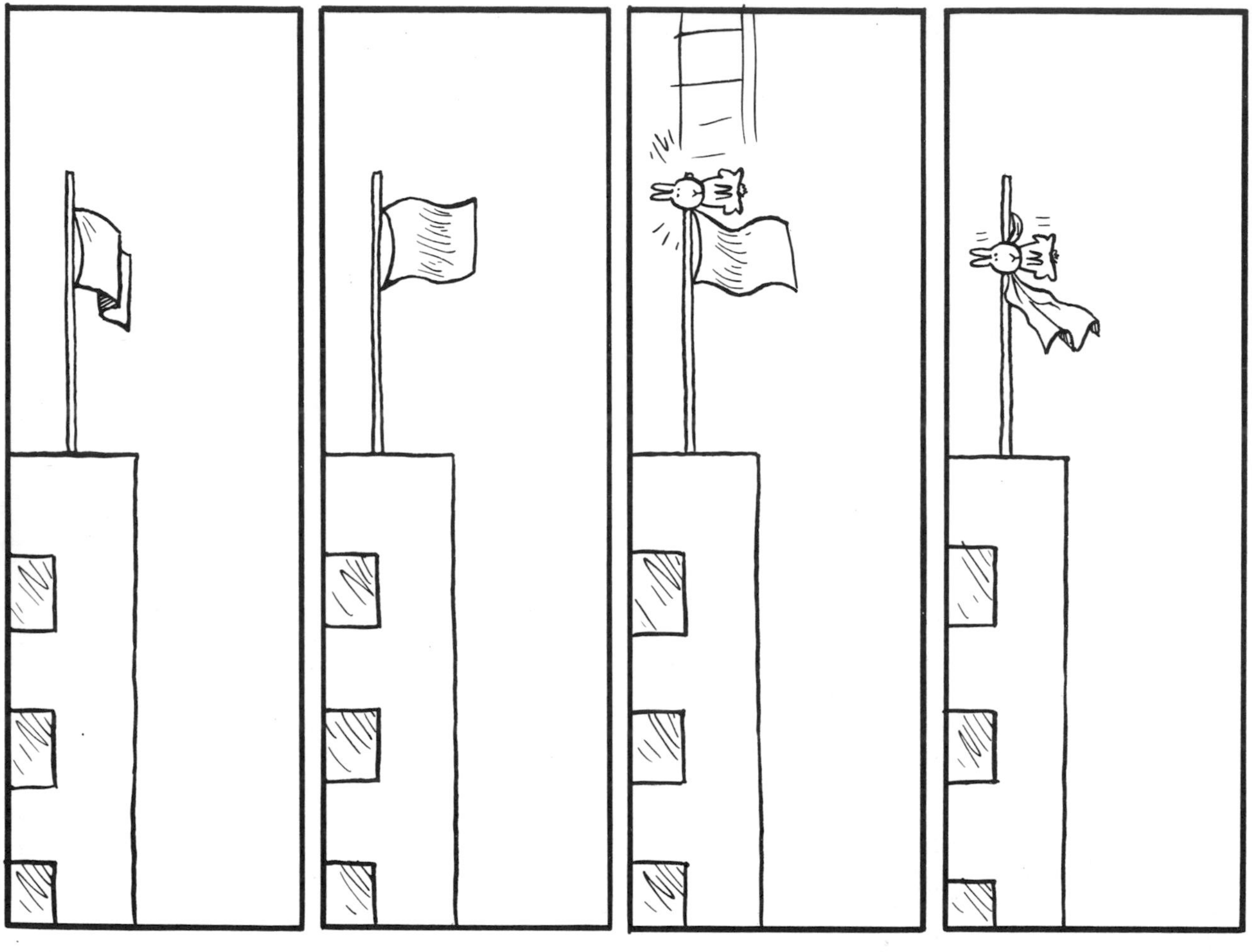

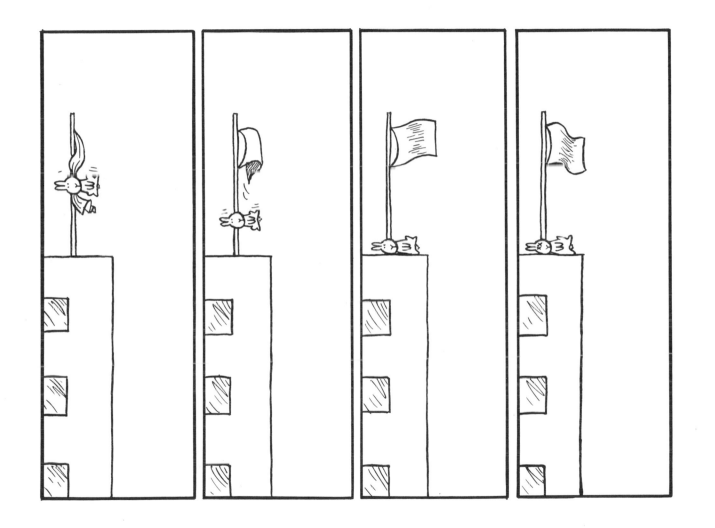

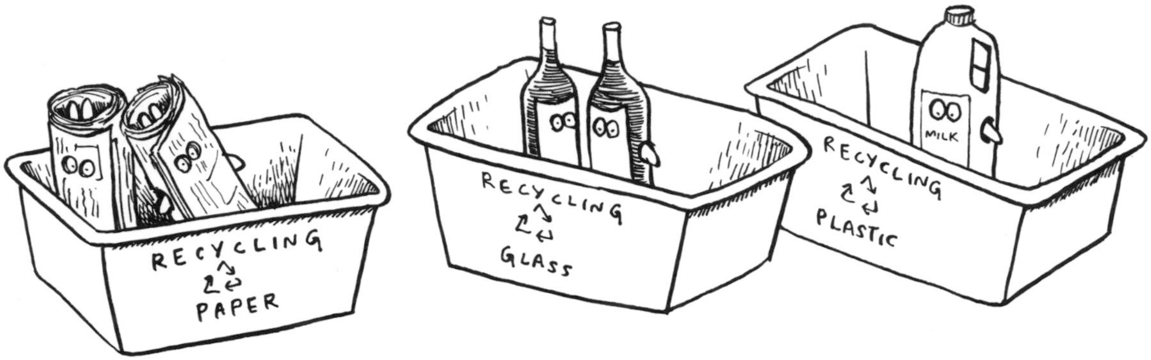
RECYCLING
PAPER
RECYCLING
GLASS
MILK
RECYCLING
PLASTIC

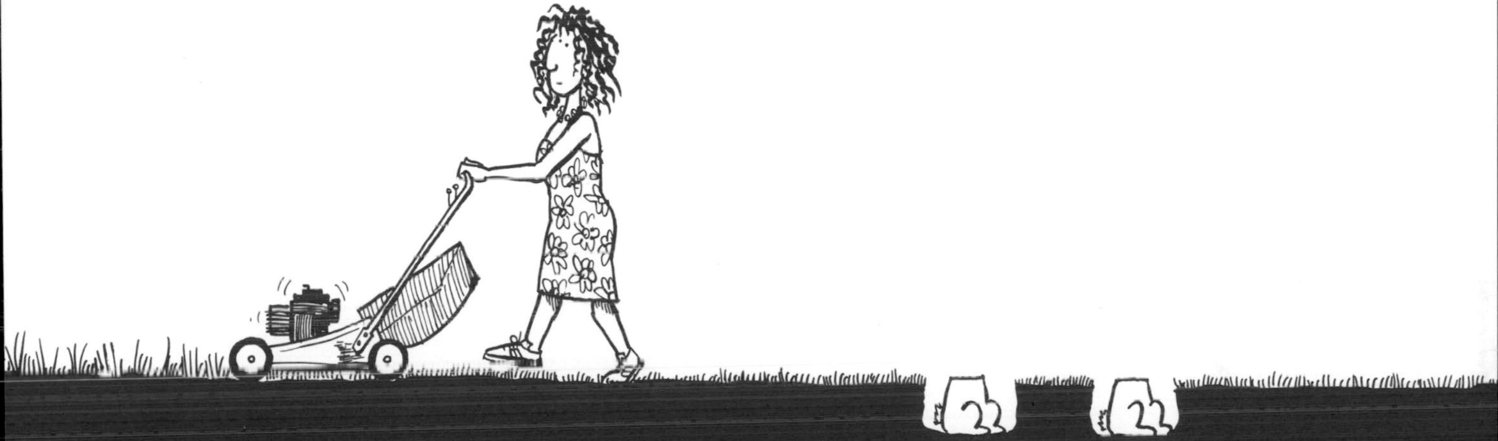
22
22

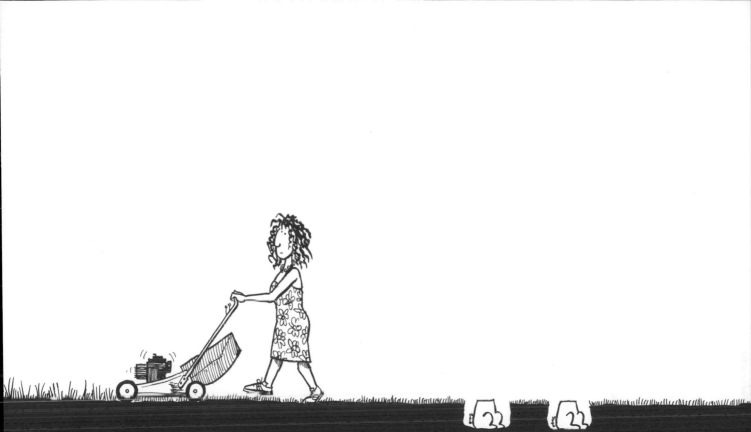

1000 W
600 W
400 W

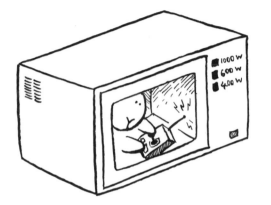

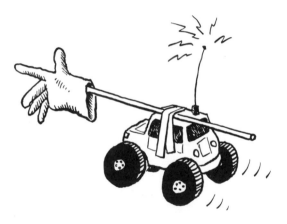

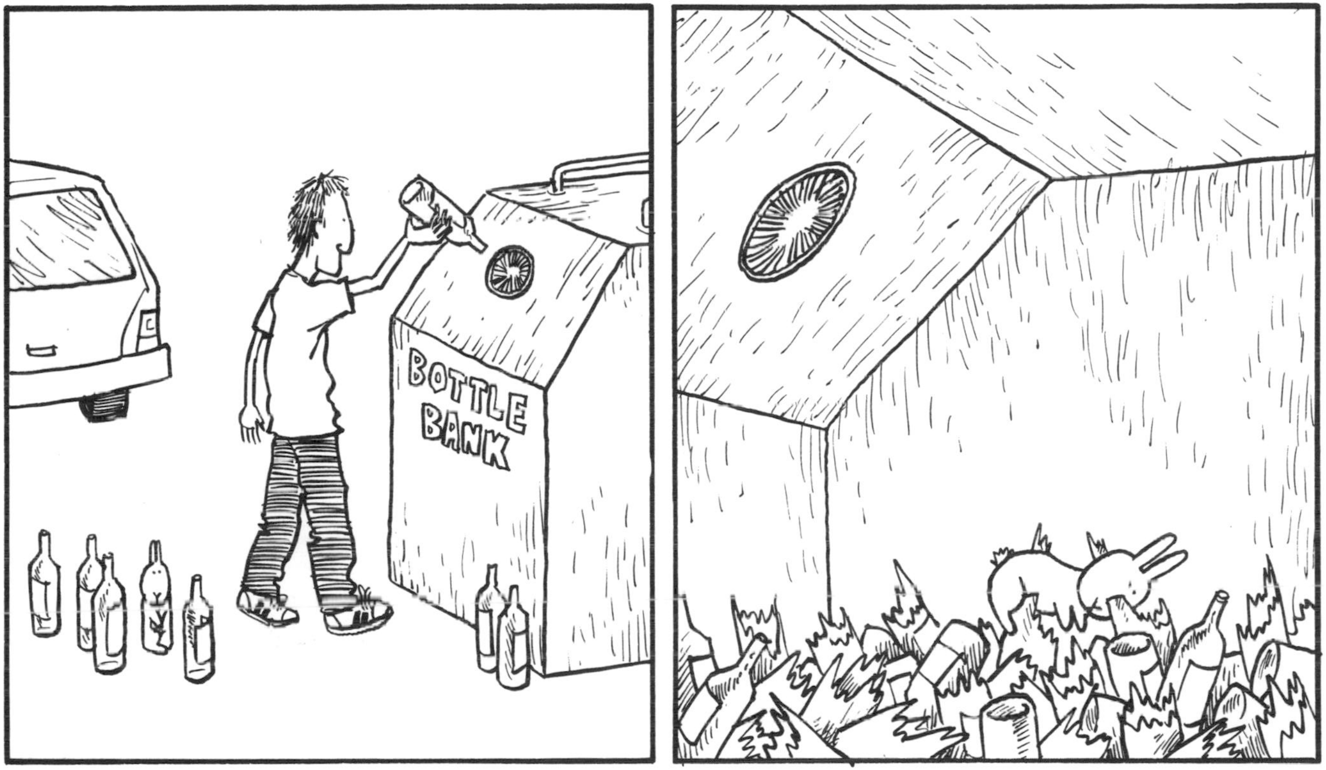
BOTTLE BANK

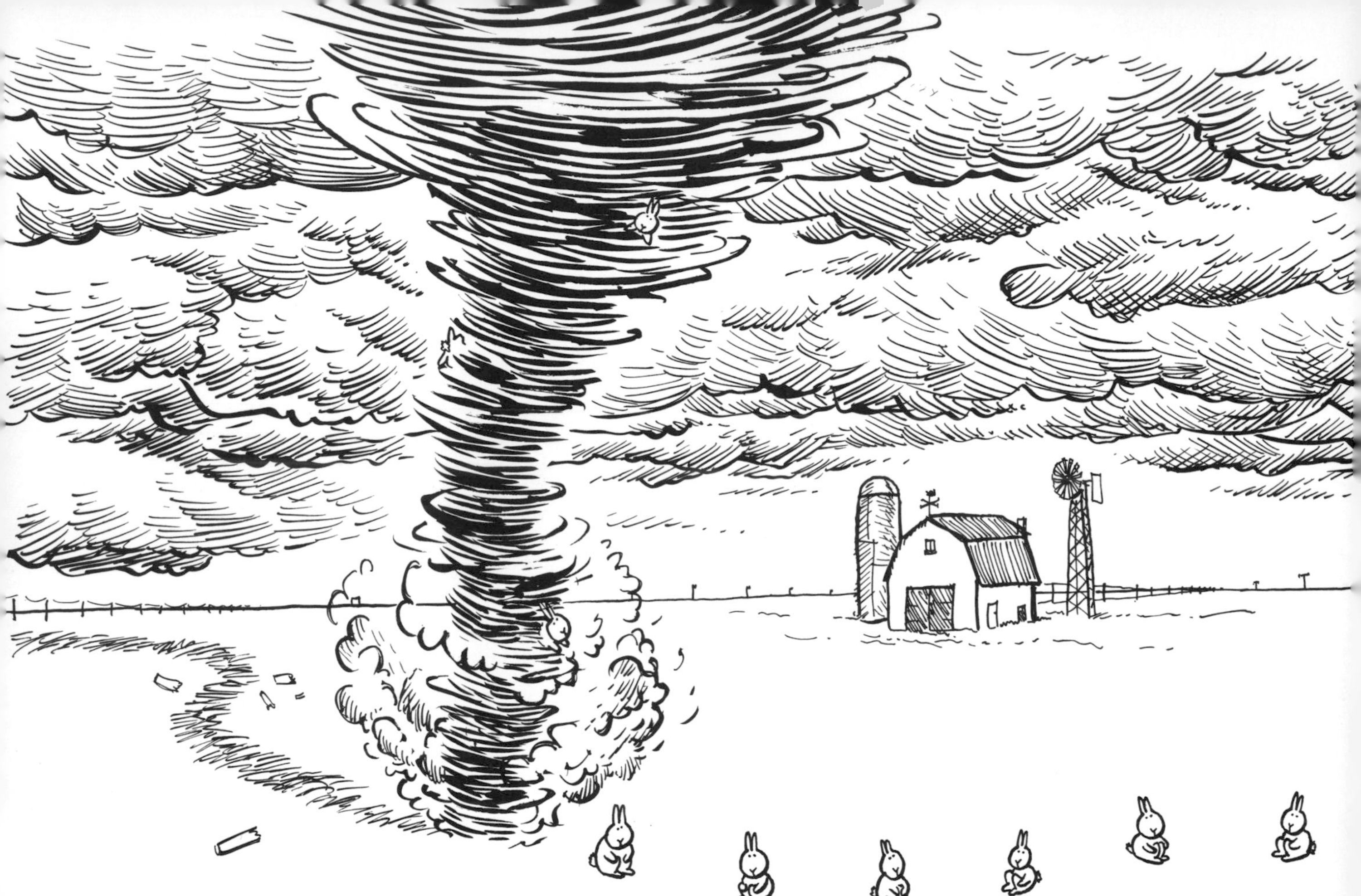

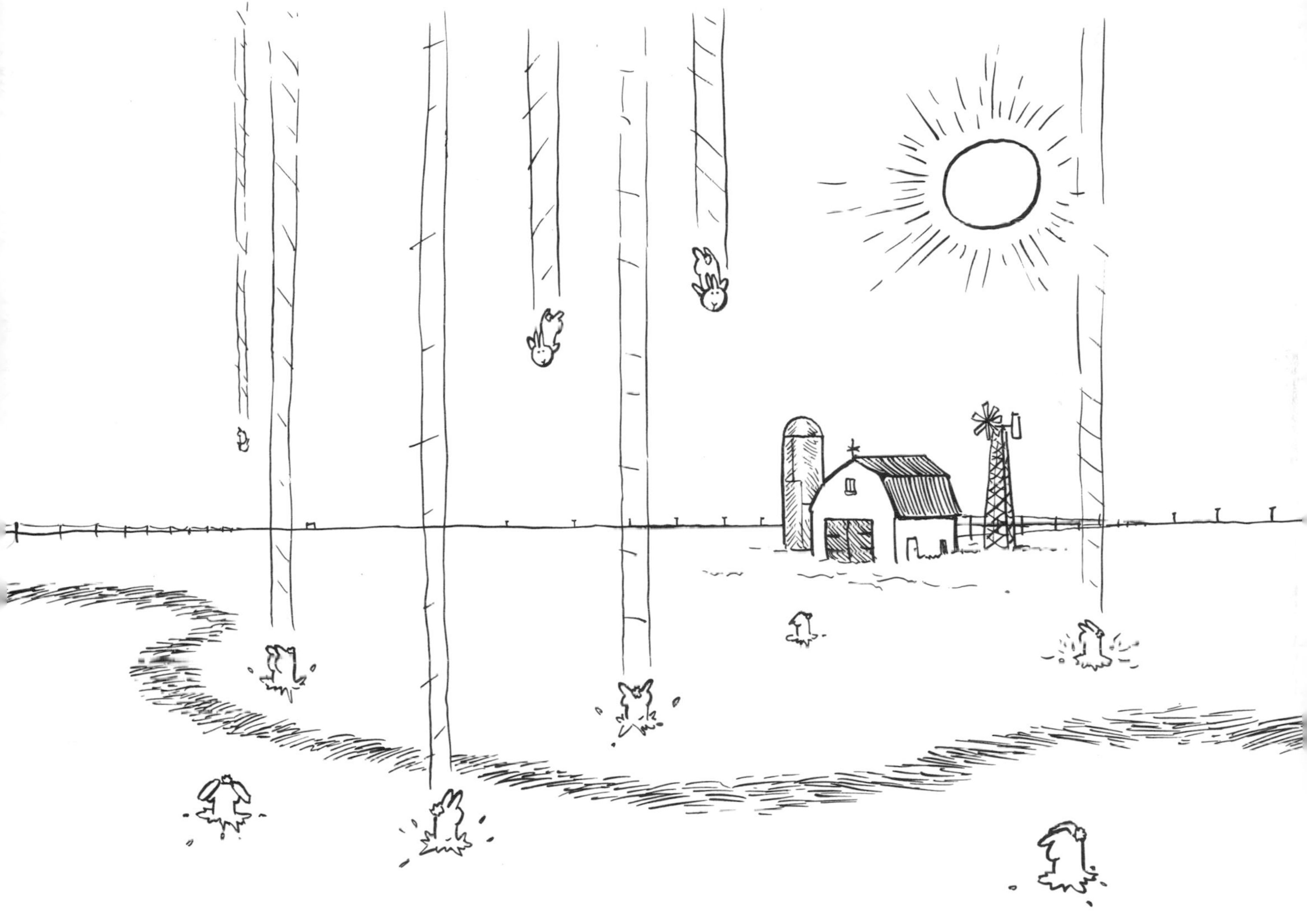

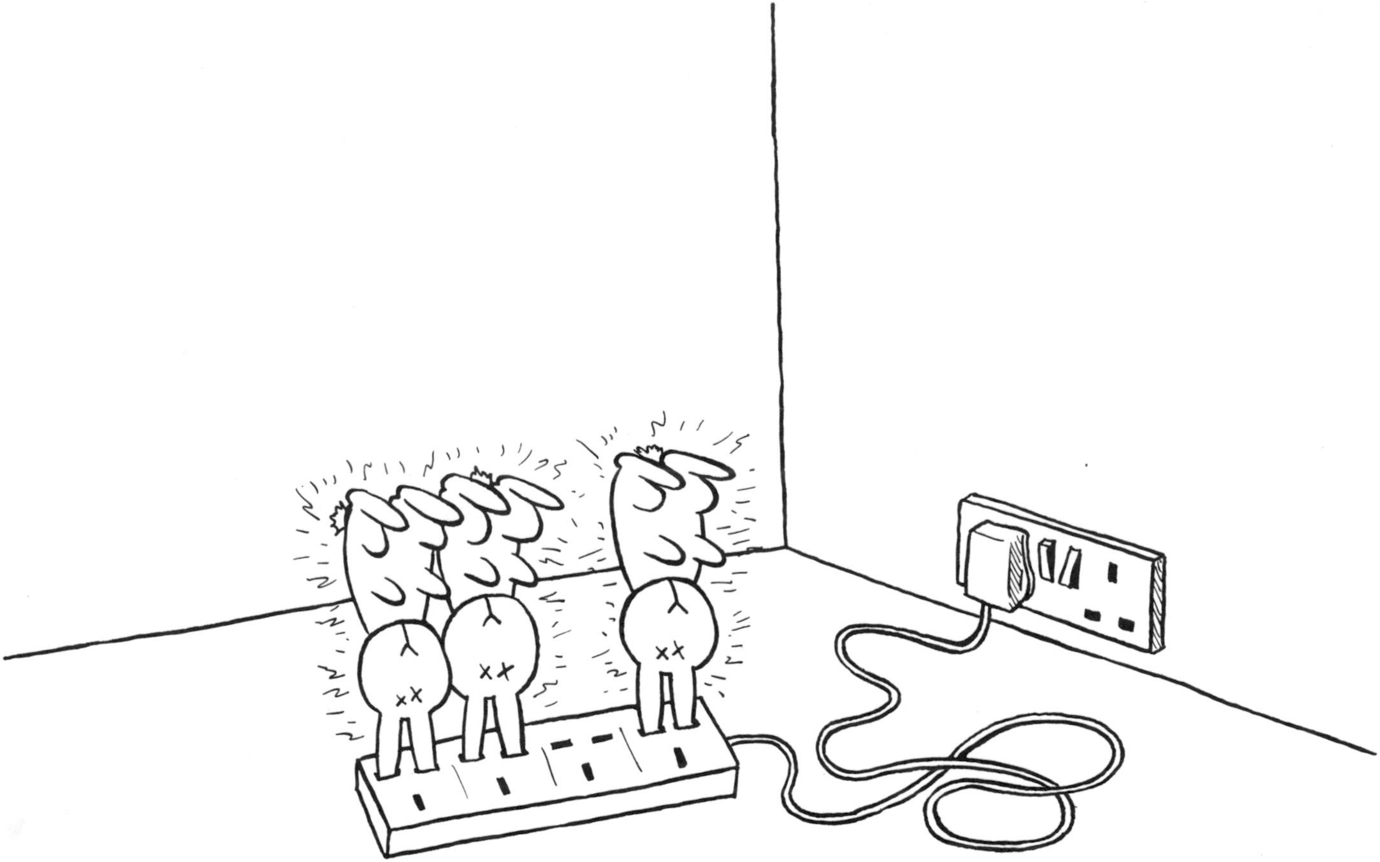

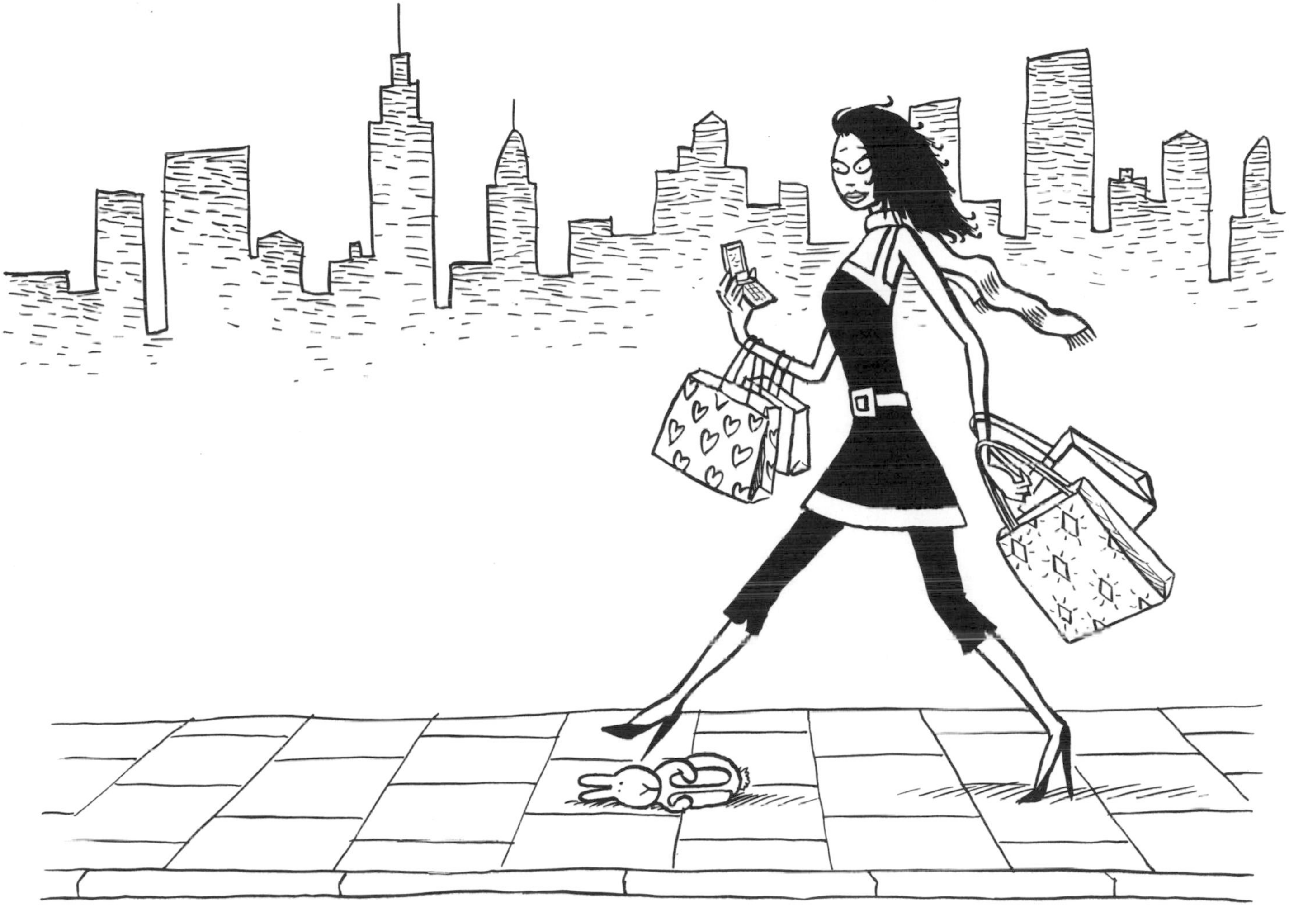

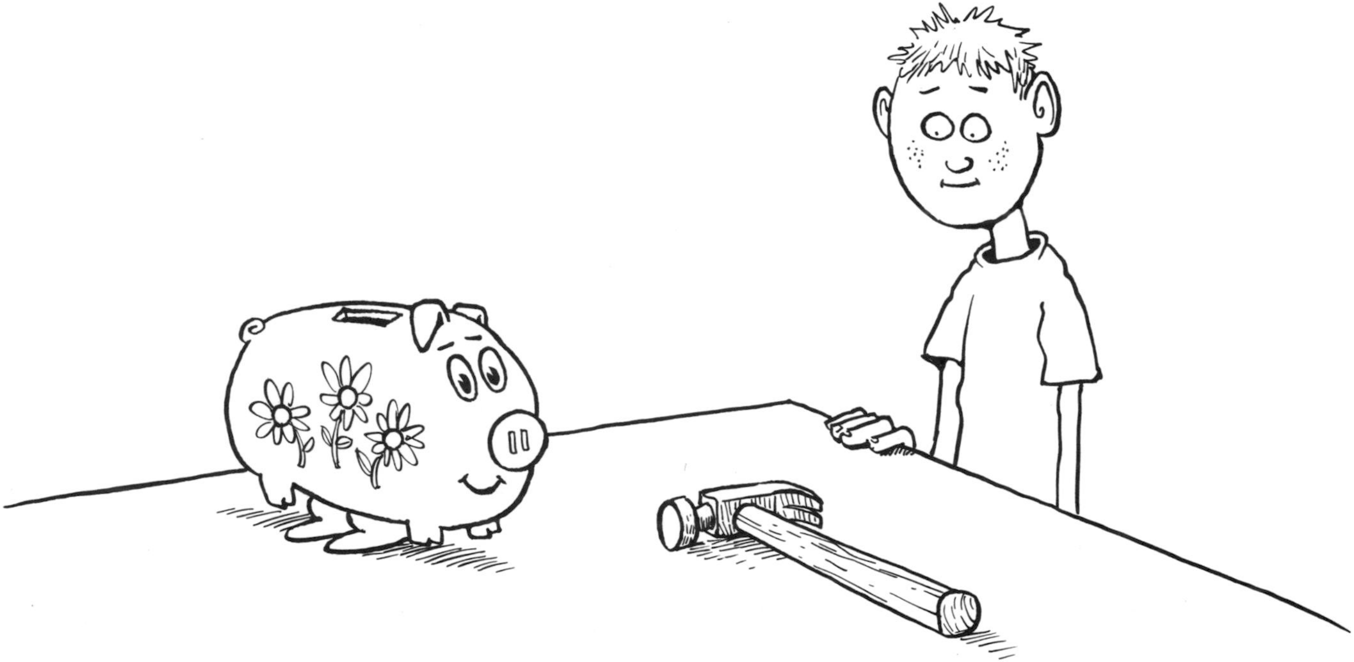

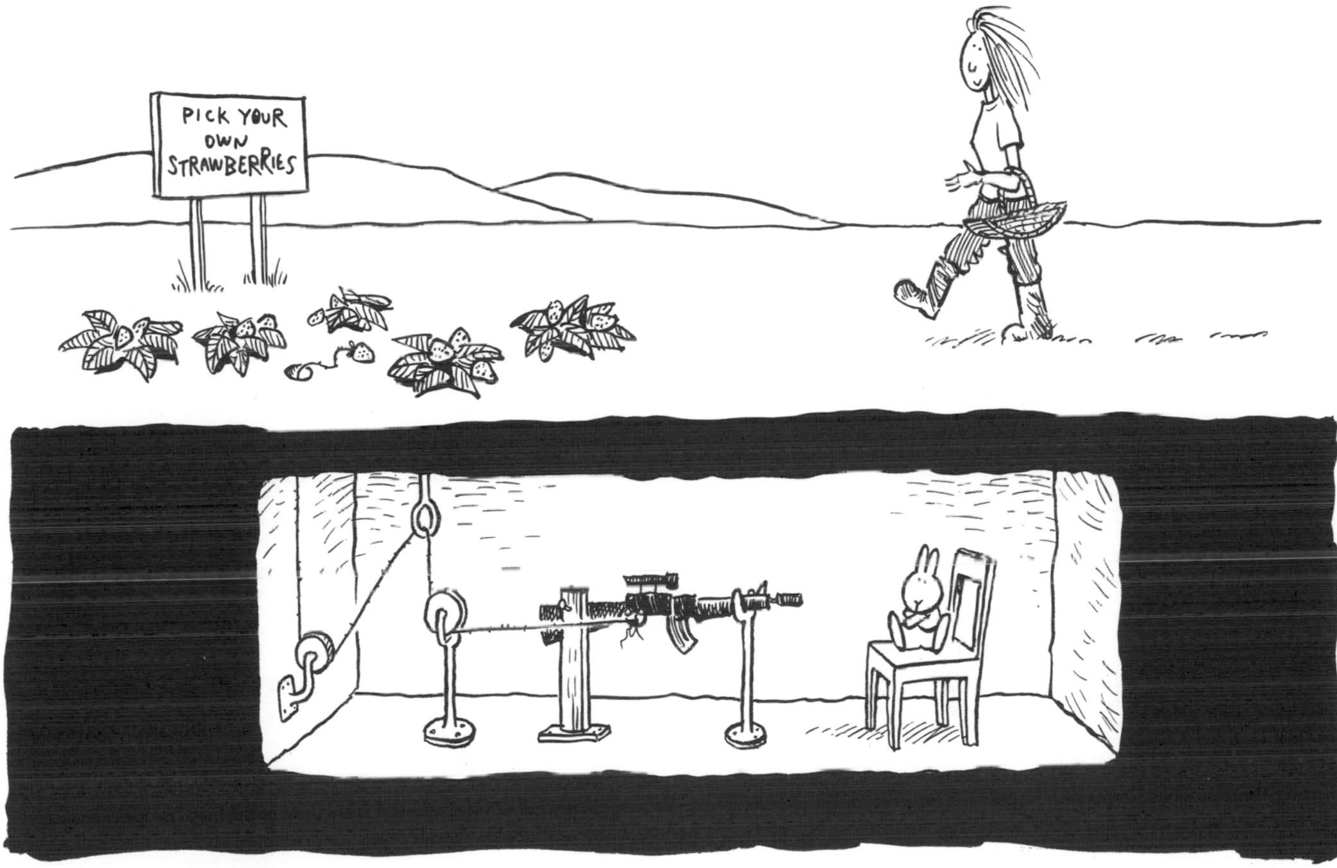
PICK YOUR
OWN
STRAWBERRIES

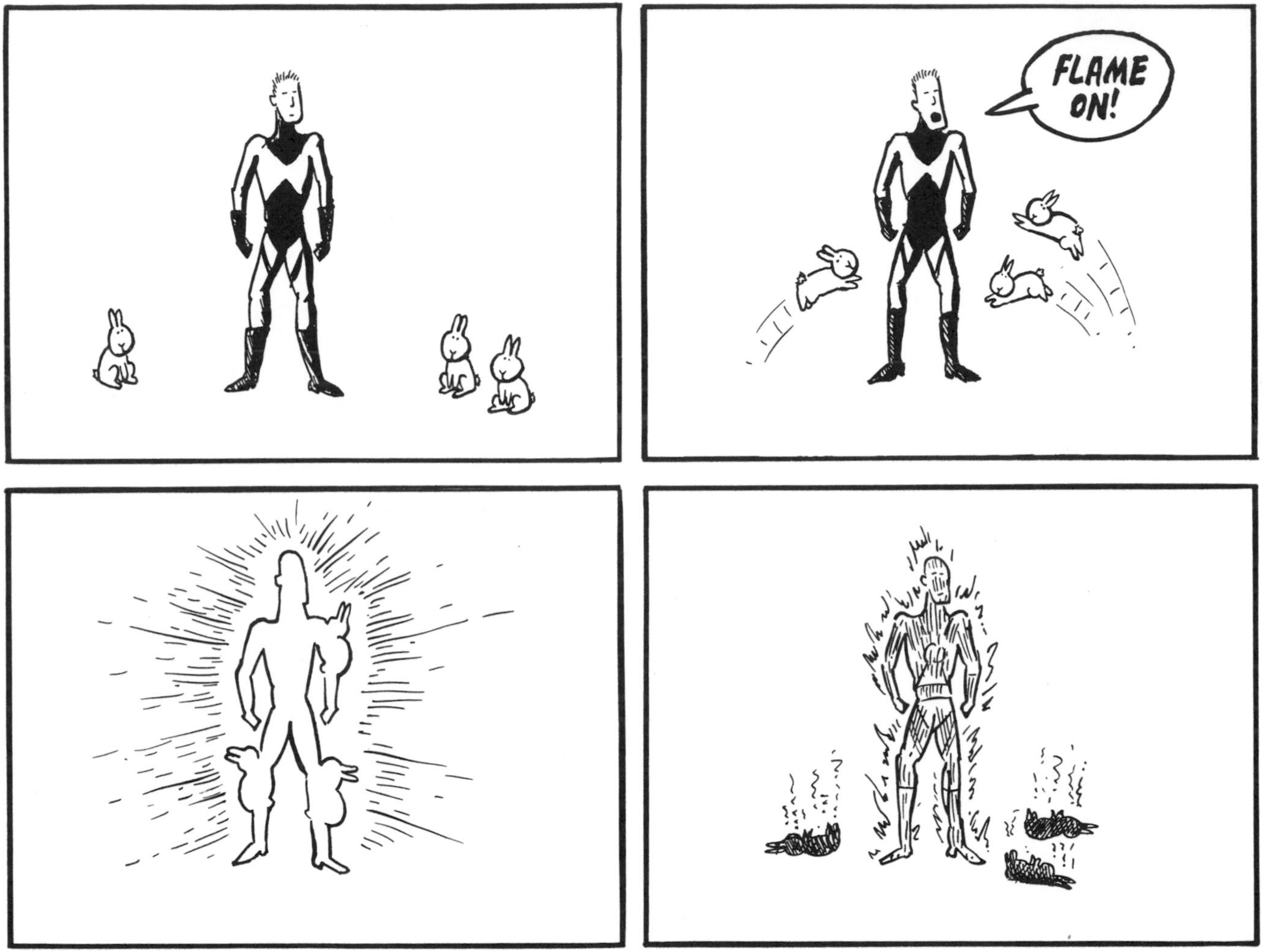
FLAME ON!

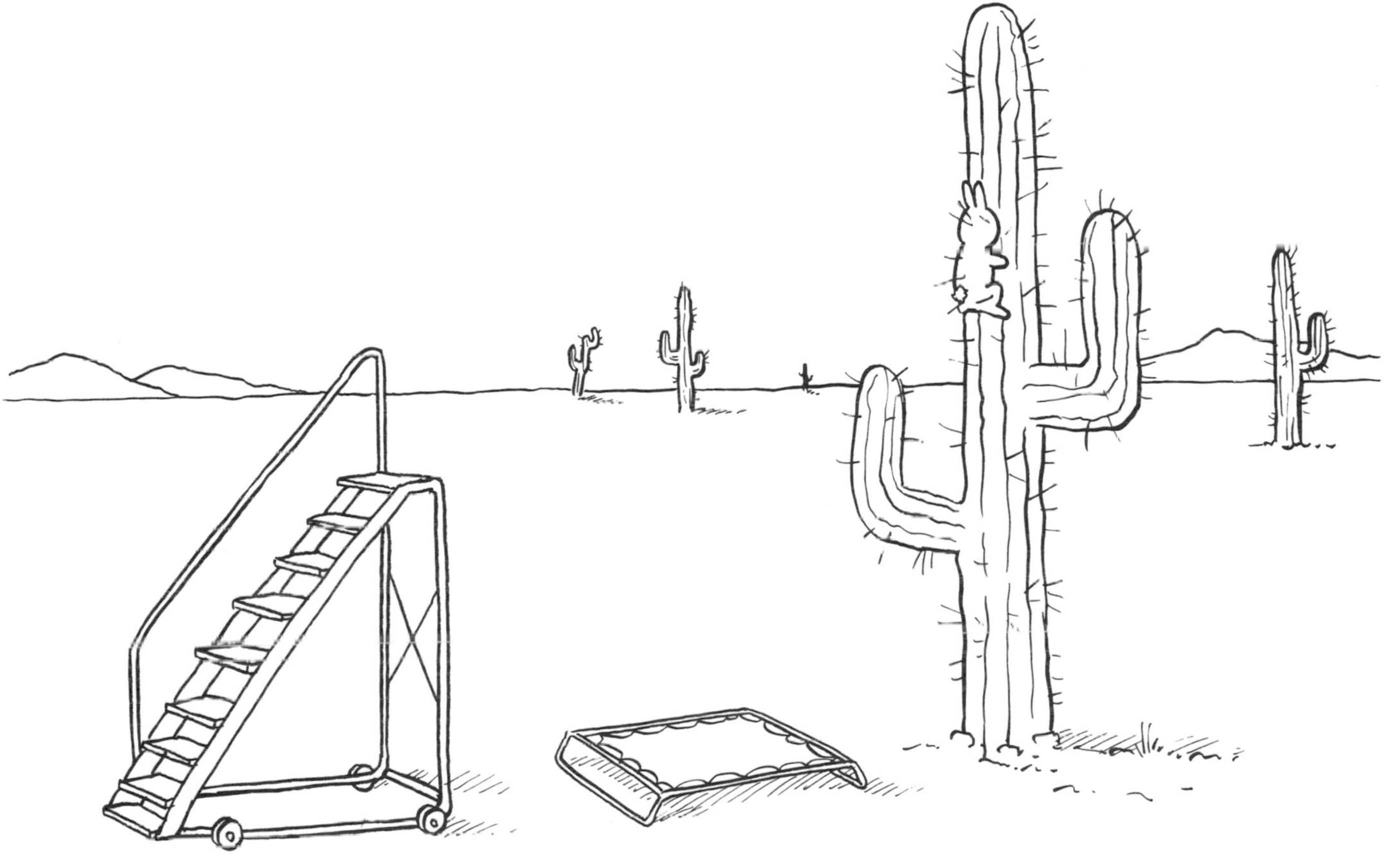

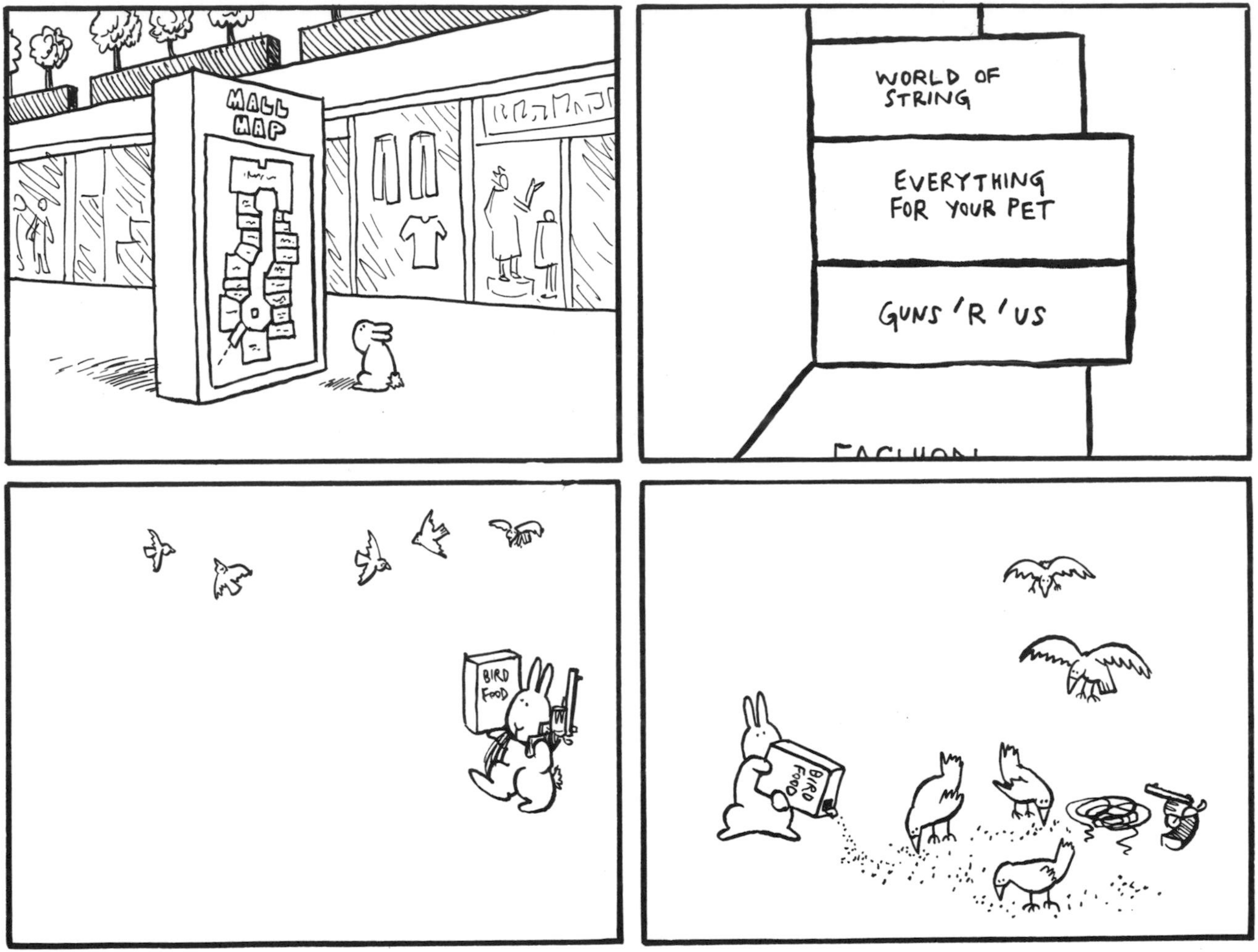
MALL MAP
WORLD OF STRING
EVERYTHING FOR YOUR PET
GUNS 'R' US
BIRD FOOD
BIRD FOOD

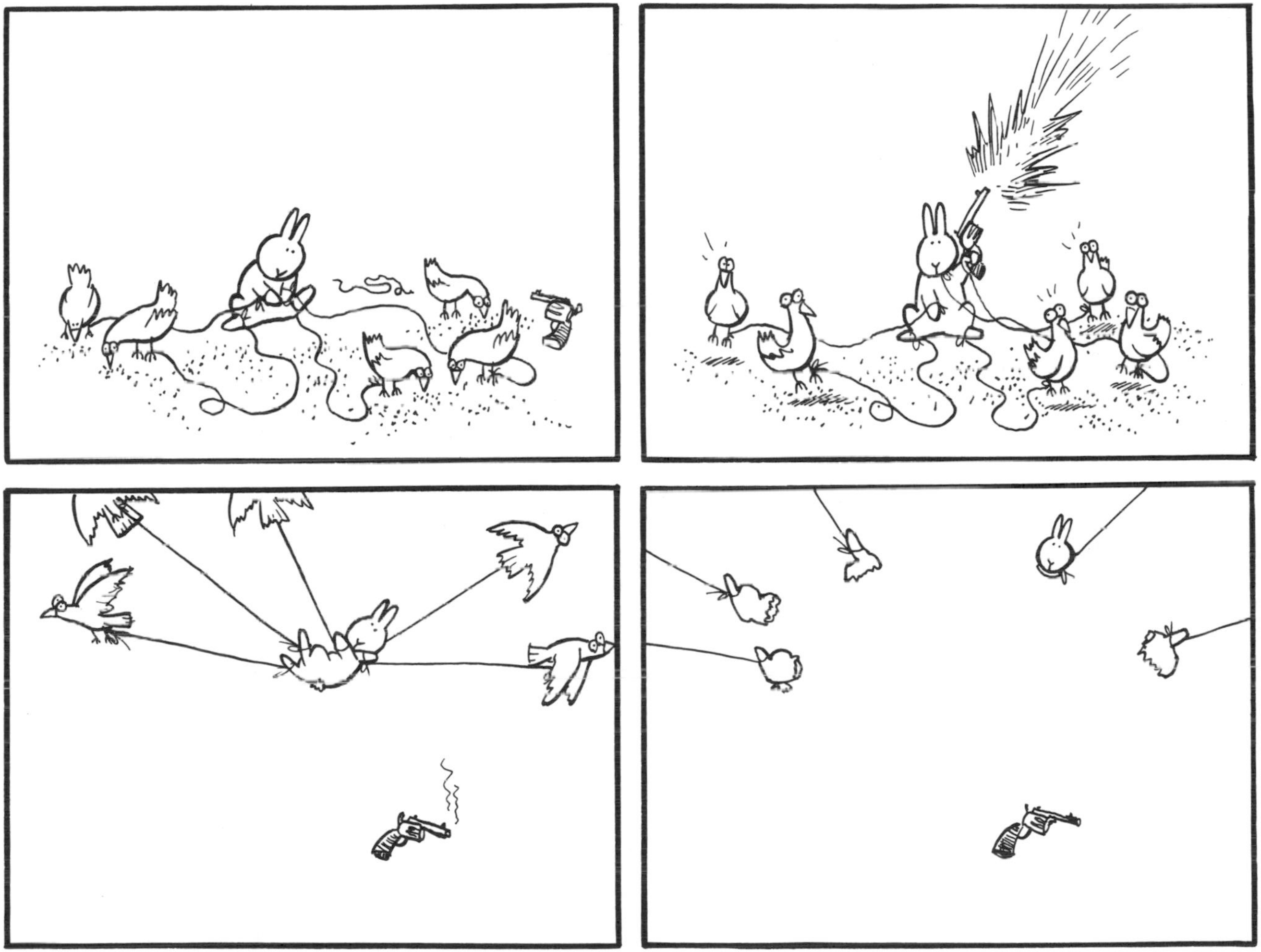

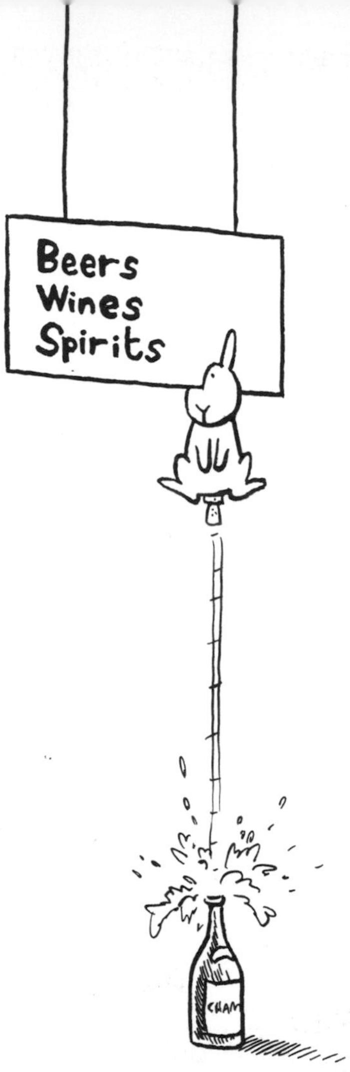
Beers
Wines
Spirits
CHAM

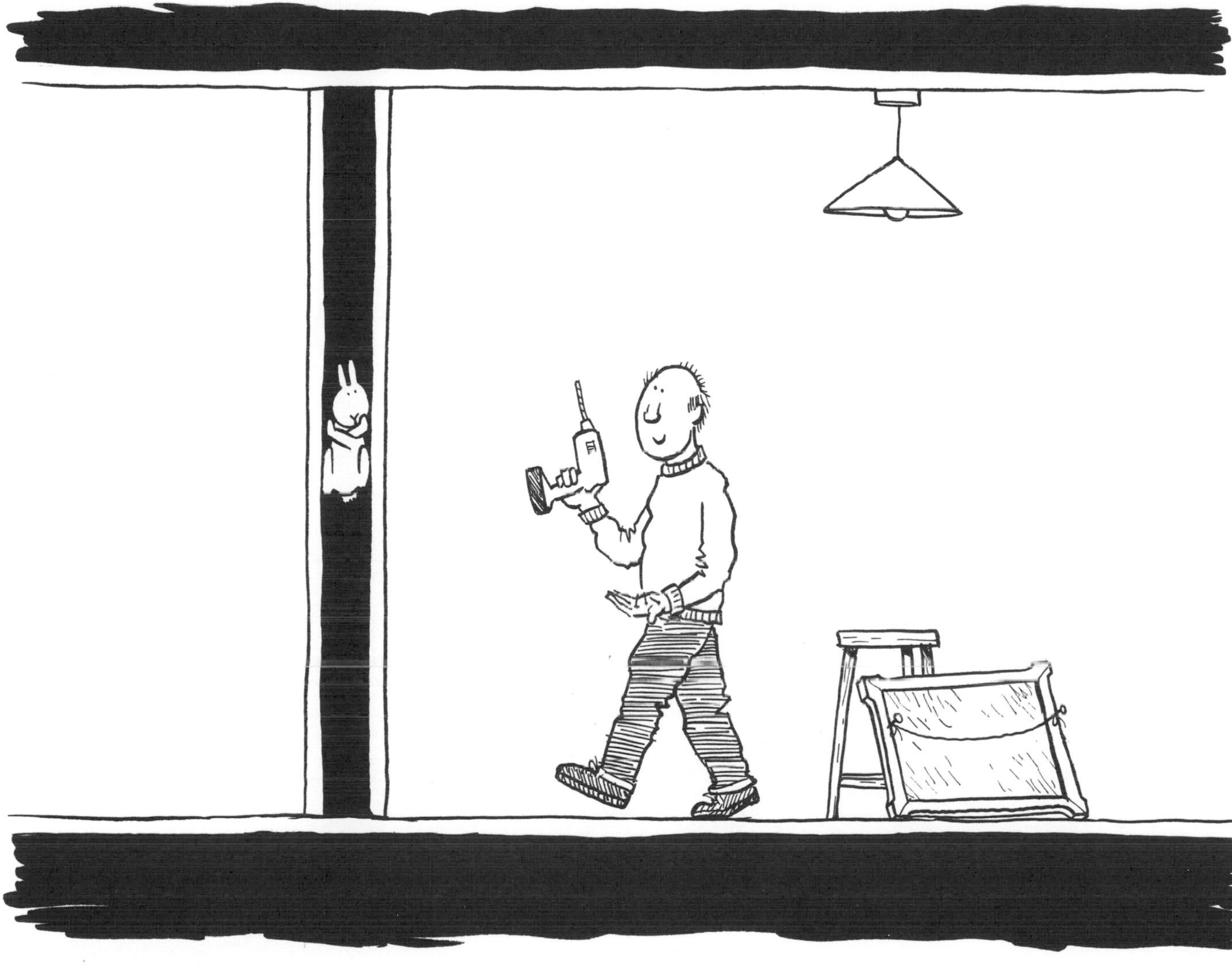

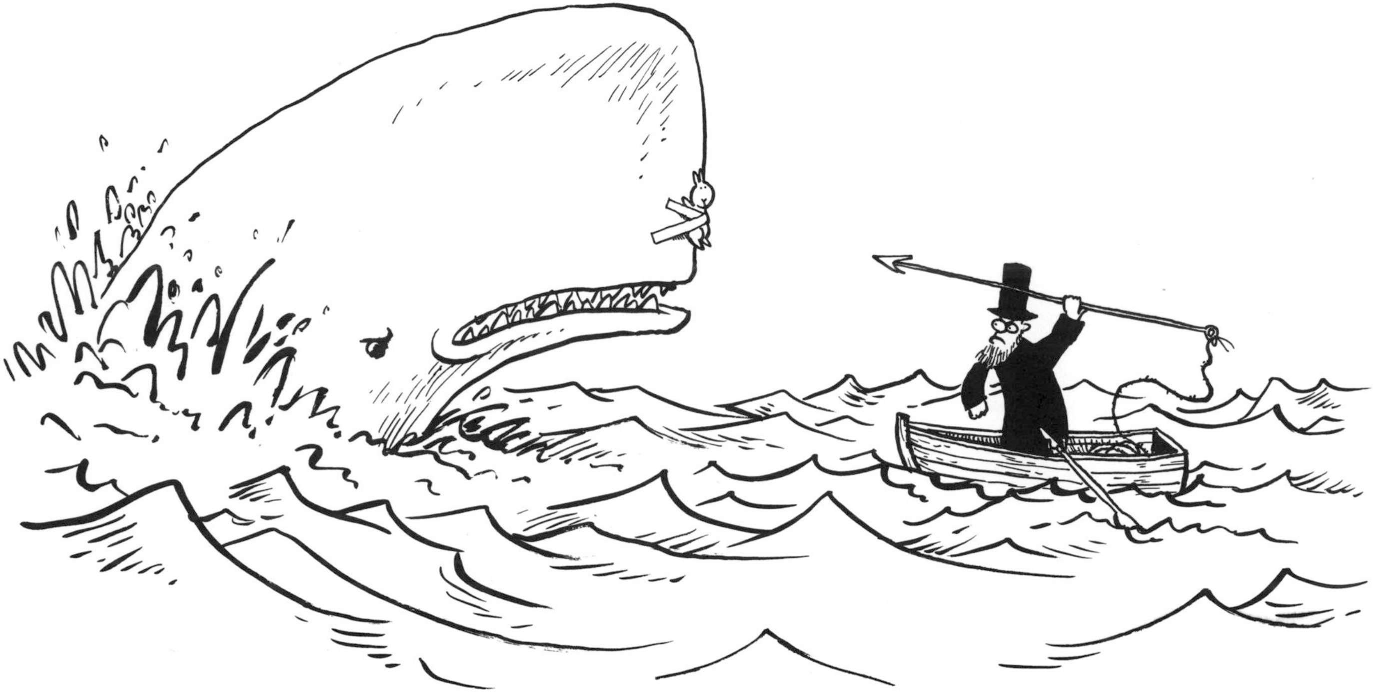

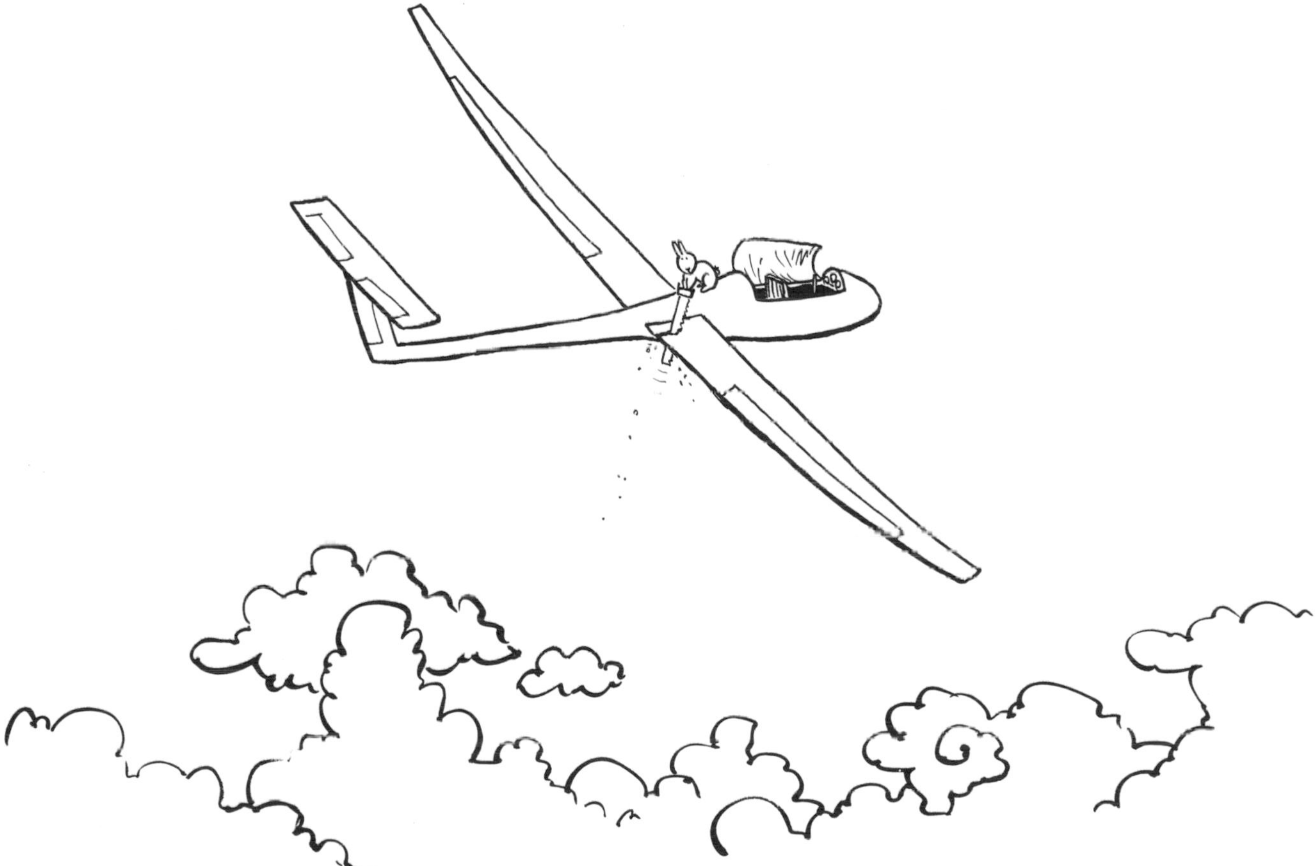

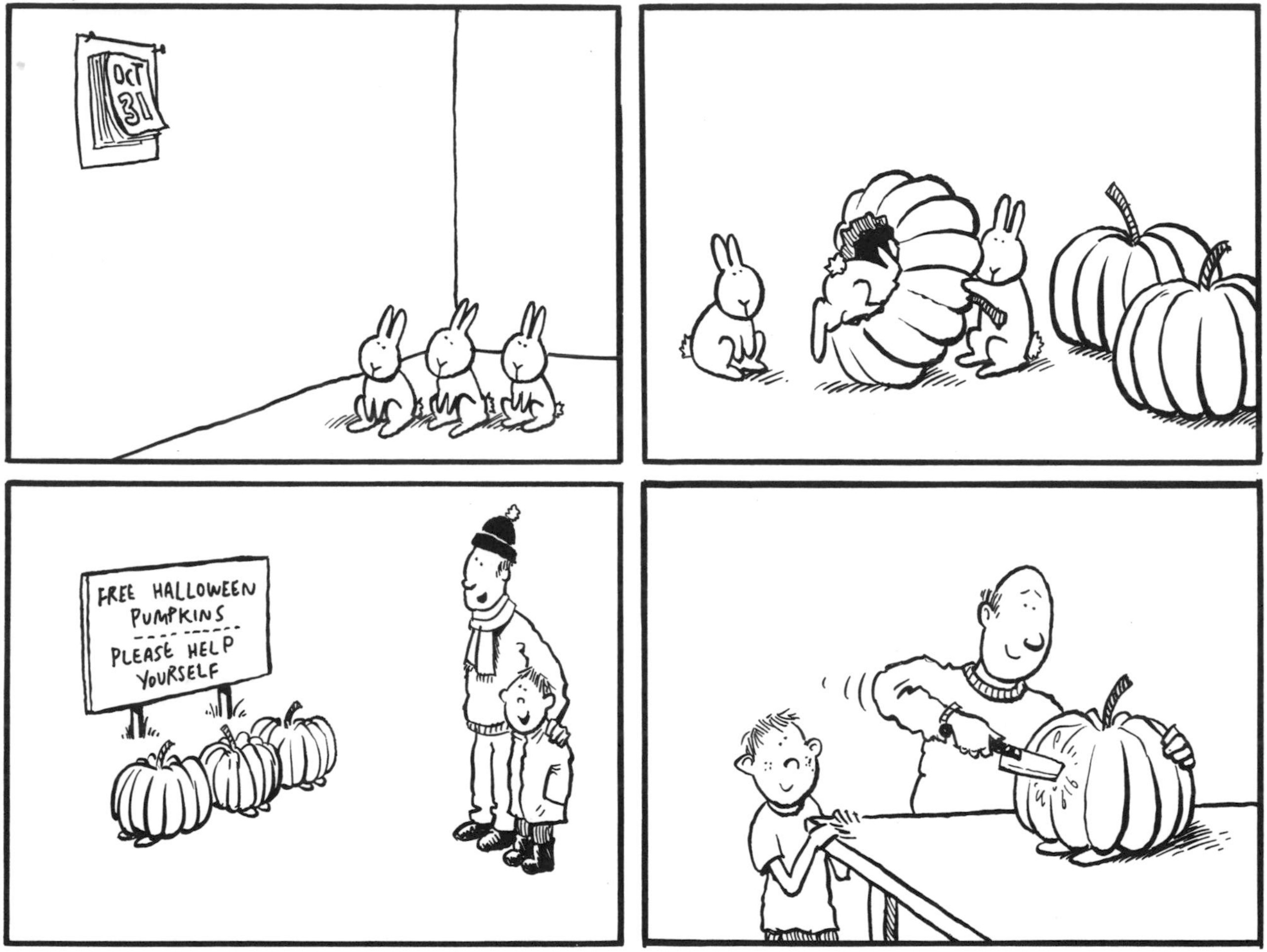
OCT 31
FREE HALLOWEEN PUMPKINS
PLEASE HELP YOURSELF

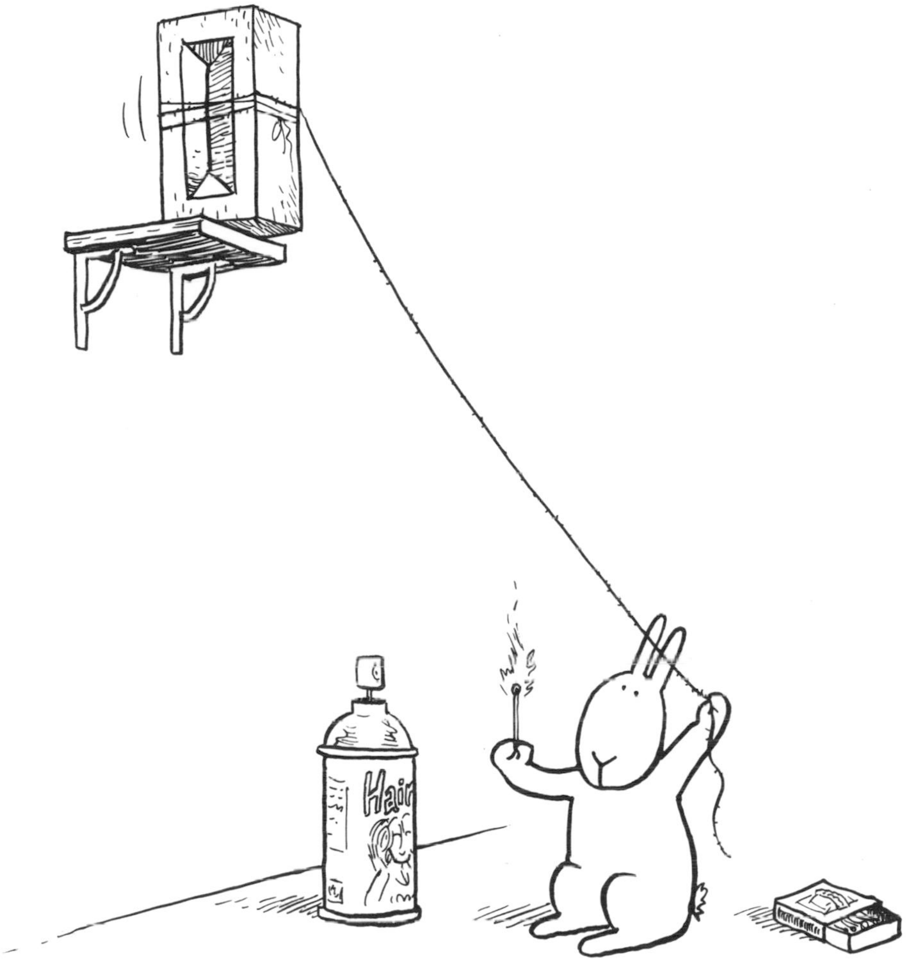
Hair

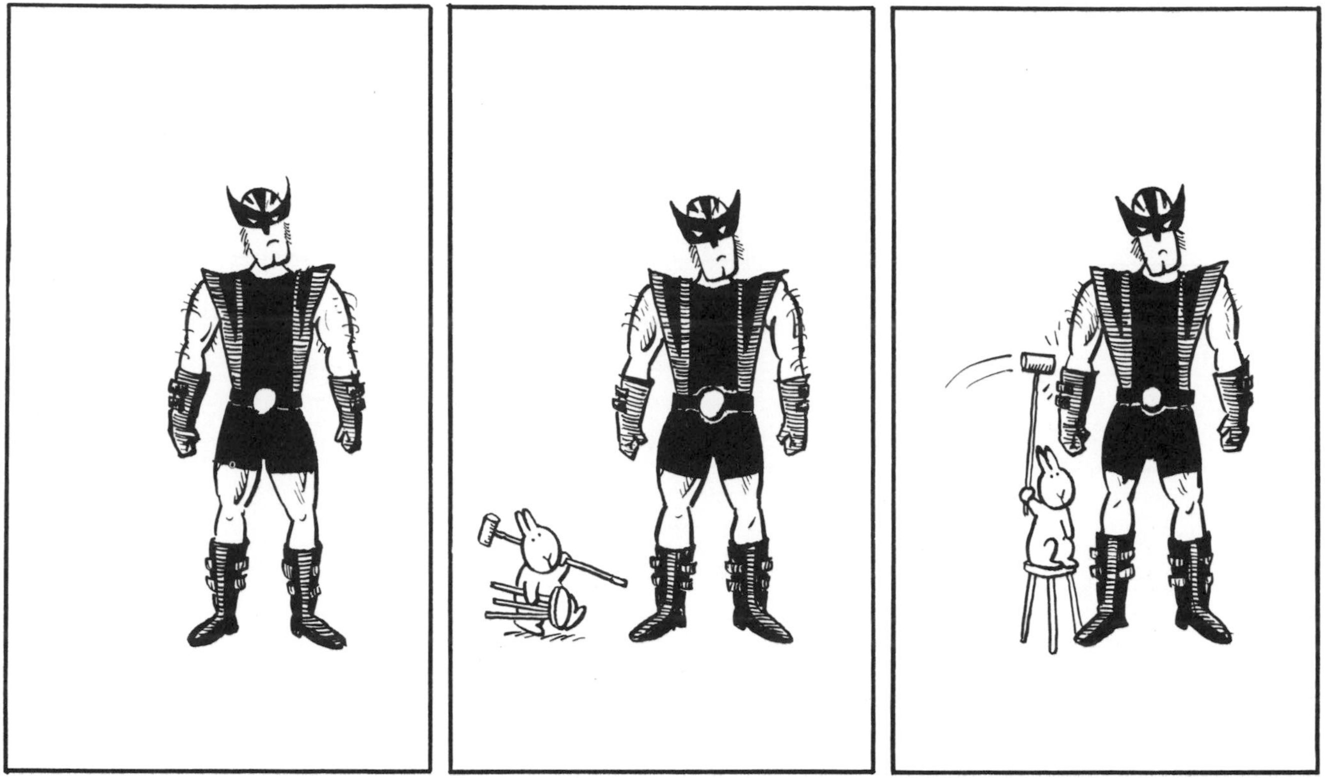

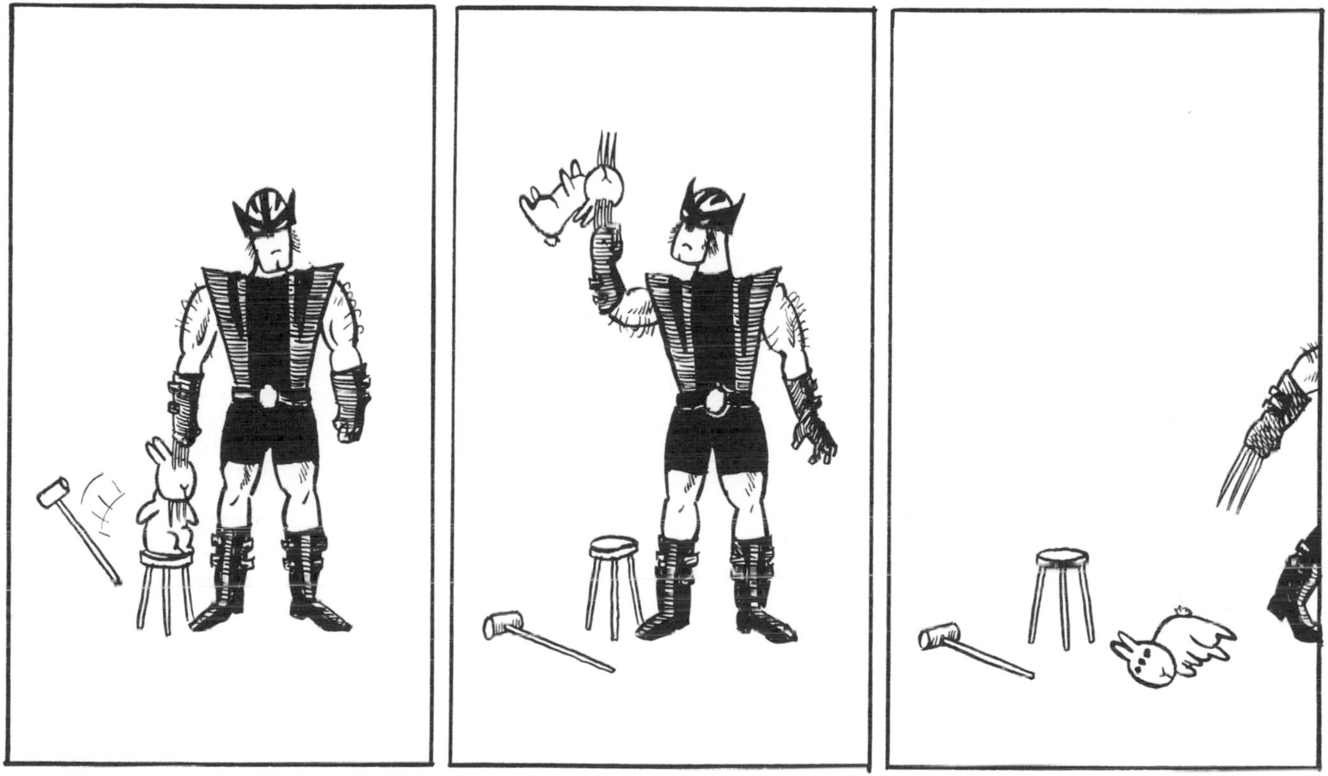

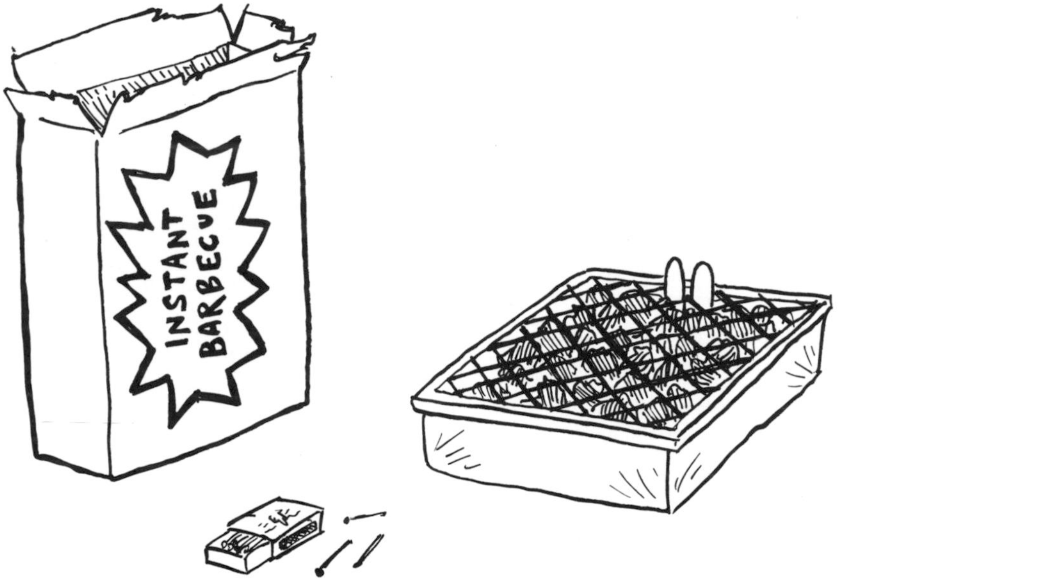
INSTANT
BARBECUE

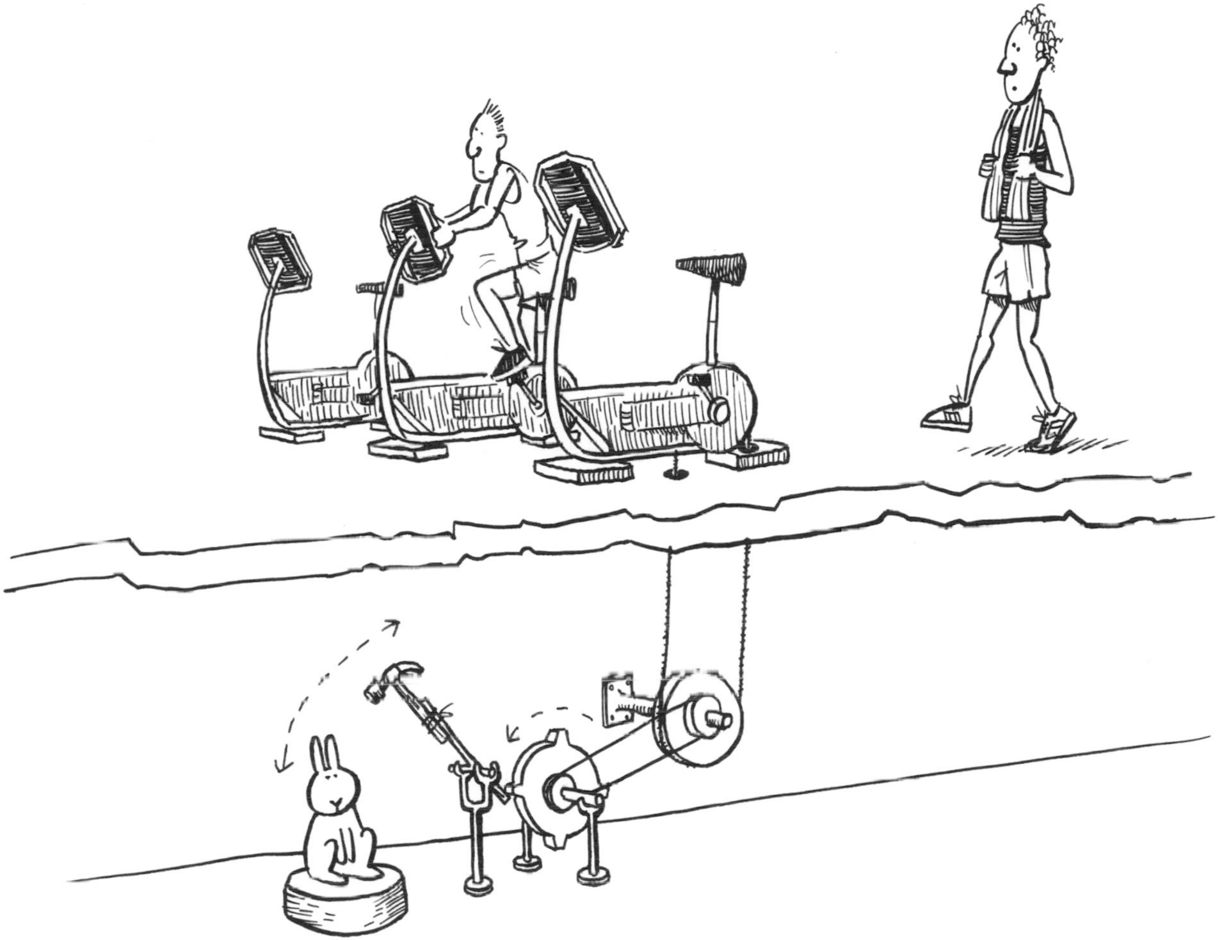

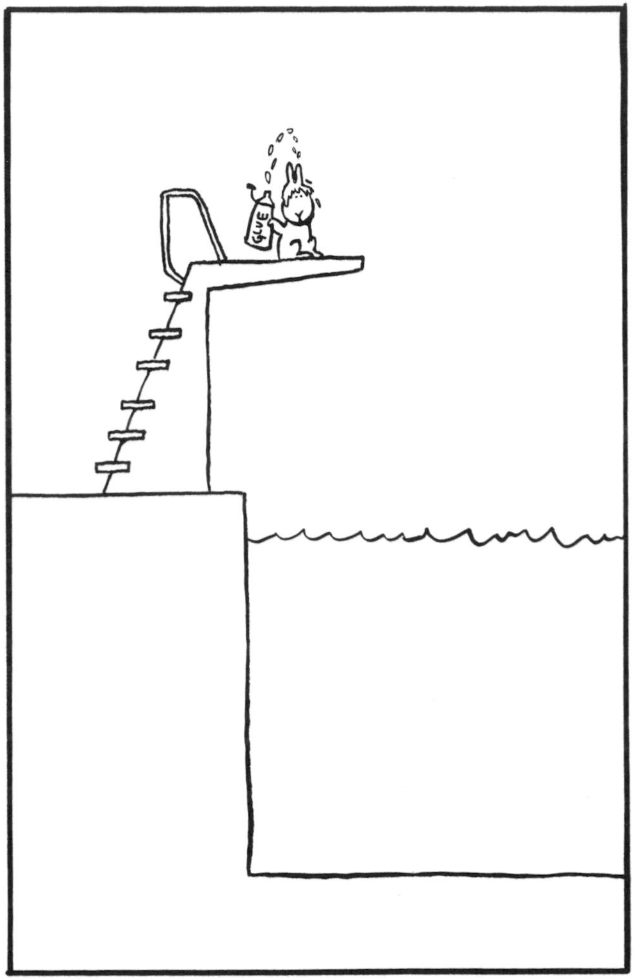
GLUE

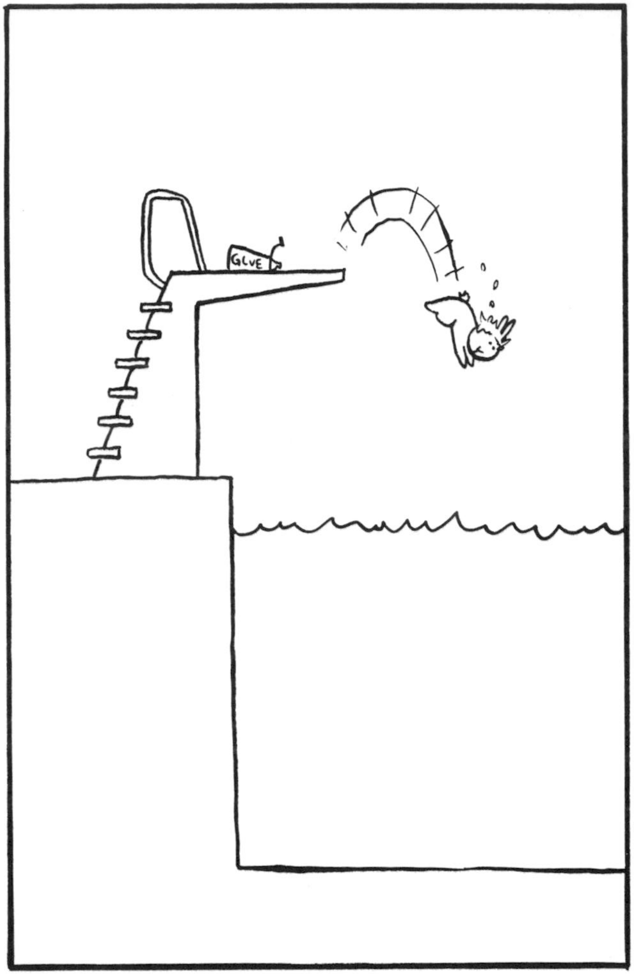
GLUE

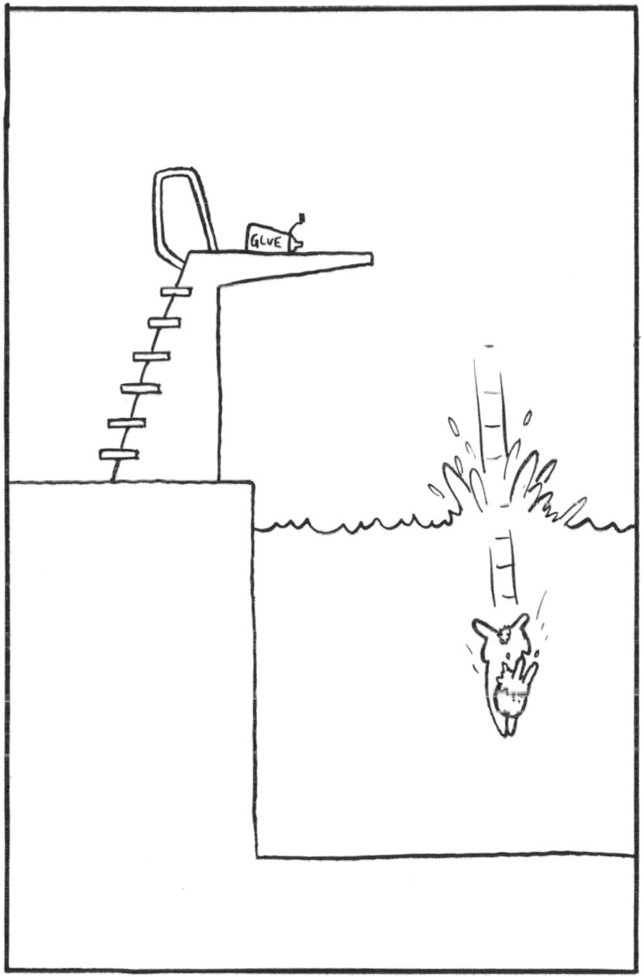
GLUE

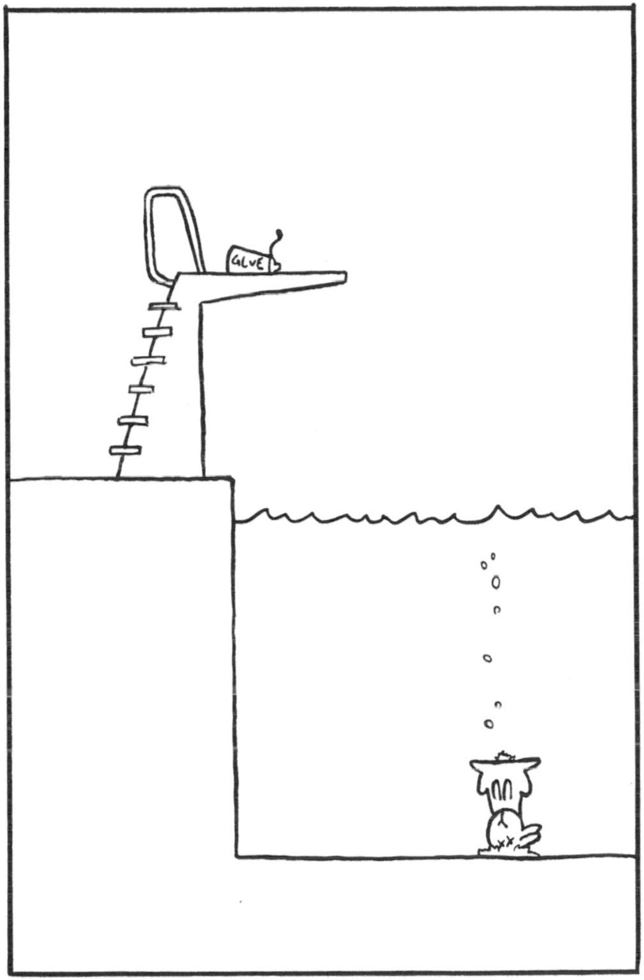
GLUE

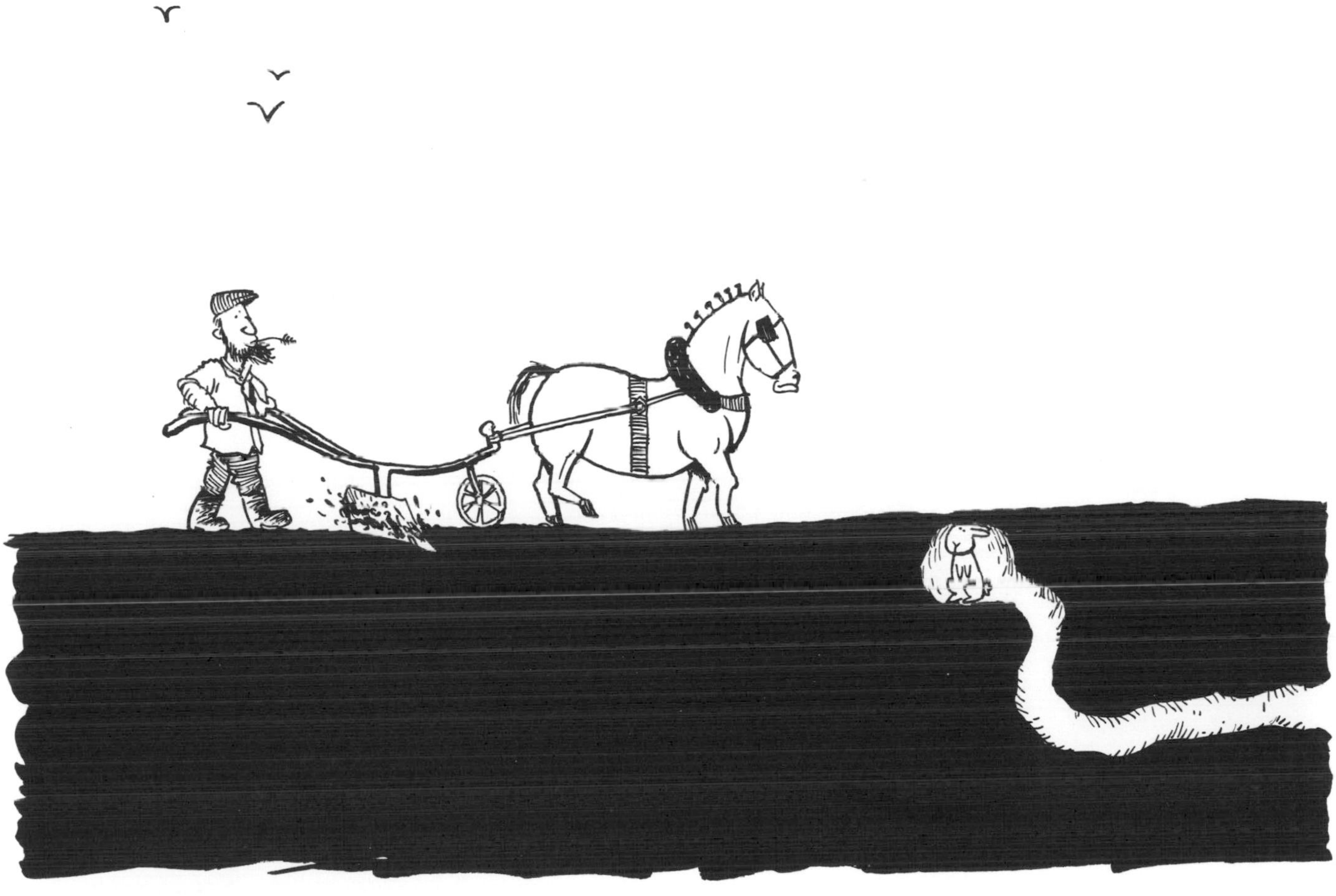

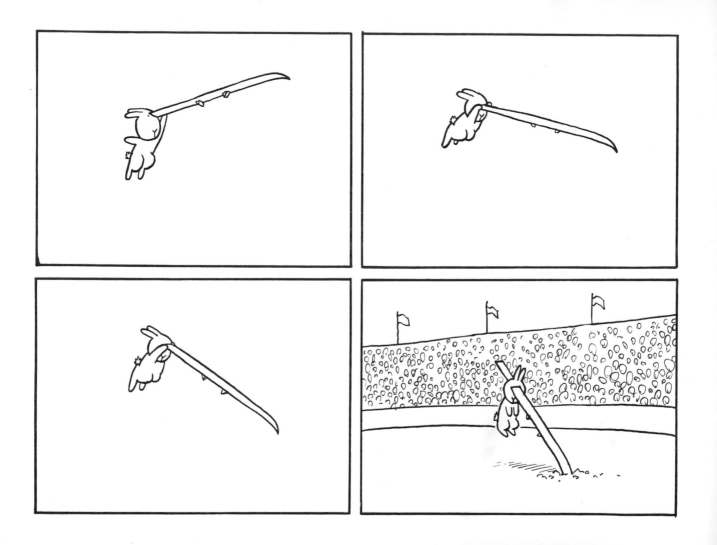

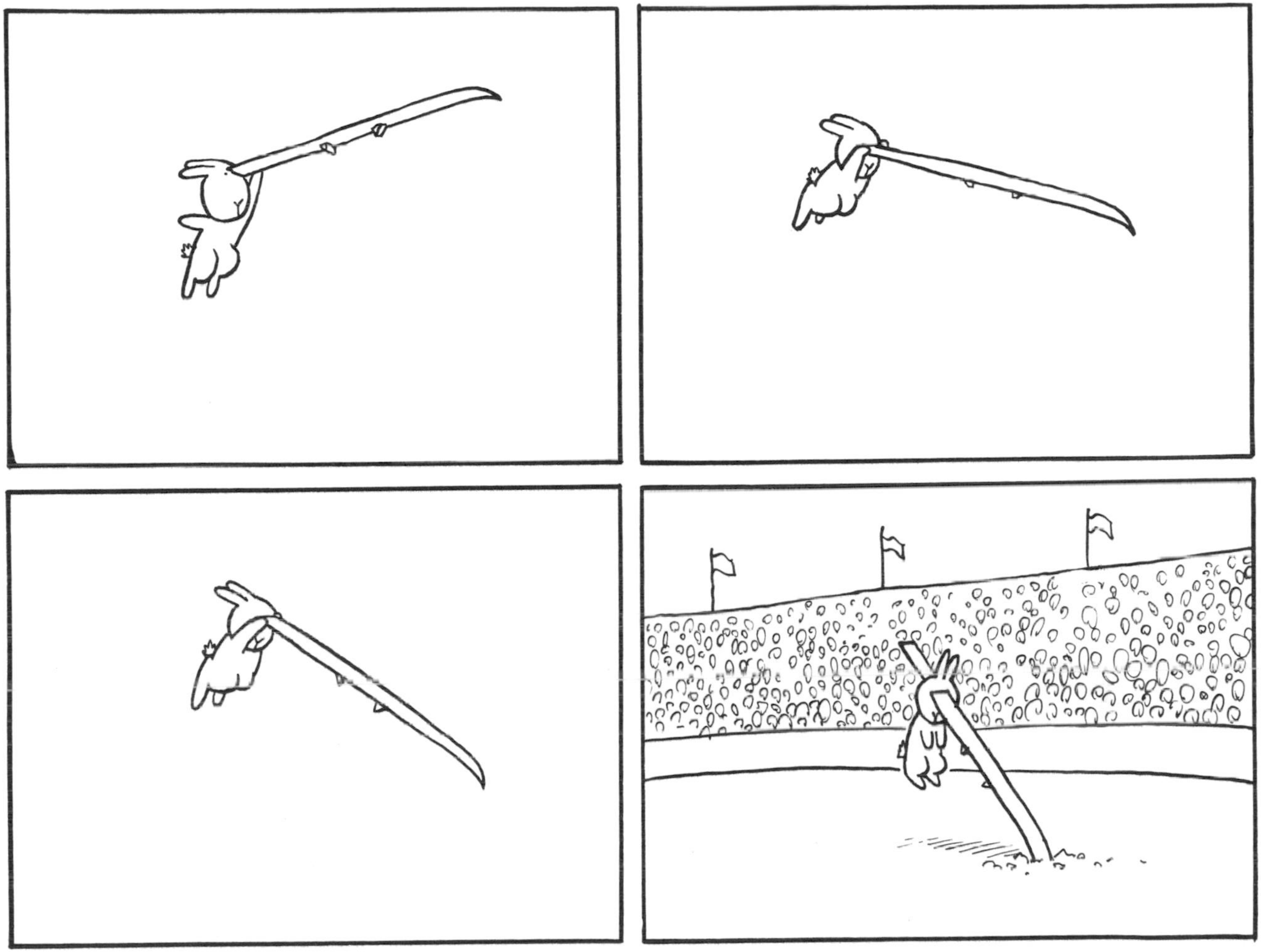

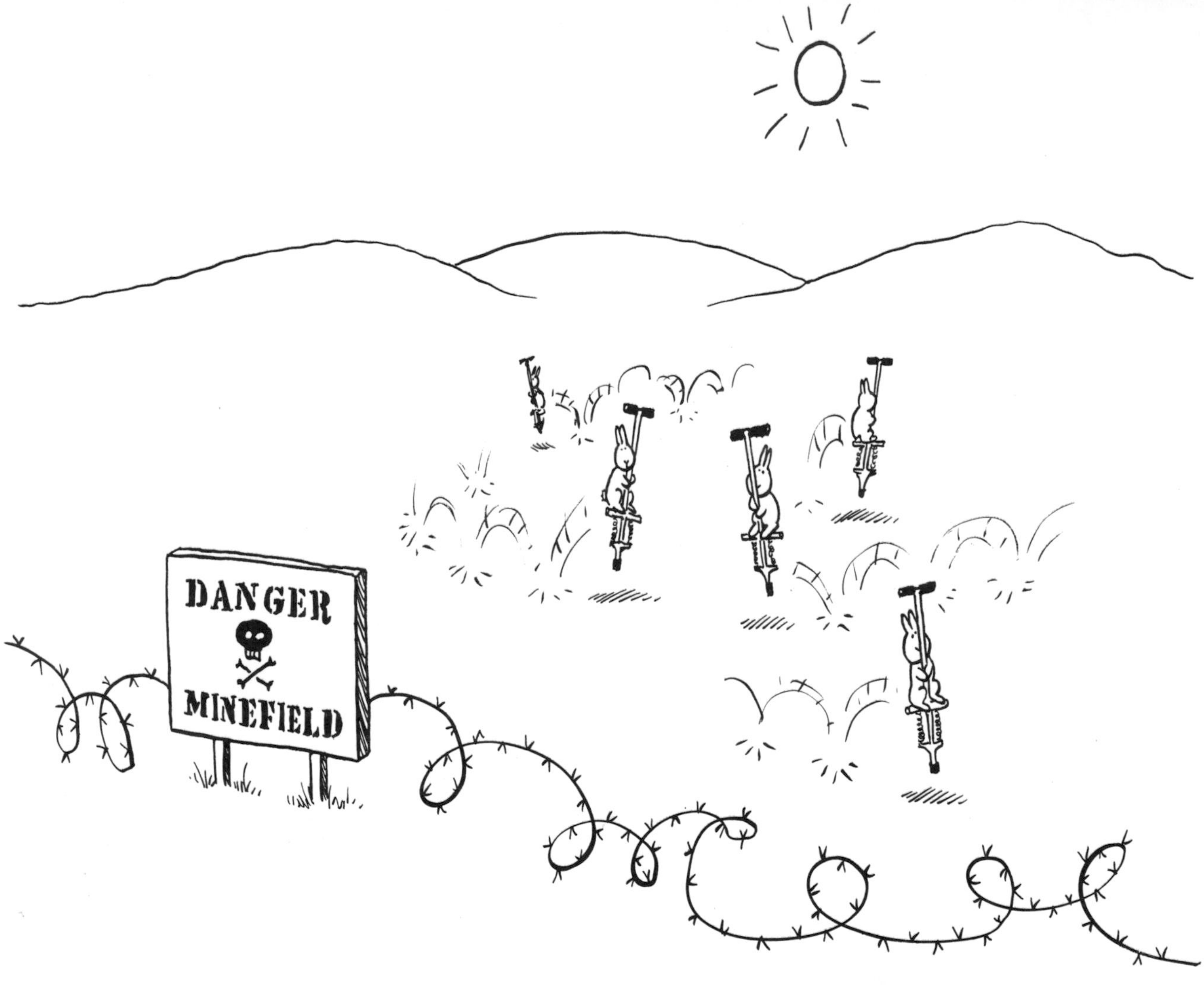
DANGER
MINEFIELD

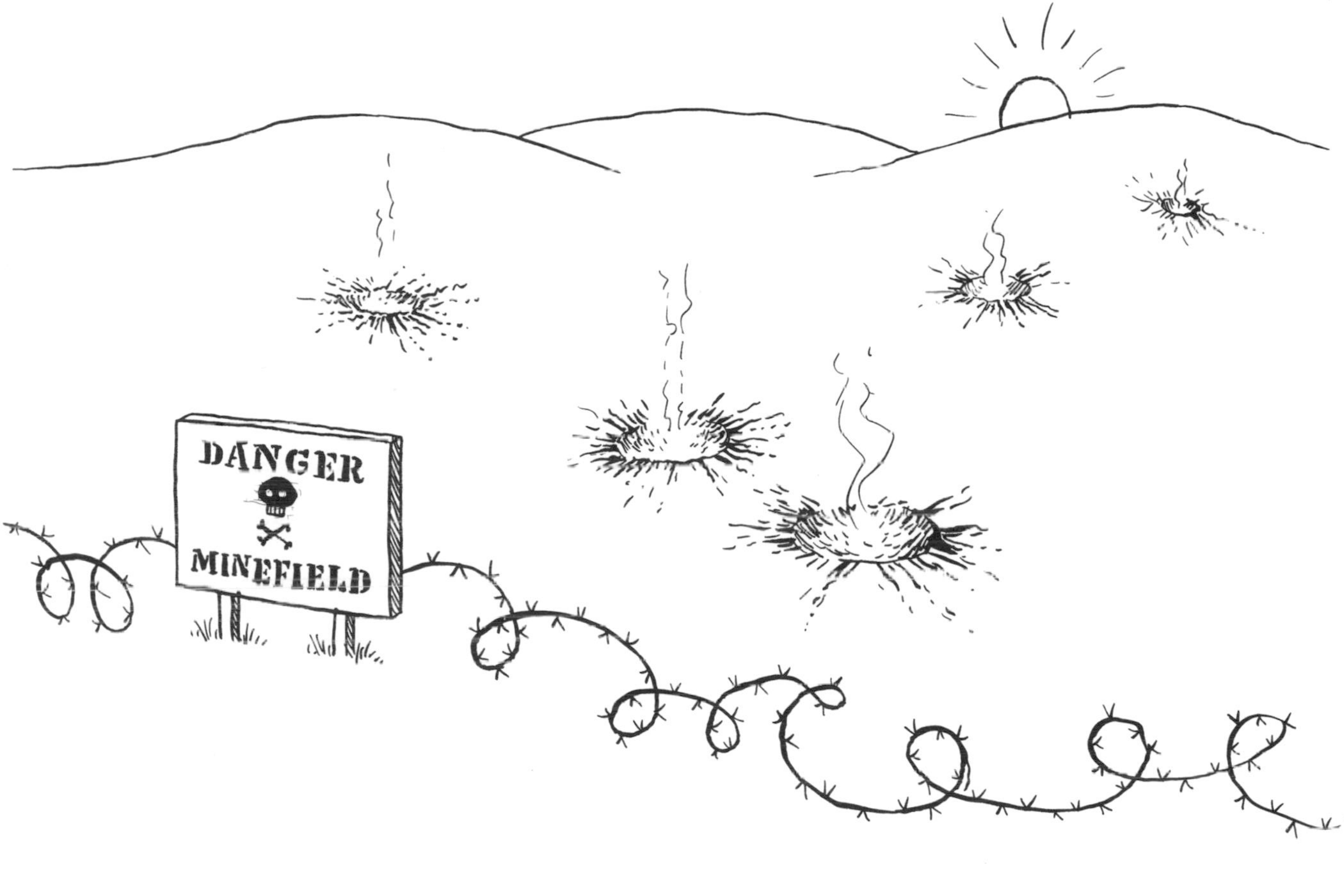
DANGER
MINEFIELD

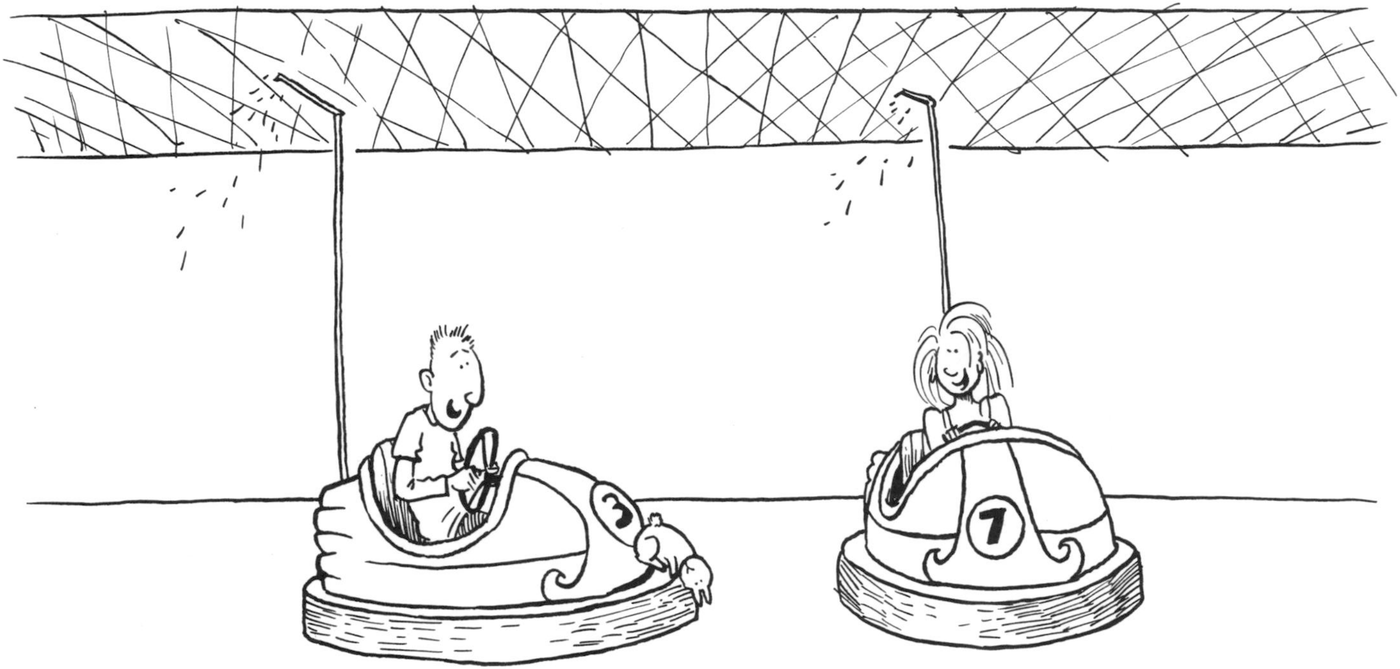
3
7

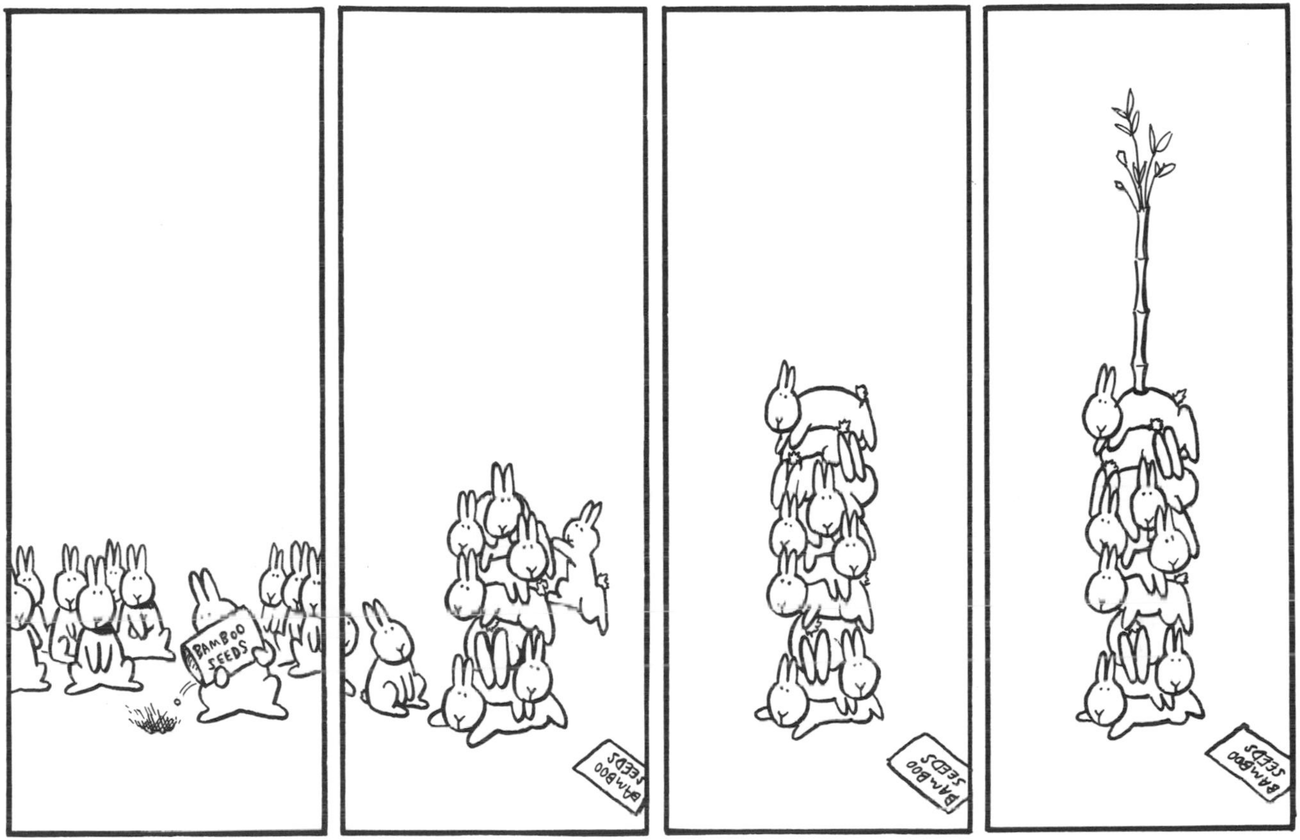
BAMBOO SEEDS
BAMBOO SEEDS
BAMBOO SEEDS
BAMBOO SEEDS

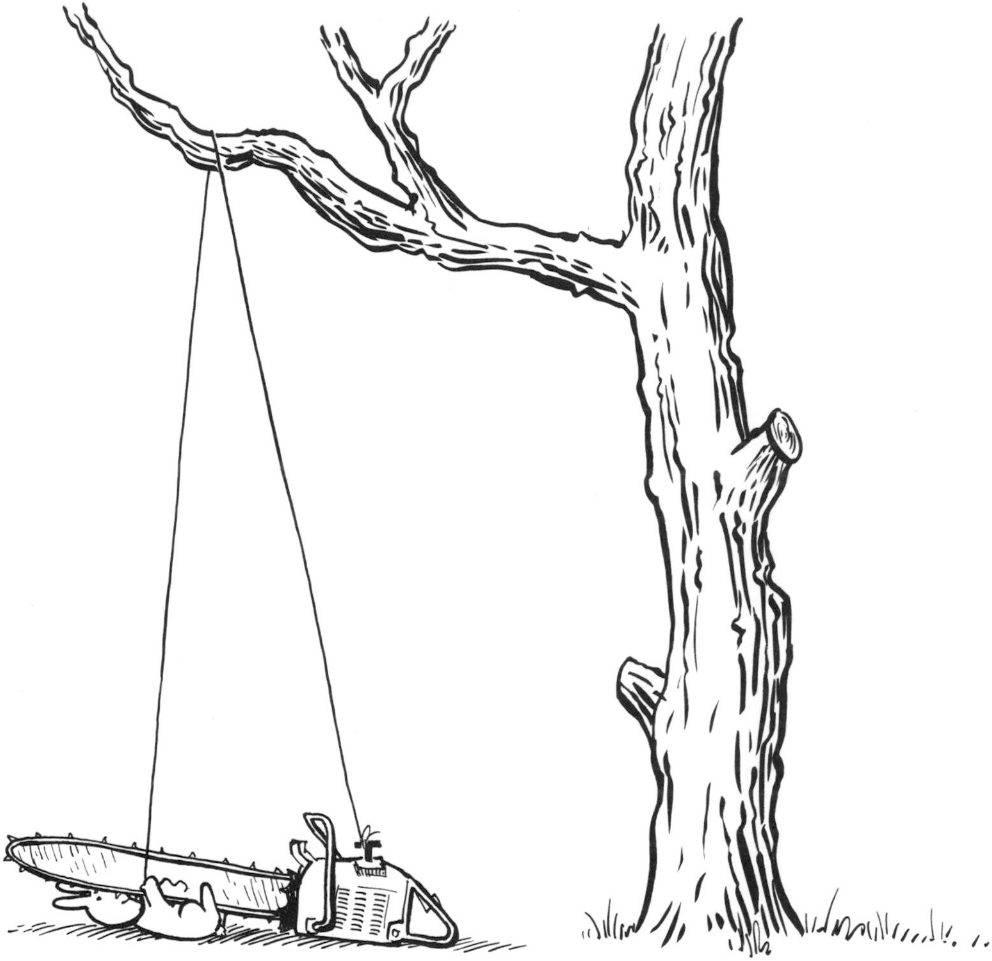

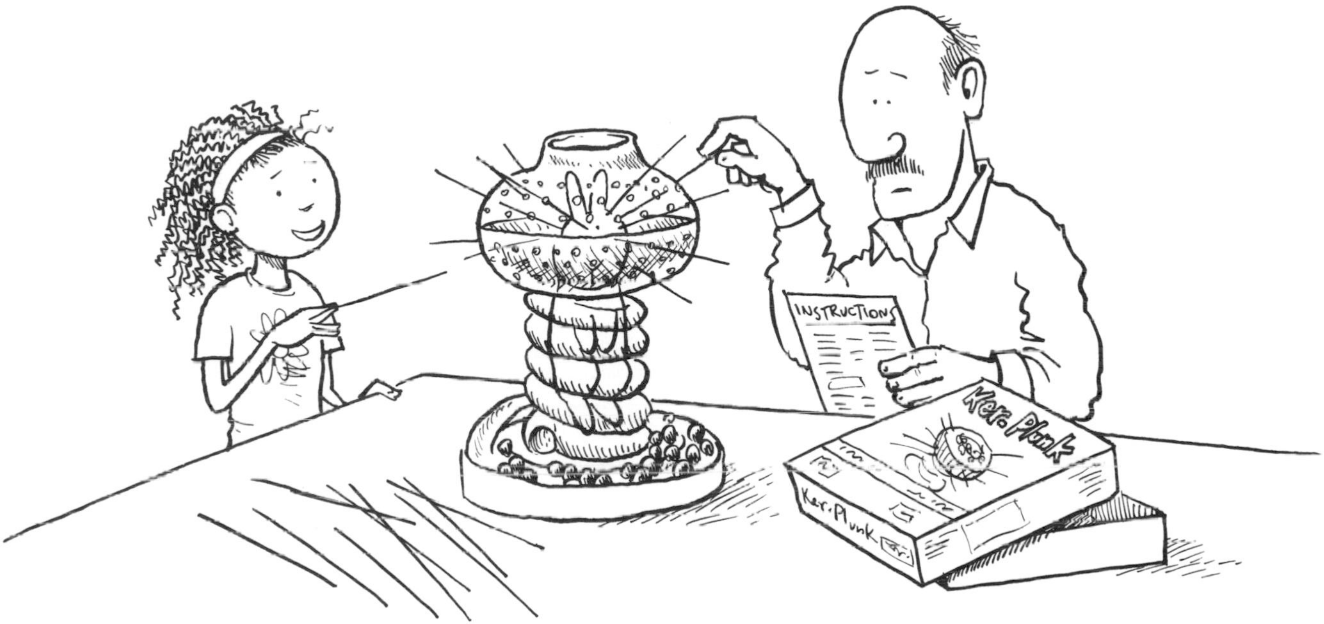
INSTRUCTIONS
Ker-Plunk
Ker-Plunk

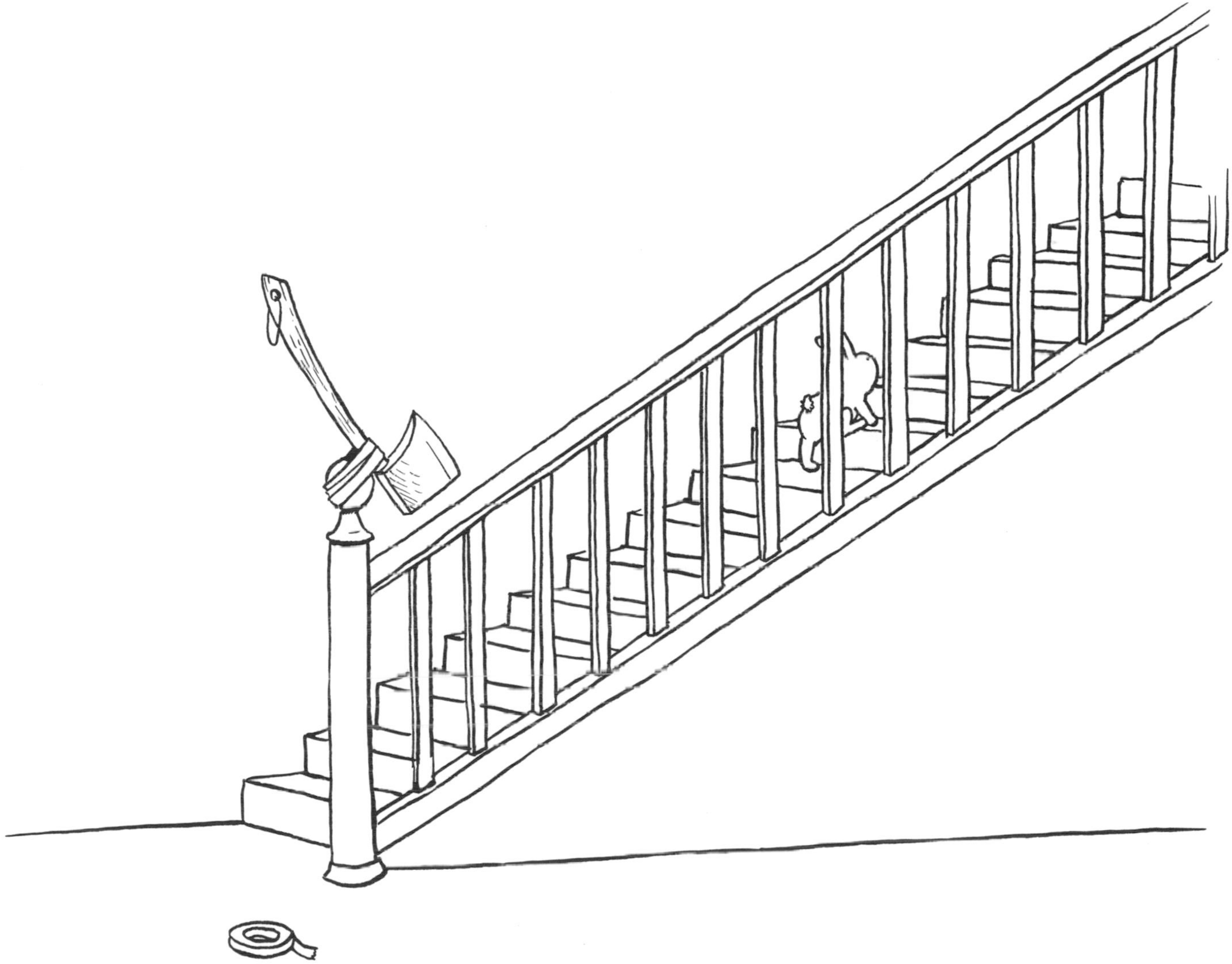

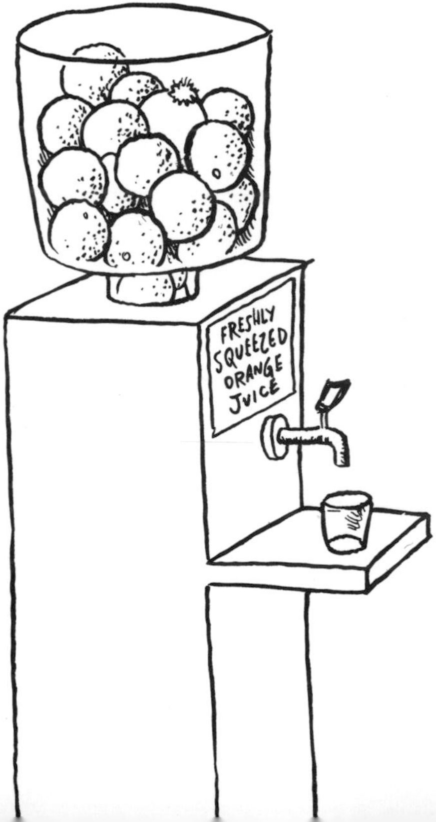
FRESHLY
SQUEEZED
ORANGE
JUICE

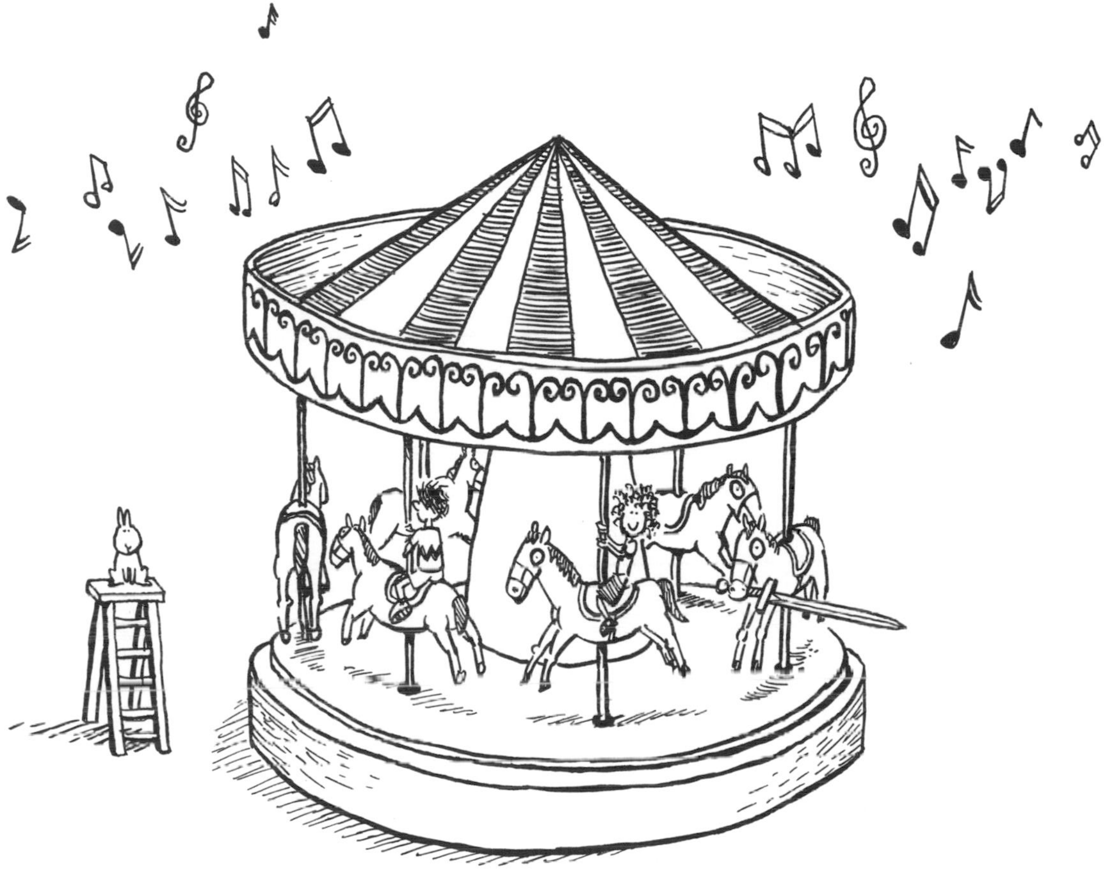

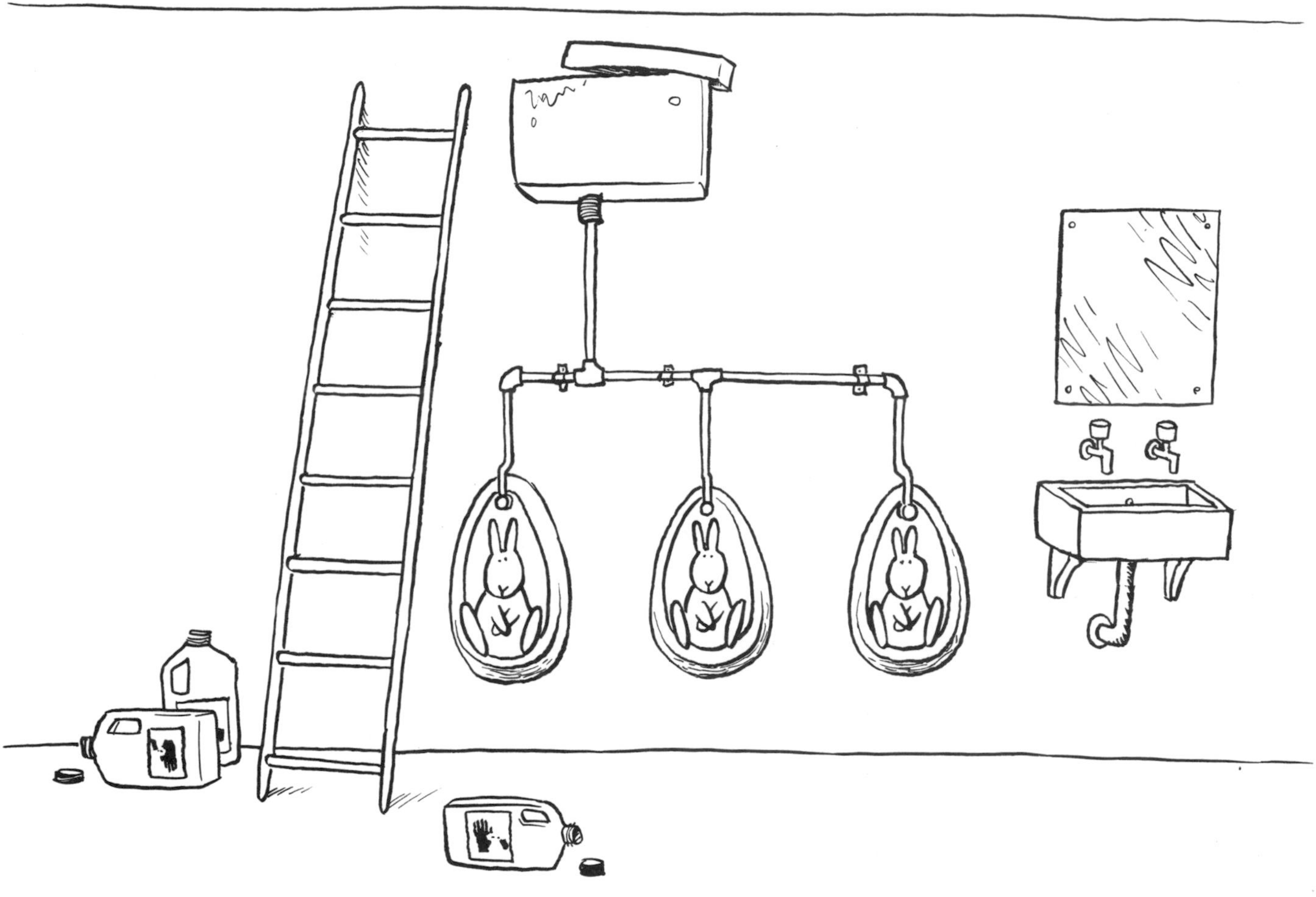

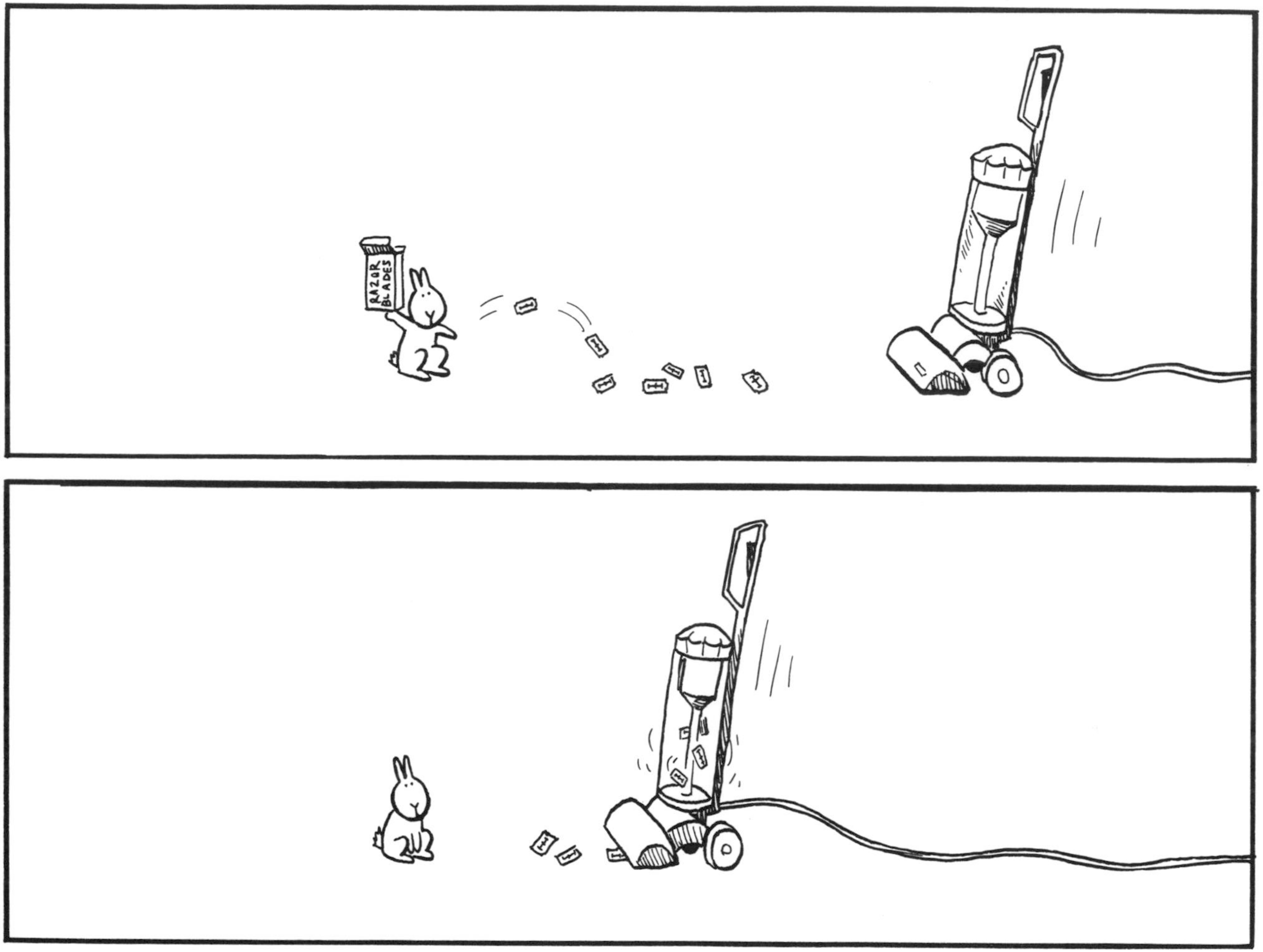
RAZOR BLADES

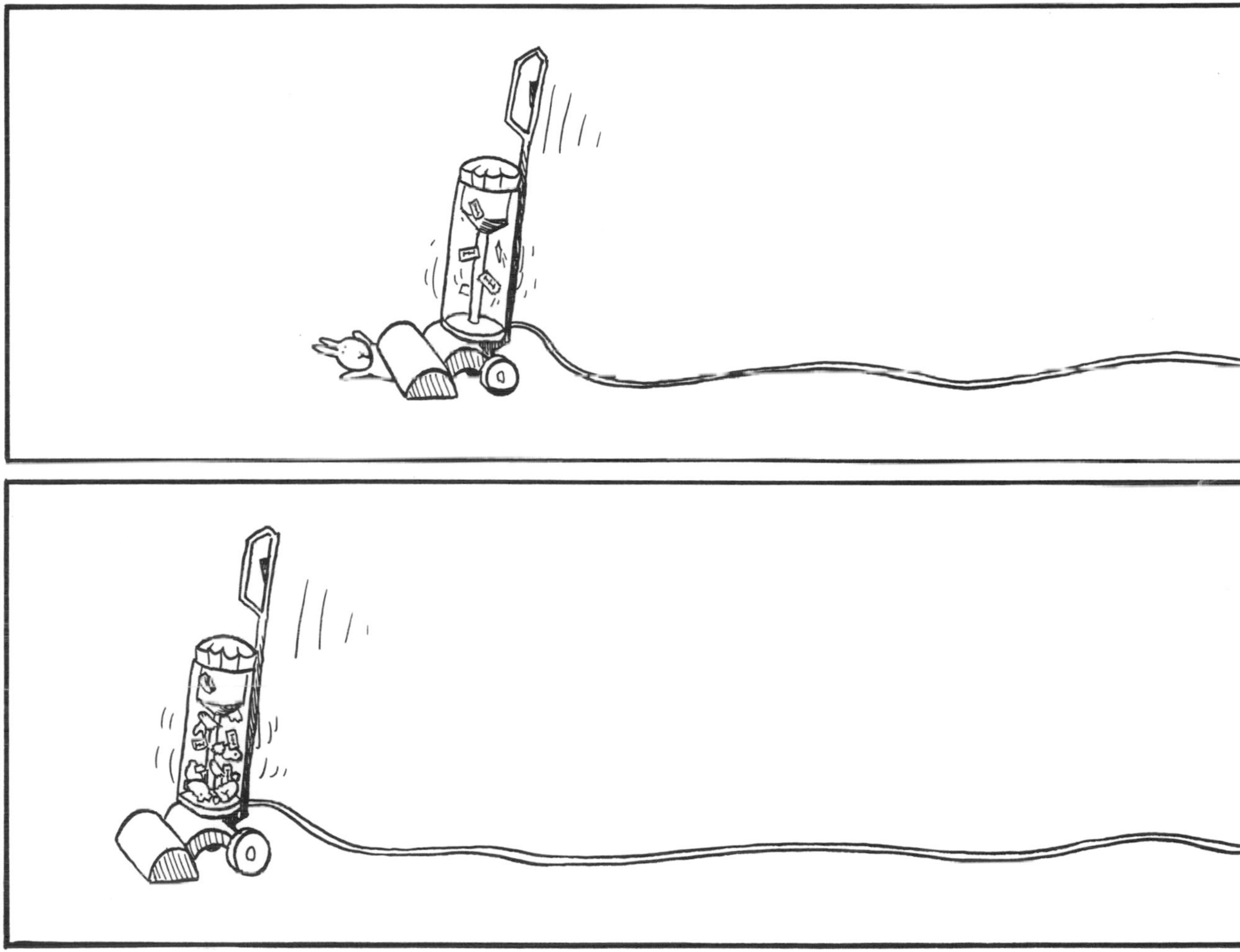

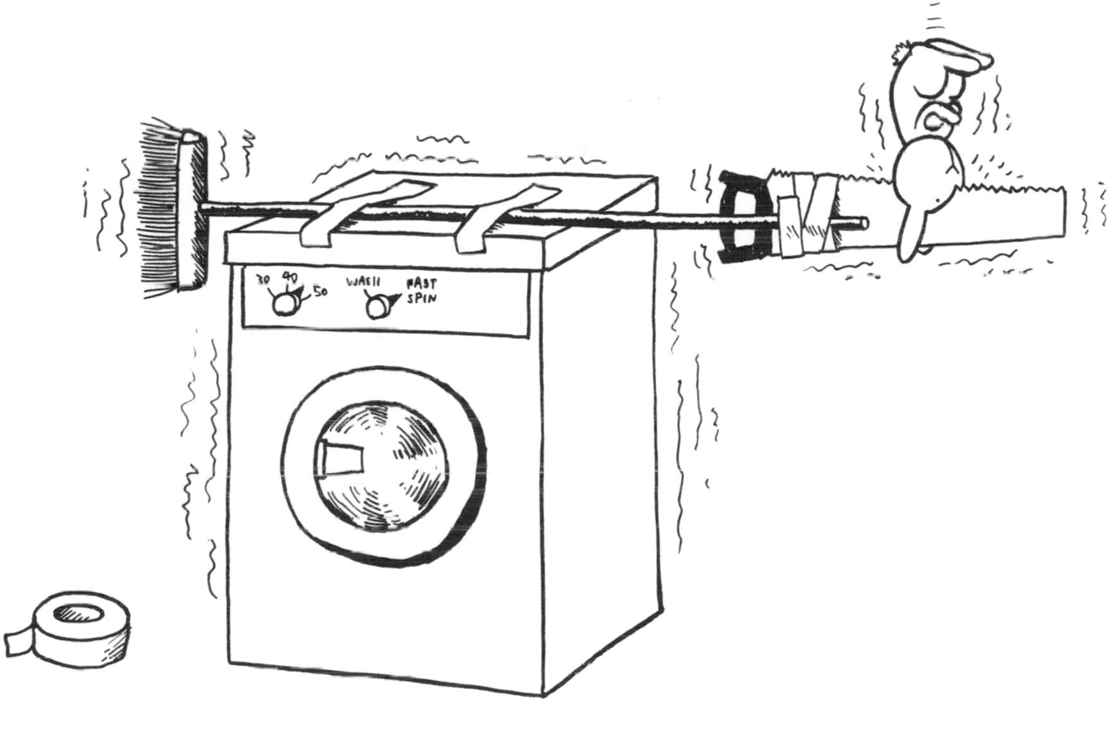
30 40 50
WASH
FAST SPIN

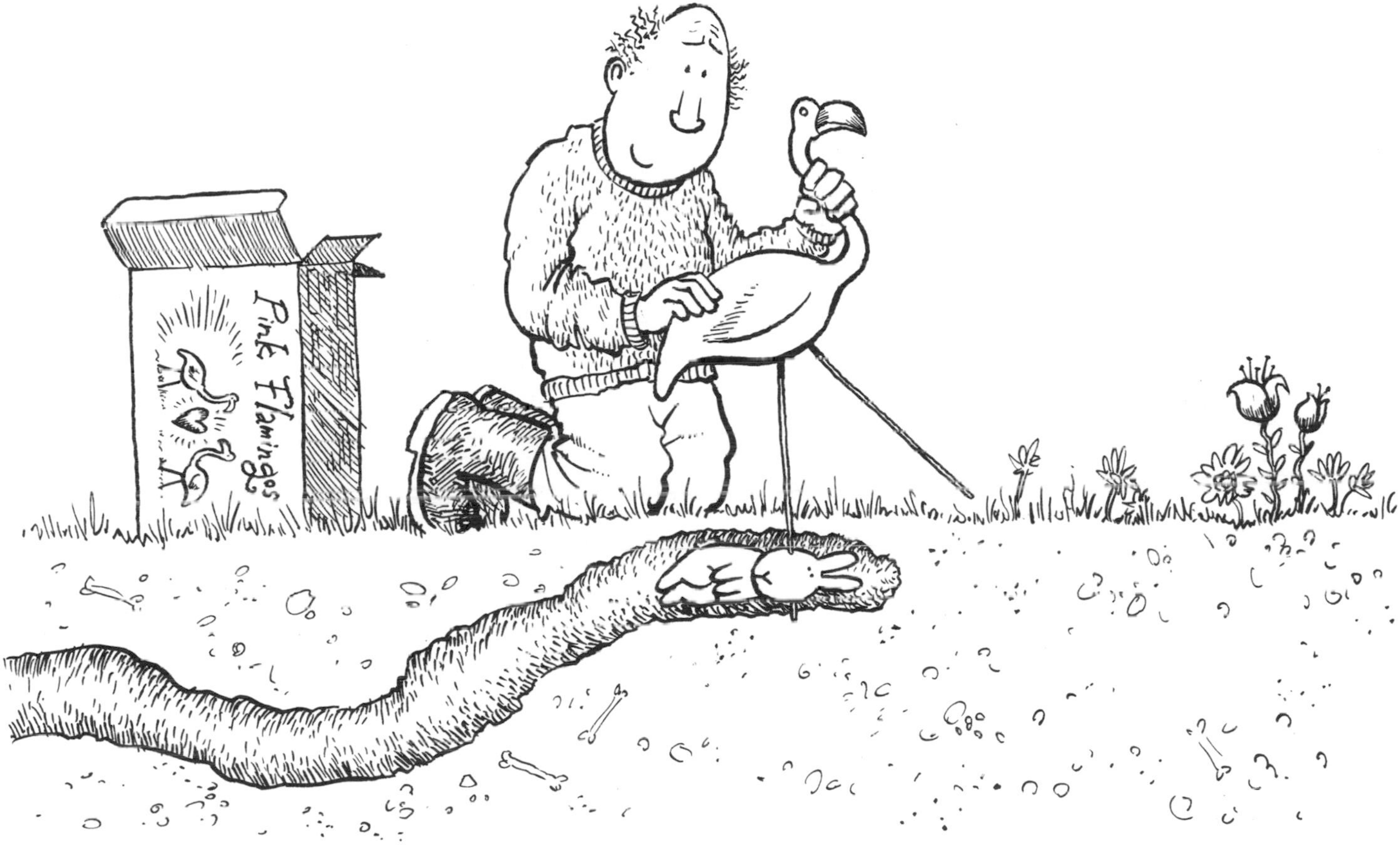
Pink Flamingos

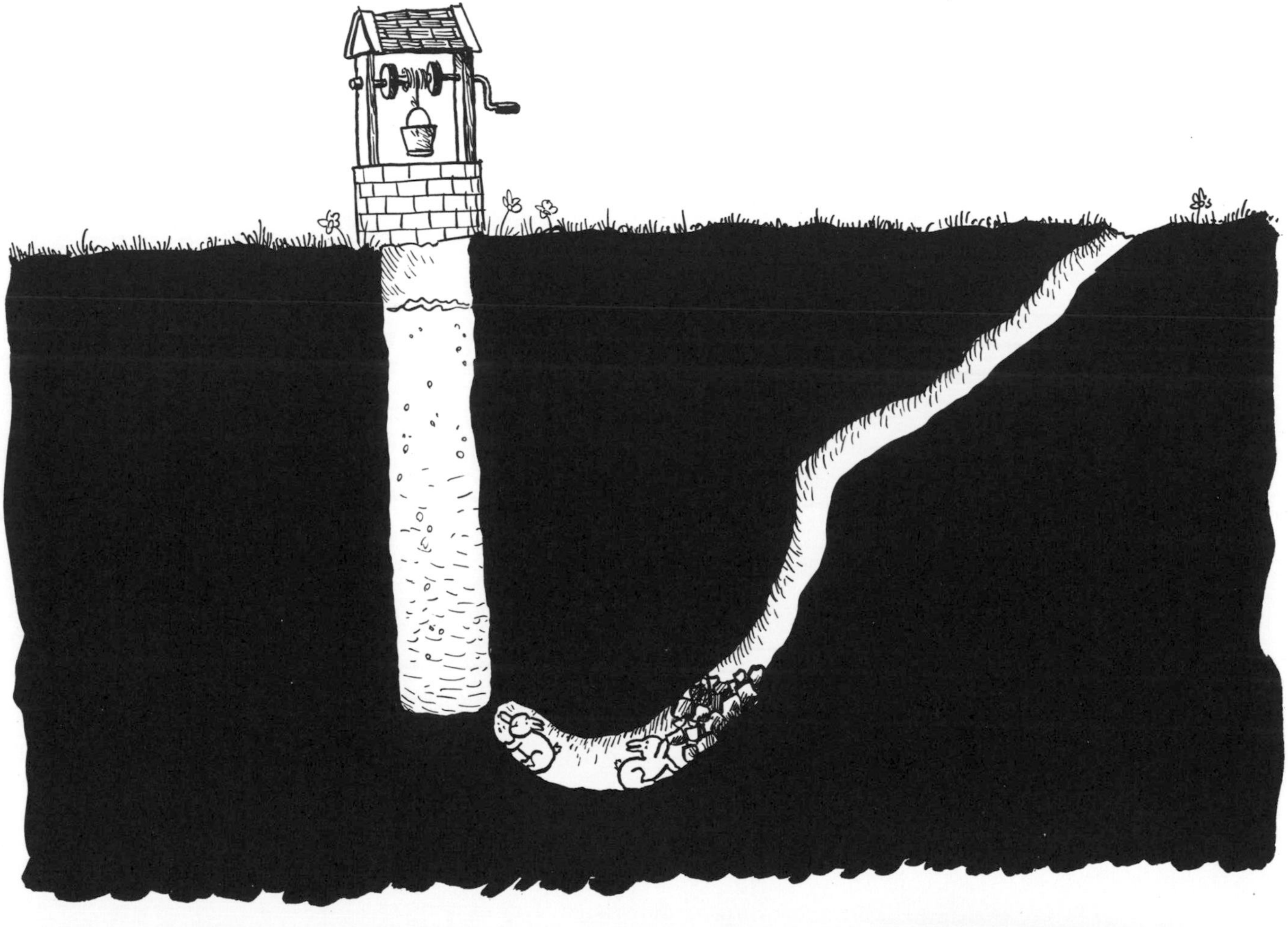

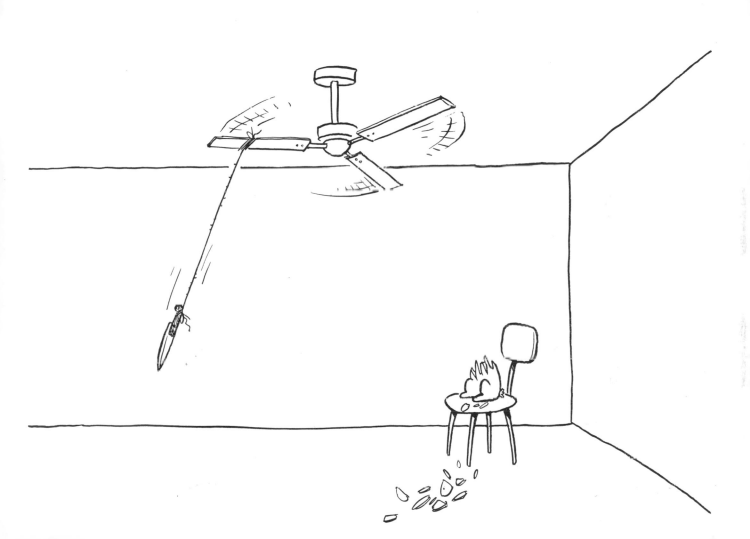

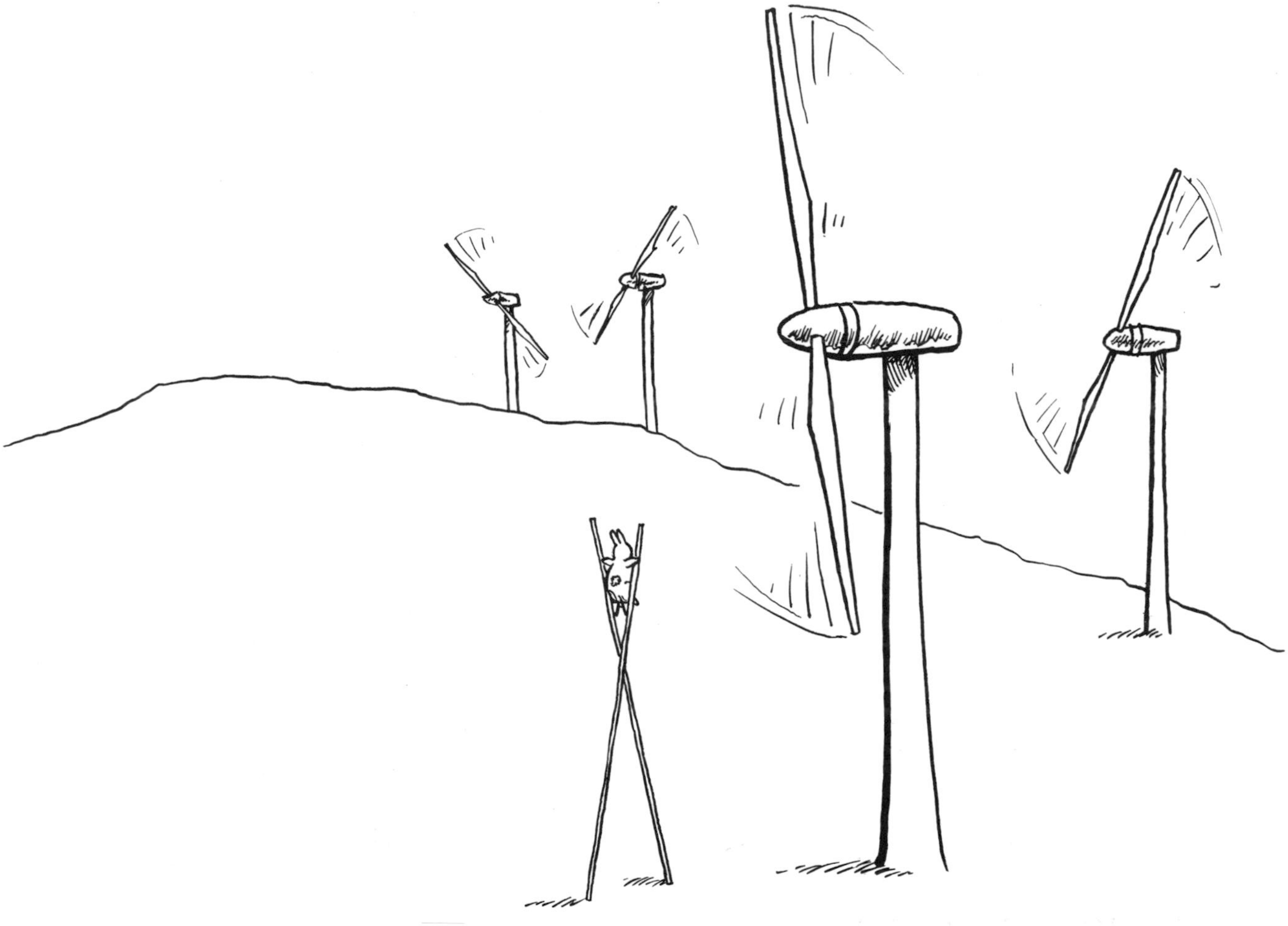

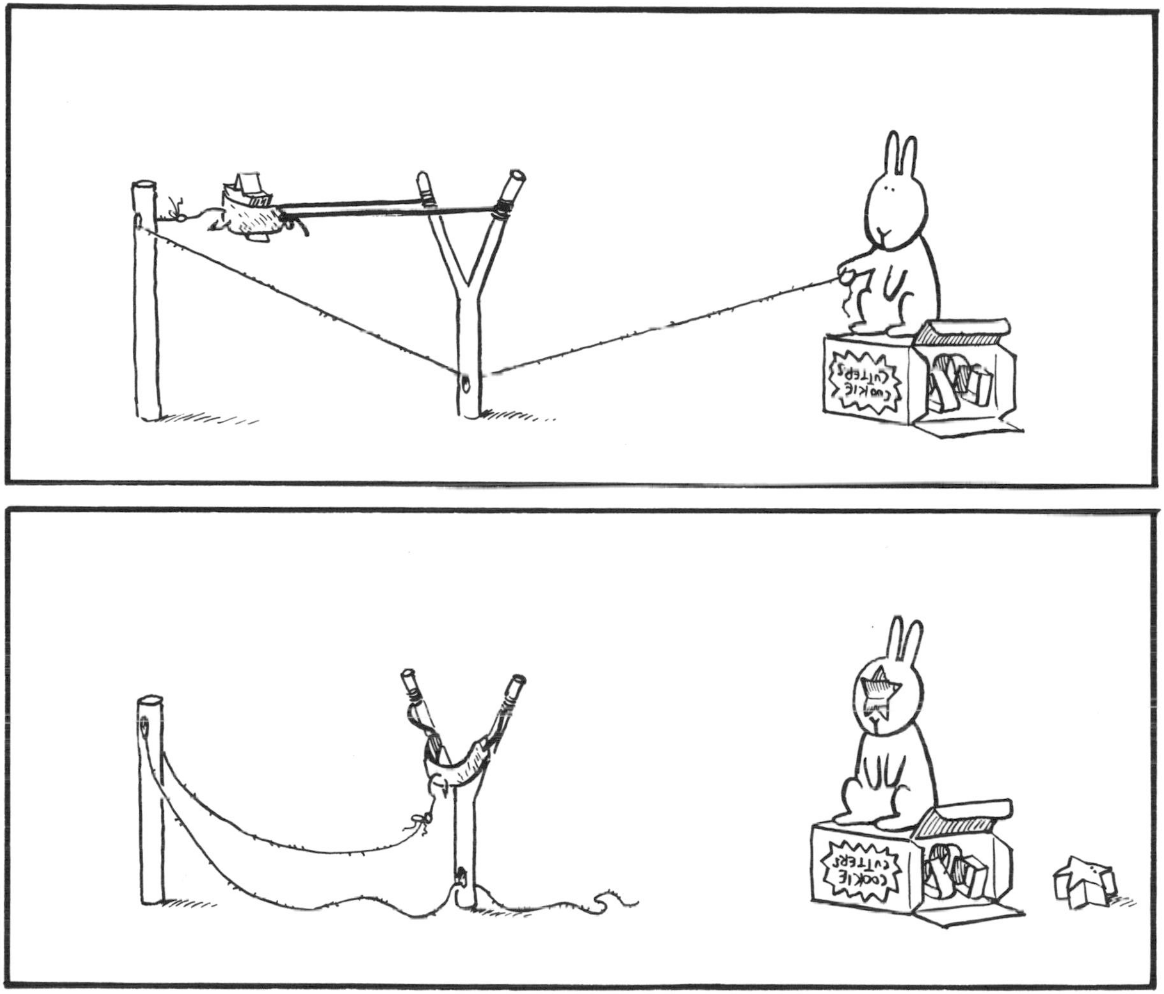
COOKIE CUTTERS
COOKIE CUTTERS

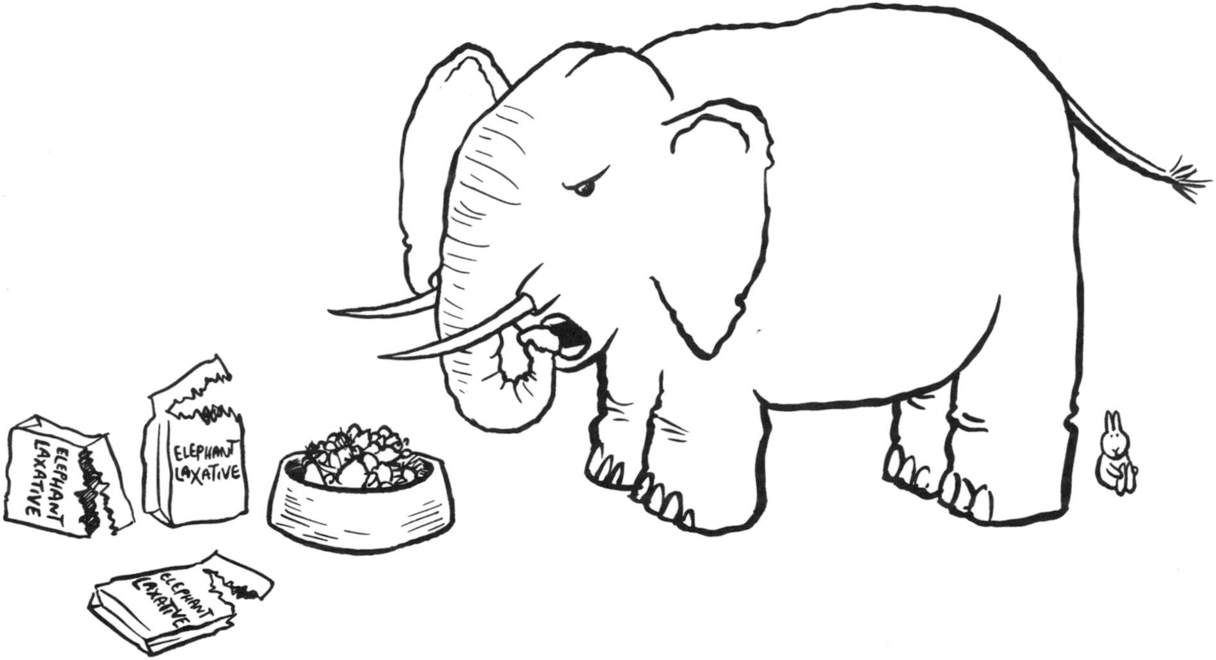
ELEPHANT LAXATIVE
ELEPHANT LAXATIVE
ELEPHANT LAXATIVE

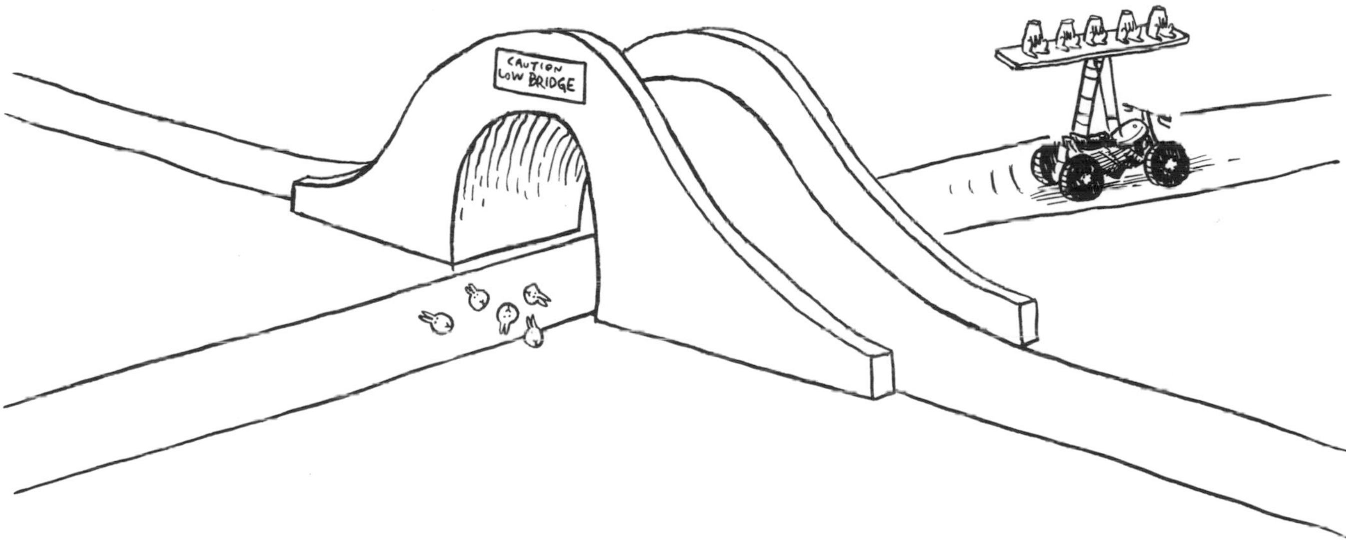
CAUTION
LOW BRIDGE

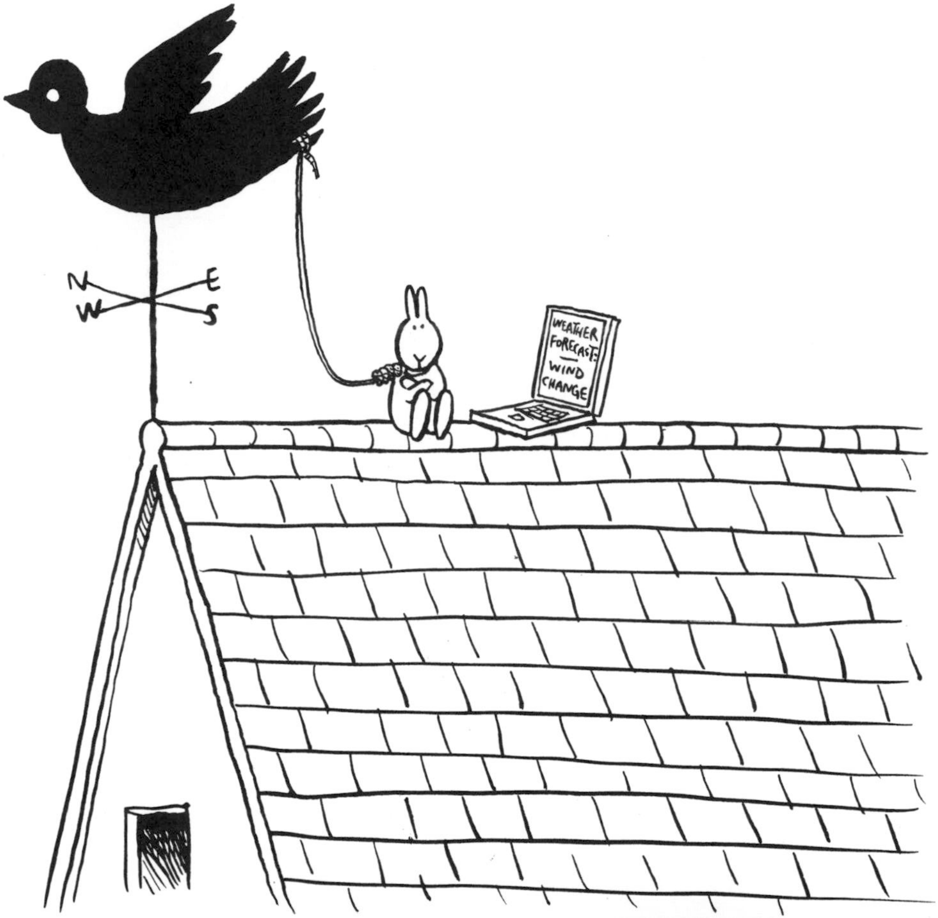
N
E
W
S
WEATHER FORECAST:
WIND CHANGE

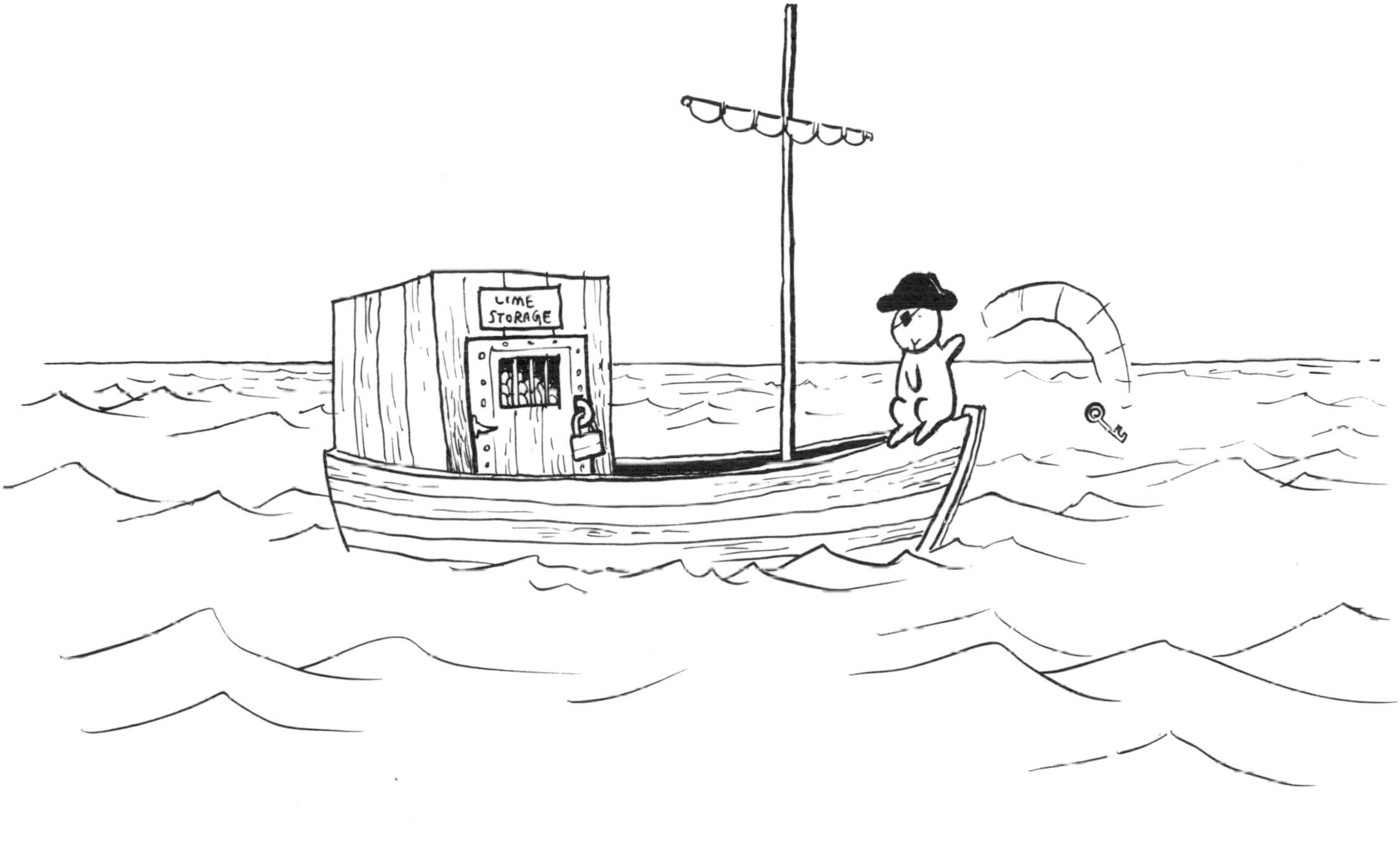
LIME STORAGE

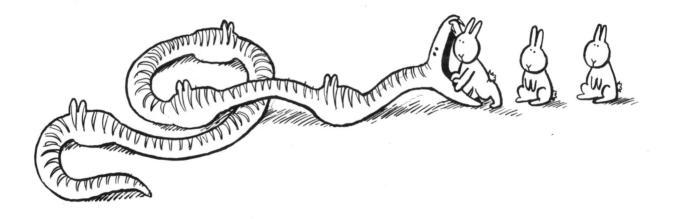

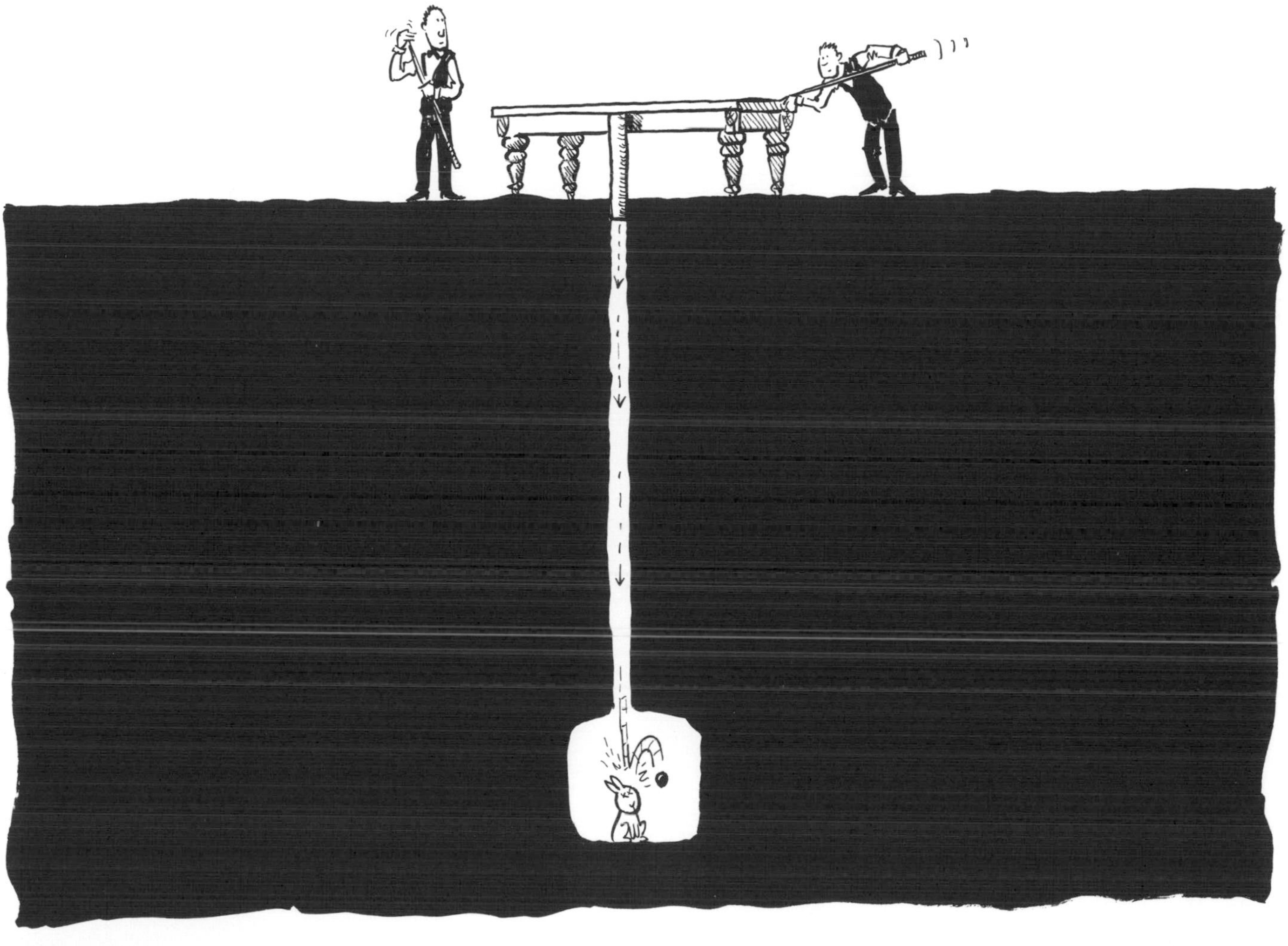

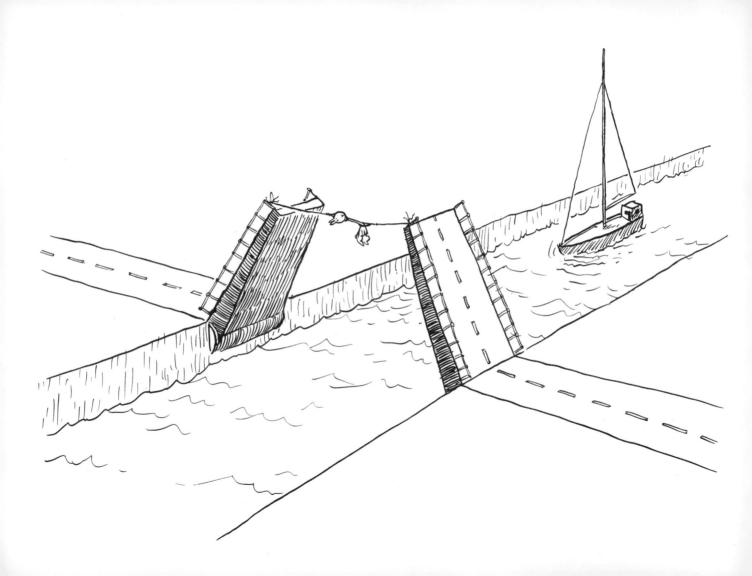

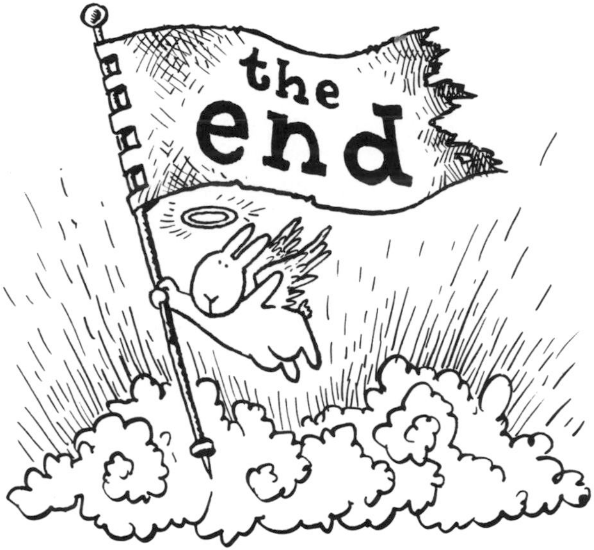
the
end

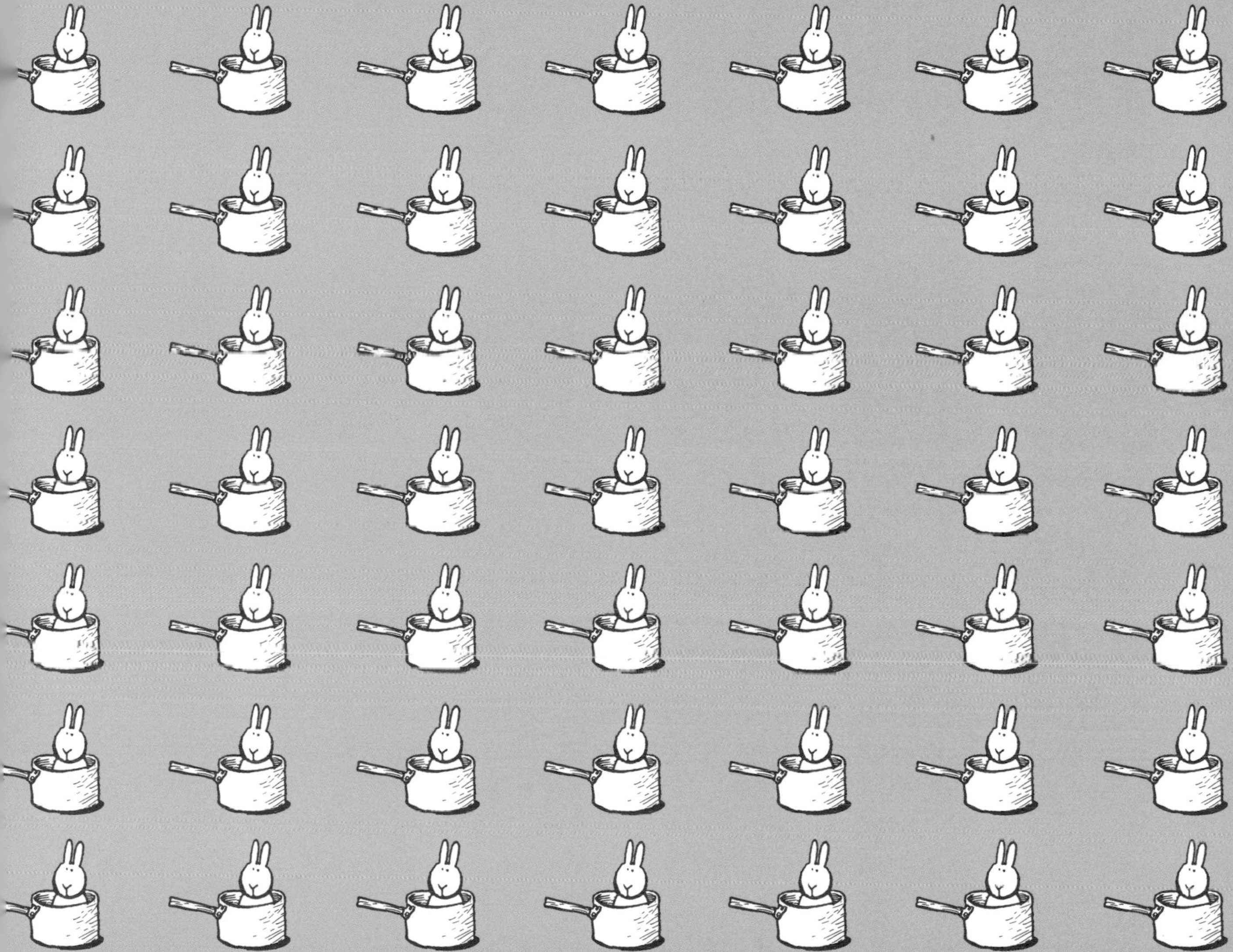

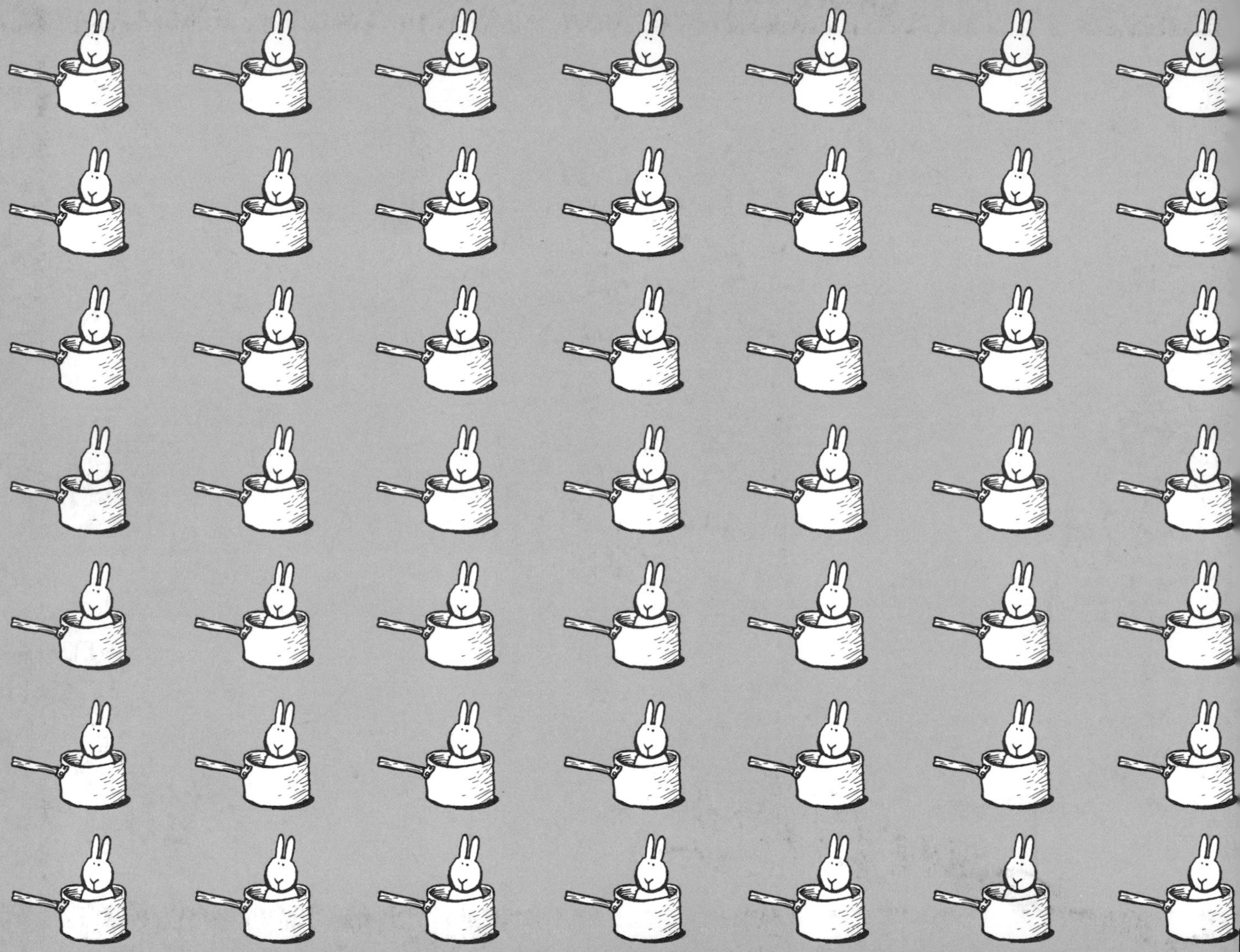